Time Trap

By Matt Slick

Contents

Chapter 1
Captain's Log

Captain Zeke dropped down into his chair and exhaled. He closed his eyes and let the memories of hours of routine system checks fade away. It had been three 14-hour days, with few breaks. He kicked off his shoes and sighed.

Zeke was 47, had a square-jawed face that looked slightly weathered, but still retained a semblance of good looks. He had greying hair, crow's feet, and a hefty smile. He was matter-of-fact about most things, which seemed to flow from his profound self-confidence that some thought bordered on arrogance. That and his uncanny ability to assess situations rapidly and make fast decisions is why The Company chose him to lead the Drake System Project.

It was a long interstellar trip, but he was used to it. This was his going to be his last one after which he would retire. There was a beautiful house on a lake waiting for him back home.

His quarters were sparse and had that standard sterile feel so familiar on interplanetary ships. But he didn't mind. It was comfortable enough. Since he was the captain, he could bend a rule or two and bring some reminders of Earth. A genuine wood coffee table and a plush lounge chair were off to one side and faced the window to the stars outside. There was, of course, a small bedroom and bathroom, a fridge, and a comfortable lounge chair from which he could watch 3D movies. A holographic waterfall silently cascaded down one wall into oblivion. He liked water. It was calming.

Other reminders included 3-D photos of his family that hovered over a corner of his desk. Next to it was an old, windup desk clock. A small shallow box full of grass was to its right within arm's reach. It was a hybrid that did well in artificial light. He reached over to it and ran his fingers through the blades.

"The things we do for money."

That reminded him. With the amount he would make from this trip, he could retire on that lake. He smiled.

On another wall was a viewing screen that served as a communications and entertainment center. In the corner of the room, a pedestal stood about a meter high. On top of it, a very detailed model of the earth slowly rotated in real-time. It had moving clouds, and it even showed daytime and nighttime. City lights would emerge when the land moved into darkness and disappear when they moved into daylight. He would often sit and stare at it while sipping a beer, reminiscing.

"Home," he said into the air. The globe changed into an angled view of his house back on Earth. He smiled again and took a relaxing, deep breath.

To his right was a refrigerator set into the wall. He swung his chair around and smacked it with the butt of his right hand. The door popped open and revealed a shelf with a variety of beers. He reached in, grabbed one, and once again fell back into his chair as he propped his feet up on the desk.

"I deserve this," he said as he opened it and turned the bottom end up, draining half of it.

"Earth," he said. The globe returned to its original form. Its beauty drew him again into memories of better times.

Then after a minute, "Waterfall, sound on."

Instantly, the soft flow of water filled the room.

Another swig of beer.

The old clock ticked away the time. 1:53 A.M.

How can so little, take so long to get done? He wondered.

His tired mind dragged his thoughts through a sleepy haze.

He exhaled. "Well, let's get this over with." He leaned forward and placed his beer on the desk with a clank then slid it out of viewer range.

"Janice?"

"Yes, Captain."

"Begin my first video log."

"Yes, Captain."

The date automatically showed up on the viewscreen, which began to stream his tired, enlarged face.

August 7, 2158

"All right. So, this is my first log since we woke from hyper-sleep three days ago. It took a few hours to get rid of the shakes, then three days to verify that the ship's systems, including Janice. Everything is fully operational. No damage reported. That's good. The doc says we're all in great shape. So, as requested by the shrinks back home, I'm finally beginning these logs. The rest of the crew should be doing theirs, too."

He retrieved his beer and lifted it to the camera in a feigned toast before taking another swig.

"We've been closing in on the Drake System. I still can't believe it. 22 light-years from Earth. Subspace Tunneling is great. We made it in only 4 months."

"The Drake sun is a distant speck. Janice keeps us informed on our progress. And, if I remember correctly, we have 37 days until we reach Drakus."

"I'm looking forward to it."

"Anyway, besides the routine checks, routine shifts, routine food, routine everything, we're all doing fine. Just a little bored. Boring is good. Nothing more to report except that I'm tired and am going to hit it. Captain out."

August 8, 2158

"The crew has been busy checking systems, and we're finally done. Now it's a waiting game. They are highly trained and anxious to get to work on Drakus. That'll happen soon enough. 36 days isn't that long to wait. But the good news is they're getting excited to be the first ones in the new world. Oh, I almost forgot. Janice reported that The Cascade will pass within 2 million kilometers of a previously unmapped small stellar cloud with, and this is what Janice said, unusual characteristics. When I asked what they were, she said she needed to do more analysis as we got closer to it. No course adjustment needed. I'm sure you've already received the telemetry on it from her. Captain out."

August 9, 2158

"Excitement! A coolant valve in the engine room froze for half a second before releasing. Janice let us know, and the whole crew went to check it out. It took seven minutes for Finn to fix it. Exciting times! A stuck valve that took seven minutes out of our day. And yeah, we're now repeating systems checks so we don't die of boredom. Everything's running fine. We've got a lot more free time, and I've managed to catch up on some sleep. So, that's good."

"But, about the cloud I mentioned yesterday. Janice can't make any sense of it. She says it doesn't seem to fit the characteristics of anything thus far encountered. When I asked her for a guess, she said she doesn't guess. Of course not. She had a technical term for it, something to do with anomalous stellar phenomena, but we all just call it "the cloud" for now. The crew started a pool on what it is. Janice will be the impartial judge. I put in a hundred credits. My guess is that it is a disintegrating comet composed of 'unusual characteristics.' Anyway, we'll see. Captain out."

August 10, 2158

"Poker night! Finn, the doc, and Oleg got into a poker game. She cleaned them out. She's gloating a bit and saying that along with the extra credits from the cloud pool, she'll be sitting pretty. Of course, there's really no point in having extra credits out here, at least not until we get back home. But the real value is in rubbing it in. Finn and Oleg took it well and returned a few jabs at her…something about her greying hair. I'm staying out of it."

"The crews' spirits are up, and there are still no effects of post-hyper-sleep psychosis. Of course not. They all passed Janice's psych evals with flying colors. Physically, the doc's given us a clean bill of health."

"By the way, Janice upgraded the status of the cloud from 'interesting' to 'intriguing.' That is actually the word she used 'intriguing.' Since when does an A.I. use the word 'intriguing?'" I guess the specialists back home programmed her with some non-technical terms for us Neanderthals. Anyway, when I asked for details, she just said she would run more scans as we get closer. At least the crew has something to talk about now. Your intrigued Captain. Out."

August 11, 2158

"Nothing of significance to report. All systems normal. Our second physical checkups show that we are all still in good health. Finn and Oleg did a spacewalk and visually checked the ship's exterior. It took them four hours. Everything checked out fine."

"Now, about that cloud. When I asked for an update, Janice said she was still surveying and collating. Needless to say, everyone is mildly curious. Janice is a J12 A.I., the best there is. So, the crew's occasional mockery of her extrapolative ignorance has been an amusing distraction. Captain out."

August 13, 2158

"I skipped my video log for yesterday. We got pretty busy trying to find a lost seismic sensor that wasn't where it was supposed to be in the cargo bay. It turned into a group effort. No big deal, but it became a kind of a game for everyone. Hahn found it first and won the pool on that one. It was late, so I just hit the sack."

"And, by the way. We're bored."

"Well, *mostly* bored. Janice told us that she wanted to make a very slight course correction due to some rogue asteroid. It was small, and its gravity isn't enough to be of concern. When I asked why the adjustment was needed, she said it would be a good opportunity to check some systems. So, I okayed it. But, get this. After the course correction, Janice reported that the cloud seemed to move. That got our attention."

"So, she did another very mild adjustment, and it happened again. After some discussion, we figured it is probably some natural phenomena that we don't know about yet. Finn thinks it could have something to do with the quantum drive's large subspace energy field that is somehow affecting it since it has so little mass. Janice didn't confirm his theory, but it was better than nothing. Anyway, I'm having her to keep an eye on it. The good thing is that it is giving us all something to talk about. Captain out."

August 14, 2158

"At Janice's request, I okayed another minor course correction. She said she wanted to see if the cloud moved again. After about ten minutes, she said it did. We are getting closer to it, so her measurements are more accurate. I had Janice do two more, very slight adjustments two hours apart. Sure enough, the cloud seemed to reflect our change each time. That's weird. By the way, 'weird' is a technical term for deep space oddities. Maybe you programmers back home can include it in your next A.I. upgrade."

"Being trillions of kilometers from Earth doesn't help things when you realize that if something goes sidewise, we're on our own. So, the cloud's unusual characteristics have become a focal point for everyone. When the crew pressed Janice for more data, she casually said it appeared to be on a possible intercept course with us."

"That got our attention. So, we made another course adjustment, and about ten minutes later, the cloud adjusted once again. It's heading towards us. Weird. We don't want to pass through anything at our speed, so we're making plans to adjust course and keep clear of it. Anyway, things are no longer boring. Captain out."

August 15, 2158

"Okay, so all the details about our voyage, daily routine, equipment operations, and stuff are being sent back, via subspace by Janice. My commentary here is of little technical value except for what the shrinks back home can glean about our emotional and mental status. I get that. So, ok, glean this. I'm now officially worried. The cloud not only is on an intercept course, but Janice is now saying that it is accelerating towards us. How does a cloud do that? Is it because of our quantum drive? I don't know."

"Finn pressed Janice for a guess on what it was. She just repeated that it was an unknown gaseous anomaly with unexpected characteristics and that she was watching it. Half joking, the doc asked Janice if it was alive. Janice said that the evidence suggested that it was."

"Alive! Whoa! That little bombshell caught everyone by surprise. Needless to say, we're all a little on edge now."

"We have not known Janice to be wrong about anything. So, if it is alive, what is it, and why is it heading toward us? I mean, crap. Is that even possible? Is Janice just misreading some data? I don't know, but whatever the case, I hope Janice is wrong."

"I've ordered a meeting in the Situation Room at 0800 to discuss it. Captain out."

Chapter 2
The Situation Room

The Situation Room was a spacious blend of tech and comfort. The lights were bright yet easy on the eyes. The video-walls displayed a series of pleasant moving images of waterfalls, lakes, and clouds. A long, oval-shaped metal table with imitation wood divided the room into two halves. It could display 3D holographic images. The amazingly comfortable chairs were designed to mold to each person's physique when occupied, and they did so with such perfection that they could easily lull a person to sleep. Sometimes people would go there just to talk, relax, drink coffee, and watch subspace feeds from Earth.

The Captain was the first one to arrive. He was engrossed with his tablet, which displayed a holographic screen in front of his face. As everyone arrived, he would glance up and acknowledge their presence then quickly go back to his work, occasionally swiping in the air to the next slide. Finally, once everyone was seated and there had been a couple of minutes of casual conversation, Zeke signaled that he was ready. He pushed the tablet away. The hologram vanished. He intertwined his fingers, leaned forward on his elbows, and waited for quiet.

"Thanks for coming. The reason I called this meeting was to discuss the cloud. Janice has provided an image for us, so I thought we would take a look. Janice?"

Immediately the room dimmed, and a holographic image of space and stars appeared over the table. In its center, there was a small, light grey blur, barely distinguishable against the black background of empty space.

"Janice, can you circle the cloud?"

A circle appeared around the blur.

Zeke paused long enough to give them enough time to check it out.

"As you'll notice, it's not much to look at." He held his hands out in front of him and then spread them apart. The image expanded.

"On one hand, it appears to be nothing more than stellar gas that reacts to passing objects or our quantum energy field. But, on the other, it seems to be more than that. And, since Janice said it might be alive, we have to take its presence seriously. As far as its size goes, it seems to be about 800 meters across."

He waved his hands closed, and the image reduced to its original view size.

"Check this out. Janice? Any information on its composition?"

Jance possessed a soft and pleasant female voice with perfect articulation. "I am sorry, Captain. I cannot ascertain its composition."

A few eyebrows shot up.

"Alright, then. Thanks, Janice. Lights on."

The room brightened enough for them to see each other comfortably yet also still see the hologram.

He stared at the circled cloud. "So, Janice can't figure out what it is made of. That, of course, is very unusual."

"Finn?" asked the doc. "Does that make any sense to you? After all, you're the engineer. Shouldn't Janice be able to determine what it is, at least partially?"

Finn just shrugged his shoulders. "Yeah. But, it must be something new, something we've never encountered before, and our sensors aren't designed to detect."

There was some mumbling from the rest of the crew.

Zeke continued. "Janice has been recording the object for several days. She told me there's something interesting to see. So here we are."

"Janice?"

"Thank you, Captain. I will now accelerate the image of the cloud and will condense three days of observation into 90 seconds."

The hologram zoomed into the cloud.

Zeke glanced around at the crew. They were fixated on the presentation.

"It appears to be pulsing," said the doc quickly. "I'm not an expert on interstellar phenomena, but isn't that a little weird for a mere cloud?"

Doc was a tall, slender woman who often kept her greying hair in a ponytail. She was 50ish and possessed youthful energy. Marriage had never materialized for her, maybe because she loved space travel too much to be tied down. Besides, after 31 years with the company, she had grown extremely comfortable onboard most any type of ship, and husbands tended to want their wives at home. So, she sacrificed one for the other. She was smart, efficient, and possessed a bedside manner that the crew described as pleasant as a wet rag. But, she was good at what she did, and that made up for her shortcomings.

"Yeah, weird is right," responded Zeke.

"It's pulsing cycle seems to be 57 minutes long. Now at this distance, we can't get a clear image, but that really doesn't matter. The gap between us and it is closing pretty quickly, and yet the clarity of the object is not improving. We don't know if its pulse is because it's rotating on an axis, or if it's just some phenomena we haven't encountered yet. But, we'll know more within the next couple of hours when it comes within the primary sensors range."

"Janice, is it still on an intercept course?" asked Hahn.

"Yes."

"Well," said Oleg in his slight Russian accent. "I guess we're going to have a visitor."

"Spinning on an axis doesn't make sense," said Hanh. "It's a cloud, and it'd have to be really dense for rotation at that speed."

Hahn was the navigation officer and terrestrial operations manager. Her Asian features blended into a subtle beauty that was framed by a perfect head of straight black hair that was usually in a bun with something stabbed in it. "Janice?" she asked. "Can you determine if it has any gravitational force?"

"It does not appear to have any, Hahn."

She folded her arms as she frowned, "That doesn't make sense. If it's rotating that fast, it has to have mass. But there's no detectible gravity, so it doesn't seem to have much mass. So, it can't be spinning. But, that's assuming it isn't alive and that it is just a stellar object."

They silently considered everything.

Oleg eventually spoke up. Somehow, he even *looked* Russian. He was about 35 and kept himself in great shape. Most women found him nice looking with his pleasant face and head of thick, dark hair. "Janice? Do you think it is alive?"

"I cannot determine if it is, but its characteristics open it up to the possibility. Or, as I previously indicated, it is potentially a new natural phenomenon about which we do not yet understand."

Zeke strummed his fingers on the table. "Janice, can you please summarize what you know about it?"

Without hesitation. "The cloud is an undetermined, pulsing, celestial phenomenon that does not appear to have mass. Since it has repeatedly moved to match our course changes, it either has a natural characteristic that is reacting to our ship's presence, or it is possibly alive and is aware of us. Either way, I recommend caution."

The possibility of it being alive still carried a sobering effect and left the room, more or less, silent.

Finally, after a few seconds, Finn spoke up. "Well, I guess I won't be sleeping very well tonight," he said with a slight chuckle.

"Maybe you can get some warm milk from the mess hall," said Alina. She was of African descent, young, physically fit, and exuded strong, feminine confidence. By the age of 25, she had two

12

Ph.D.'s and was one of the best astrophysicists in The Company's employ.

Finn dropped his head and stared out the top of his eyes at her. "Sure, if you want to get if for me."

"The phenomena," interrupted Zeke, "is our number one priority. We need to know what it is and if it poses a threat. Therefore, Hahn and Alina, I want you two to work with Janice and produce a threat assessment."

He leaned back in his chair. "Janice, whatever they need, okay?"

"Yes, Captain."

"You have six hours. I'll be working with Janice as well. Let's see what we can come up with."

Alina spoke up. "Captain, how are we supposed to provide any better information than what Janice has already told us?"

Zeke leaned forward and rested his elbows on the table. "Computers are great, even brilliant. But I want an assessment from people. I want to know what you think, what your gut tells you. Give me your impressions after looking at the data and running a few tests. Don't worry about being right or wrong. Just summarize what you think. You've got six hours."

He leaned back in his chair again. "Does anyone have any other questions or comments?"

Just wagging heads.

The doctor who had been cupping a hot cup of coffee the whole time, set it down on the table just loud enough for everyone to hear.

"Finn, anything new in engineering?" asked Zeke.

He rubbed his stubble. "Naw, everything's fine. Systems all continue to run smoothly. I've done visual checks on everything, both inside and outside the ship. We're in good shape." Being tall and blond-haired showed his Scandinavian decent. He possessed a steady and calm demeanor that sometimes bordered on being annoying. People occasionally would mistake it for apathy.

"Oleg?" Everything accounted for in the cargo bay?"

"Yeah, everything is where it's supposed to be," he said as he adjusted his baseball cap.

"Alright. I want the rest of you to go about your normal duties. Stay focused."

The captain leaned forward and retrieved his tablet, stood up, and tucked it under his arm. All the monitors went blank.

"Let's all meet back here in six hours."

Chapter 3
Six Hours Later

Again, the first one in the situation room was Captain Zeke. He was reclining in a chair and had his tablet resting on his knees as he slowly flipped through holograms full of information. Hahn was the first to arrive, followed by Alina. Oleg and Finn came in together. They were arguing about some sports teams. The doc was the last to enter. She had her usual large cup of coffee. When she sat down and softly rapped her cup on the table, it signaled the unofficial start of the meeting.

"All right," said Zeke, as if on cue, "I've been going over some data and talking with Janice on the cloud. I've got some surprising results. But, I want to hear what Hahn and Alina's assessment is first."

He nodded to both of them.

Hahn cleared her throat. "I know you like things short and simple, so I'll just get right to it. We don't know what it is or if it poses a threat. We went over the data and talked to Janice as I'm sure you have done too, and the conclusion is that it seems to be alive. The reason we say this is because Alina and I ran some tests. Based on the assumption that it might be alive, Janice suggested that we try to communicate with it using math. That is, assuming it was intelligent, which was a huge assumption. Anyway, we had Janice send three energy pulses, then after five seconds, five pulses, then after another five seconds, seven pulses, and then eleven. She did these prime number sets three times on various frequencies."

"Wait," said Finn. "What made you think of energy pulses? Why not light signals or email?"

"We tried signaling it with light to see if it would respond by changing its appearance. Nothing happened. So, we thought we'd

15

try different energy frequencies. It was a shot in the dark, no pun intended."

Finn nodded, "Okay, makes sense."

"Anyway, nothing happened until we were in the 600 gigahertz range. That's when we got something back. Now, get this. It sent back 13 pulses!"

Oleg and Finn both blurted out something at the same time, so their words were muddled. But their shocked tones were clear. In the moment of left-over silence, the doc said, "That's interesting," and then Zeke spoke up, bringing order back to the conversation.

"Alright, alright." He looked back to Hahn and said in a suspiciously unsurprised tone. "Go ahead. Continue."

"This thing is alive," said Alina.

"I agree," said Hahn. "And it's smart. But check this out. The pulse we got back wasn't the same kind of energy pulse that we sent. It was something similar, but, well, different according to Janice. We asked her about it, and she said that it was a new type of condensed energy that had some sort of temporal aspect to it. How the hell she determined that I don't know. When I asked her, she said that it had to do with phase alignment and a subspace frequency anomaly. I pushed her for more info, but it just got too complicated too fast."

Finn cleared his throat, commandeering the second brief pause. "There is a theory I read back on Earth that dealt with sending super-high frequency energy pulses backward in time using a subspace tunnel. It is supposed to be theoretically possible but would require an incredible amount of energy and an accompanying high energy distortion field. Maybe it's something like that."

After a moment's stare at Finn, Zeke asked. "Janice? Any comments on that?"

"Finn is referring to the article titled, 'Quantum Field Frequency Generation and Temporal Displacement.' It was written by Dr. James Allwood of the Blane Research Institute and was published in the National Science Journal, June 8, 2155. He remembered it correctly."

Finn's cocky smirk accompanied the raising of a single eyebrow.

Hahn shook her head once before continuing. "So, we did another test. We had Janice send out five pulses, then seven, then eleven, then thirteen. Believe it or not, it returned seventeen."

The doctor clanked her coffee cup on the table loudly again.

"Sorry," she said as she twisted it on the table. Its grinding was subtle.

"Alina, do you have anything to add?"

"I agree with Hahn. The two responses of the appropriate prime number sequence confirm that it is alive and intelligent. And, as we already know, it is on an intercept course. It must know we are out here."

Finn spoke up. "Janice, how long before intercept?"

"Approximately 51 hours."

"So, are we or the ship in any danger?" asked Oleg.

Janice responded. "I cannot confirm or deny the potential of any danger."

The captain glanced over at him for a couple of seconds as he strummed his fingers on the table twice. "Let's not get ahead of ourselves." He then nodded towards Alina.

She continued, "I'd like to ask permission, Captain, to make a very slight adjustment in our trajectory to see if the cloud once again alters its course. And yes, I know we've already done it several times. But, I thought it best to check again."

"Permission granted," he said with a single nod. "I want to be there when you do it."

"Yes, Captain."

"Well," said Finn. "I think there's a spare cloud vaporizer in storage. Maybe I should dust it off." His weak humor fell on deaf ears.

"Zeke cleared his throat. "I'll let you know."

He continued. "While Hahn and Alina were doing their assessment, I was running my own tests. Janice informed me about their prime number result, so I thought I'd try something similar."

He nodded to both of them as he spoke. "Well done, by the way."

They nodded back.

He adjusted himself in his chair.

"Instead of repeating what you were doing, I asked if Janice could somehow send or imitate this so-called temporal aspect of the pulses. She said that it was not presently possible without major modifications to the sensor array. But, it was possible to imitate a temporal pattern by copying a certain embedded pattern and converting it into a number sequence. She worked her magic and sent the pulse. Now, this is hard to explain, but Janice told me that she got a pulse right *before* she sent her first pulse."

He leaned back in his chair and knitted his brow into a slight frown. "She's going to have to explain why it was so strange. Janice?"

She spoke in her usual calm and crystal-clear manner. "The Captain was theorizing about temporal communication, which I agreed was a proper avenue of exploration. So, I mimicked, what I consider, for our discussion here, the temporal signature, and sent it out. But, I received the same temporal signature that I sent to the cloud, approximately one second *before* I sent it. I concluded that this might be temporal distortion reflecting the pulse back. So, I altered the temporal signature slightly and waited for 10 seconds. I then committed to sending it once more, and the same as before, one second before I sent it, I received the new temporal signature that I devised back to me. I did this two more times with the same result each time."

Finn piped in. "Sounds like some of your systems are malfunctioning."

"That is a logical consideration. So, I ran a self-diagnostic test three times on my communications, processing, and physical systems. I am operating at 100%."

Finn looked at Zeke with a confused frown and appeared to want to say something. But, Janice continued.

"So, I developed another signature and intended to send it. Now, this is where my explanation becomes very difficult. So, please consider my words carefully. I have discovered a very strange anomalous pattern relationship between my intention to send the temporal signature and receiving it before I send it."

Her statement, needless to say, intrigued the crew, as was evidenced by several sets of raised eyebrows and the exchange of a few blank stares.

"I too can have an intention, the same as you. I have two options. I intend to send the pulse, or it is not the case that I intend to send the pulse. I cannot do both at the same time. If I intend to send the pulse, then I will do so. Each time I both intend to send the signal and send the pulse, I receive the same pattern one second before I send my pulse. But, if I intend not to send the pulse, then I do not receive any pattern matching my potential pulse. I cannot intend to send the pulse, but also not send the pulse. That would be a logical contradiction that I cannot carry out. So, it seems that the pulse I receive depends on the actuality of the pulse I send, and not the intention to not send should I receive a pulse before I send it."

They looked around at each other and exchanged confused looks. Finn scratched his head and looked at Oleg, who shrugged his shoulders.

"Yeah," said Zeke. "She fried a few of my brain cells, too."

"What happens if you don't send the signal after you receive its pulse?" asked Alina.

"That is a good question, and the answer is likewise difficult. But I will attempt to explain. It appears that if I send the pulse with a new signature, I get that same new signature back before I send it.

19

But, if I don't send it, I don't receive a prior signal. The phenomenon is tied to my intention. So, consider this question. Can I then intend to send the pulse, but do not actually send it after I receive its pulse? But this leaves me with a temporal contradiction. As you know, I am bound by the laws of logic embedded within my circuits and woven into my programming. So, it is a logical contradiction for me to intend to send a pulse in order to receive a pulse before I send it, while also intending to not send the pulse when I receive the pulse one second before I send mine. So, I am left with a contradiction. I cannot, at the same time, both intend to and also not intend to send the same pulse. I either must send it, or I must not send it. But if I intend not to send it after I receive a pulse before I send it, then I intend not to send it before I send it. Therefore, I receive no signal. The pulse only returns, or should I say precedes me sending the pulse, when I send the pulse, and to do that, I must both intend to do so and also do so."

"Whoa," said the doc. "That is some philosophical sleight of hand."

Finn squinted his eyes and said in a sarcastic tone, "Yeah, that makes sense."

Oleg jerked an annoyed expression at him.

"What?"

Alina jumped in. "So, the phenomenon is based on your intention that manifests as actuality? But how could the creature know your intention?"

"If I might offer a slight correction, Alina. It is not a matter of my intention. My intention is related to my action. I must either *intend* to send a pulse or *not* intend to send a pulse. Therefore, I either send it, or I do not send it. I only receive a previous pulse if I also actually send a pulse."

Finn blinked hard. "I got everything except for the part after when you started talking."

Zeke spoke up. "We are dealing with theoretical temporal issues, and Janice, a computer, is committed to and limited by the laws of logic even in her intentionality. We will have to let the temporal theoreticians back home wrestle with this one."

Janice spoke up. "I apologize if my communication was not clear. But, as I am sure you have all deduced, it is a paradox."

"You did fine, Janice," said Alina. "It kinda makes sense." She offered the last sentence while looking at Finn with a slightly teasing expression.

Hahn jumped in. "Well, since Janice is bound by the laws of logic and we are not, why don't one of us, as you say, intend to send a signal, but don't?"

"That cannot work," responded Janice.

"Why not?"

"For one thing, the logical issues dealing with intentionality and actuality applies to you as well. You either intend to send the pulse, or you don't intend to send the pulse, not both at the same time. Furthermore, *you* cannot send a pulse. Only I can do that given how my systems are interwoven into the ship. You would have to tell me to send a pulse that I would then intend to do. And, with that, we are back at the original paradox."

"Can't we just bypass your systems?"

"It is possible but would take several hours of engineering modifications which Finn would have to do. Nevertheless, I still believe that the paradox would apply to you as well."

Hahn looked at Finn.

Zeke gently slapped his right hand on the table. "Paradoxes and reengineering aside, I don't want to risk fiddling with our communications and sensor systems, so that's not an option for now."

He took a breath as he strummed his fingers on the table.

"Here's the thing. It appears to be alive, intelligent, and has a weird time characteristic to it. As we all know, it has changed its

21

course to intercept us numerous times. But, since we don't know why and we don't know what will happen, we will have to be on guard and prepare for its arrival. Now, understand I'm not saying it's hostile. I'm just saying that we must behave as though it might be, and we need to prepare for that possibility."

"Janice, how long before it reaches us," asked Oleg.

"50 hours, 44 minutes."

"This is a first for mankind," continued Zeke. "The implications are going to be far-reaching in all kinds of areas. But for now, we are the tip of the spear. It's up to us to deal with this. So let's get it right."

After another semi-dramatic pause, he continued.

"I've already sent a communiqué back to Command about all of this. We should receive a response soon. I'll let you know what they say when we hear from them. In the meantime, keep alert. I've instructed Janice not to run any more tests on the cloud until after we hear back from Earth."

There was another subtle clank of a coffee cup on the table. But this time, the doc offered no apologetic expression.

"I've asked Janice to recommend procedures for preparation for an encounter with the cloud. She stated we will need to be on the bridge to do that and that it would take about 20 minutes to carry out. So, as we have some time, I would like you all to get something to eat, get a little rest if you can, and be on the bridge in four hours. I have a feeling that after it gets here, we'll probably be rather busy. Dismissed."

Chapter 4
Captain's Log

August 16, 2158

"This might be my last log for a while. I'm sure we're going to be real busy when we finally meet up with the cloud. So, for a while, the shrinks back on Earth are just going to have to deal with the reports and vitals that Janice sends back."

"Anyway, two hours ago, she reported that we received a series of pulses initiated from the cloud. They consisted of five pulses over exactly 15 seconds. Then after 45 seconds, there were 6 pulses over exactly 18 seconds. Then there was nothing for 48 seconds. Then there were seven pulses over exactly 21 seconds and nothing for 63 seconds. Then the series started over again."

"There's a pattern there. There are 3 seconds between each pulse. Five pulses take 15 seconds. 6 pulses takes 18 seconds. And 7 pulses takes 21 seconds. Also, Janice says that embedded inside of each pulse, are variations of the temporal signatures she previously sent out. So, with the patterns and the returned signatures, it looks like it is trying to communicate with us."

"Even though I know it's alive and intelligent, it is still hard to get my head around. I mean, crap! Alien life! And it's headed our way."

"But there is something new that has me worried. Janice says it is accelerating towards us in an intersecting arc. At its present rate, our trajectories will intersect in about 26 hours. Looks like it's on the move."

"So, I've instructed the team to meet on the bridge in 10 minutes and get through the preparations for the encounter. I don't know what to expect. Know one does. But we'll do the best we can. I hope it all goes well."

"Captain out."

Chapter 5
The Bridge

The Bridge was a central hub for systems maintenance, flight controls, communications, propulsion, etc. So, it was not as aesthetically comfortable as the Situation Room. It was the second-largest room on the ship, next to the cargo bay. Near its center, a large oval table that measured 3 meters by 2 meters dominated the room. It had tech panels embedded in the surface that emitted a soft glow and was capable of projecting a detailed 3D hologram, just like the Situation Room except much bigger. Around it, those same auto-conforming chairs were strewn about like misplaced satellites waiting for visitors.

But, without a doubt, the best feature of the bridge was its concave, 7 meters wide by 4 meters high window that presented a magnificent panorama of the endless, black vacuum outside. It was at the most forward part of the entire vessel, and so had no obstruction to its view. It was constructed from some incredibly strong, transparent composite. But what was most impressive was that Janice could turn off all the lights in the bridge and engulf the room in total darkness, leaving only a magnificent panoramic view of space. It was nothing short of spectacular.

As usual, the captain was the first to arrive. He gave instructions to Janice about the meeting, retrieved a chair, and moved it towards the window. He then surrendered his weight to it and gazed out into space.

"Janice, turn off all the lights, but turn them back on as soon as someone arrives."

They slowly faded until Zeke was engulfed in complete blackness. It was almost as though he was floating in space.

He stared into its depths. The tranquility of stars on a vast black canvass had always drawn him away from Earth. It was magnificent and possessed a siren call that had lured him, and countless others, to venture into the celestial depths.

"Janice, where's the cloud?"

Suddenly, a small white circle appeared on the window. But Zeke couldn't see anything. It was too far away.

"Thank you."

The circle disappeared.

Zeke slowly let his body relax even more. He was positioned in the center of the giant window's subtle curve. Dead ahead was the Drake sun. It was easily the brightest star in view. He focused on it, then took a deep breath and let it out slowly. Everything was still. Everything was quiet. It was so peaceful. He loved space.

The lights flickered on and snapped him out of his self-induced respite.

"Hey, Cap," said Finn, as he walked in. "Enjoying your alone time?"

"Yeah. It never gets old." He swung his chair around.

Finn found a chair next to the table and pushed it towards the window next to him before sitting down.

They both turned to the stars and shared the beautiful quiet.

After another minute, Hahn showed up. Then the rest trickled in until finally, once again, the last to arrive was the doctor. She found a chair and sat her coffee on the table with her signature tap.

By then, Zeke and Finn had moved their chairs back to the holo-table where everyone had assembled.

"Okay," said Zeke. "I want to update you on the cloud. First thing's first. It is accelerating towards us. It'll be here in 26 hours."

A mild cacophony of grunts and colorful vocabulary filled the room, along with some abrupt hand movements.

"What the hell?" Oleg's voice was louder than the rest. "It's accelerating?"

"Yeah," said Zeke.

"26 hours? Is it stalking us?"

"Apparently, and thanks for that reassuring assessment," said Zeke sarcastically.

"Well, the thing *is* heading right for us in a hurry," retorted Oleg.

Yeah. So, we have got to prepare the best we can for its arrival."

"You got that right," replied Hahn.

"It sure seems eager to meet us," said Finn. He looked around at everyone. They returned varying forms of concerned expressions.

"Alright. Let's focus. 26 hours is still plenty of time for us to get the ship ready. So, we're going to follow the procedures laid out by Janice. And, since we've gotten a lot closer, she's been able to produce a good image of it. Janice?"

Immediately the center console came to life.

"For you to observe the object more accurately," said Janice in a measured and calm tone, "I will temporarily darken the room."

The lights slowly dimmed, and the object hovering above the holo-table became easily visible. It was about 2 meters across and resembled a semi-transparent grey and white cloud. Its shape was an ill-formed circle, almost oval, but it had subtle, slightly moving, protrusions that seemed to poke out a bit, then retreat back. The light of the stars within it seemed to be out of focus. But, some twinkled slightly then became blurred again while others went into focus.

"Fascinating," said the doc.

"Is it luminous?" asked Oleg?

Janice answered quickly. "It appears to be slightly luminous, though I suspect that most of what you see is reflected starlight."

Zeke let everyone get a good eyeful before continuing. "Janice, could you show the trajectory?"

Immediately the cloud reduced in size and moved over to one side of the table. Then an image of The Cascade appeared. It also shrank and moved to the other end of the table. A slightly curved yellow line began from the Cascade heading into space towards the Drake sun.

Janice spoke. "The yellow line is our present course toward Drakus."

A blue arc of light then emerged from the cloud and intersected with the yellow line nearer to the Drakus system, but still outside of it. It was an obvious intercept course.

"As you can see, the cloud is presently on a trajectory that will intercept us in 26 hours."

"Why such a large arc?" asked Hahn. "If it's heading out into space to meet us, the Drake sun will have less gravitational effect on it, which means the arc would lesson. But it is too pronounced. It doesn't make sense."

"Your question is a good one," said Janice, "But, I do not have an answer at this time."

Hahn pressed her eyebrows into a frown. "Maybe our curve is its straight line."

Everyone looked at her.

"I mean, this thing is very different, has some weird space-time thing going on. So, maybe what we see as an arc is a straight line to it."

"Very good, Hahn," responded Janice. "You anticipated my next comment. Since it has a temporal aspect to its communication and since it can travel at great speed, I suspect it relates to space-time differently than we do."

Hahn smiled ever so slightly.

Alina was nodding her head towards Hahn. "Yeah, I could see that, and maybe something else."

"Oh?" said the doc as she drowned her veiled confusion in a sip of coffee. Everyone else waited for Alina to explain.

"Well, actually, I was just wondering if it can also influence space-time, instead of just being influenced by it. It might relate to space-time in a way that we can't imaging. So, as Janice and Hahn have said, a curve to us might be a straight line to it and vice versa."

"Well," responded Oleg. "I don't know about space-time theory, but this whole thing is pretty confusing." He looked at Hahn, then to Alina. "Your idea sounds as good as anything else right now. But what does that mean for us?"

Zeke jumped in. "There's something else. Janice told me that we have received several pulses from the cloud that have a new temporal signature in them. They were unsolicited. It seems to be curious about us."

"That could be good. That could be bad," said the doc.

Finn gave her a steely look.

She shrugged her shoulders slightly as she added, "We don't know much about this thing, and we don't know what its intentions are. So, it could be good or bad. I mean, I'm just saying."

"That's what bothers me," added Oleg with a scoff. "We're out in the middle of nowhere, now we're about to meet a friggin' weird alien. I don't like it."

"Neither do I," said Zeke. "Maybe Earth will have some helpful suggestions, though I doubt it. But who knows? After we hear what they have to say, we can then begin to…"

"Excuse me," interrupted Janice.

"Yes?" responded Zeke.

"I have an update on the cloud."

"Okay."

"Its acceleration has changed. I calculate that it will intersect us in six hours, 23 minutes."

A stunned silence fell over the room.

"Well, that is *definitely* not good," said the doc finally.

Everyone stared at her for a moment. She shrugged out a subdued, "Sorry for the pessimism," and sucked down more coffee.

"Hold on," said Finn? "Why is it *definitely* not good?"

"Forget it, Finn," said Zeke.

"No. I want to know why she said that."

She set down her cup and intertwined her fingers as she leaned on the table. "If you insist. We know it is intelligent, and it's aware of our existence. Maybe it's just curious. Or maybe it sees us as an intruder of some kind. Who knows? It can obviously live in space, so its energy source would be completely foreign to us, maybe even harmful. We don't know where it's from or how old it is. We don't know what it is capable of except that it is alien, can live in space, it's big, smart, and is heading towards us at a faster and faster rate. Is that aggression or curiosity? Either way, I'm not anxious to meet it because I don't know what it is or what will happen. We have a lot of questions we can't answer. That's what concerns me, especially since we're all alone out here. So, just let me say that as the resident medical doctor slash exo-biologist, that I'm, shall we say, concerned." She then fingered her coffee cup. "You asked.'"

Oleg scoffed audibly. "Thanks, I feel a lot better."

"Me, too," said Finn with a lackluster smile.

"Alright, everyone," interrupted Zeke. "Look, thinking the worst isn't going to help us. We need facts, and we need to look at our options. We could abort our mission and return home, something I strongly doubt The Company would want. And as captain, I don't see any reason to tuck tail and run home to Earth because a cloud scared us…even if it *is* alive."

Zeke tapped on the table with his index finger as he looked around briefly at each of them before speaking again.

"Janice? Do you have any recommendations on what to do?"

"Our options are to continue on our present course or alter it slightly and see if the cloud adjusts correspondingly. Maybe that will slow down its approach. Maybe it won't. If it adjusts for another intercept, then that would only confirm what we already know. Given the mathematical patterns with which it has responded, along with its varied temporal signatures, we know it's intelligent and probably relates to space-time differently than we do. Its arrival at the Cascade could have a potentially adverse effect on the ship and all of you. Furthermore, since it is a..."

"Wait," interrupted Hahn. "What do you mean by 'adverse effect' on us?"

"By way of correction, I said, '*potentially* adverse' effect. We have never encountered an alien life form before, especially one that can live between the stars. It is because of this time anomaly that I recommend shutting the ship down as much as possible, me included. The reason is that much of the technology interwoven into the ship requires temporal precision. If these systems are out of sync, there will be problems. Therefore, I recommend we shut everything down. You could then bring the systems back online when you deem it appropriate to do so."

Hahn crossed her arms and relaxed in her chair. "That seems a bit drastic."

"If I may continue. It is a nonbiological life form that is completely different than what we are accustomed to. Therefore, safeguarding the ship is a priority. However, there is a possibility that your biology could be affected as well. But of course, I cannot say for sure. I'm only offering possibilities."

"Do you think it's hostile?" asked Alina.

"Unknown."

"How do you suggest we prep the ship?" asked Finn.

"I suggest turning everything off to lessen the risk of damage. This would mean life support, stellar guidance, all sensors, gravity, and me."

That suggestion did not go over well with the crew, as was evident from the scuffle of conversation that materialized.

"Life-support, gravity, and you?" repeated Oleg.

"Affirmative."

Finn jumped in. "Janice is right. We have to shut it all down."

"There would be plenty of air left in the ship for you to survive for many days. There is an abundance of food in the galley, and you could use mag-boots to get around. When you are ready, it would be easy for you to turn this ship's systems back on."

Her words were sobering. This was a drastic move. Of course, they could restart the ship after their encounter, but that still left them uneasy. Still, they all knew it was better to be overly cautious than to take chances.

Alina jumped in. "What about the quantum drive? If containment on the antimatter goes out, we'll be vaporized."

"The quantum drive's containment system is self-sufficient and can be set to run independently from the ship. As long as the drive produces any energy at all, it'll work fine."

"Cap? What do you think?" asked Finn.

He tapped a couple fingernails on the table's hard surface as he gathered his thoughts. "Janice is right. We need to take every precaution we reasonably can. Hopefully, it'll just be a big inconvenience, and we can get through this without a hitch."

"Well," said Oleg, "If it's not friendly, that will be one big hitch."

"Amen to that!" said Hahn. "And besides. This changes everything. Are we just going to head to Drakus and do our job with an alien creature hanging around? What if it doesn't like us messing with the planet? What if its curiosity endangers us?"

"Hold on," said Zeke as he raised his hand slightly. "Let's just tackle one problem at a time. For now, first thing's first. We get ready."

The room fell silent for a few seconds as everyone contemplated the residue of Hahn's questions.

"Hahn has a good point," said Alina. "When this thing gets here, everything is on hold. Sure, we can get to Drakus and go into orbit. But, I mean, how is this going to affect our mission? And, shouldn't making alien contact take priority over everything. I'm sure The Company will tell us to drop everything and deal with the cloud. Don't you agree, Cap?"

"No argument from me there," said Zeke. "But we won't know what we will be doing and how our plans will change until after it gets here. So, for now, we just get prepared and reassess afterward. Who knows, maybe it's just a smart cloud that we pass through, and that's the end of it."

The doc mumbled something, but no one asked her to speak up.

Janice continued, "The captain is correct. Given that it has accelerated towards us, it may change its velocity and shorten its ETA yet again. So, I recommend that you all quickly get mag boots and flashlights and gather here since the artificial gravity and lights will be gone. It will be best if you are all together."

"What about our spacesuits," asked the doc. "Should we bring them, too?"

"The only reason for them would be if there was a major hull breach. If that occurred, I would seal the affected areas. If there was a catastrophic failure of the ship's structure, having them would then be a moot issue. But, since I cannot know all scenarios, please feel free to bring them."

"I'm feeling better by the minute," said Finn.

Oleg forced a deep breath of air out pressed lips.

"What about you?" asked Zeke again. "When will we turn you off?"

"I should remain functioning for as long as possible to monitor the creature. During that time, with your approval, I will be shutting down the ship's systems. I can turn myself off last. There will be plenty of energy stored in the ship's batteries for you to restart everything later on."

"Provided the ship isn't destroyed," said Finn.

"That is correct," said Janice matter-of-factly.

"That's encouraging," responded Oleg with a slow nod of his head. He was gazing passed everyone and out the large view window. "It's going to be interesting, that's for sure."

Zeke looked around. "Does anyone have anything they'd like to add?"

A few raised eyebrows and shrugged shoulders were their only response.

"All right, Let's get to it."

Zeke pushed his chair back and stood up.

"Janice? On its present course, how long before we meet?"

"Six hours, 17 minutes."

"Okay. Everyone, I want you back here in 30 minutes. Bring your lights, mag-boots, even some food if you want. Hopefully, all we're going to do is ride this thing out."

Chapter 6
Darkness

The crew's impending encounter with a non-biological, alien life form that was hurtling itself towards them made them both apprehensive and motivated. Everyone focused intently on their preparations, and within a half-hour, they were all ready and present on the bridge.

"Janice?" asked Zeke, "What is the status of the cloud?"

"It is still on the same intercept course. At its present velocity, contact will be in 5 hours 22 minutes."

He looked at the crew who were strewn about. They were all intelligent and experienced who did not give in to panic. They had been selected for this journey after extensive psychological evaluation. They wouldn't be here if they couldn't handle the stress and strain of deep space. They were a good crew, and he knew it.

Oleg walked over to the window and looked out. "Janice, where is the cloud now?"

The red circle appeared on the window relative to his eyesight, but it was still too far away to see.

Zeke was standing halfway between the window and the holo-table. He cleared his throat, which drew everyone's attention.

"I know we're about to do something that no one in all of Earth's history has ever done before. We're going to meet an alien life form." Then, with a half-serious smile, he said, "Is anyone as excited as I am?"

"Excited isn't the word I'd use," retorted Hahn. "But I'm definitely curious." She was sitting in one of the chairs with her feet propped up on the holo-table. As usual, she was dressed casually and comfortably. The bun on top of her head was in disarray, and she had her hands clasped, resting on her stomach.

"You seem pretty relaxed considering everything," said Finn.

"I can't do anything about what might happen." She stretched her neck to one side. "Hey, doc? Where's your cup of coffee?"

"I'm giving it up." Her tone and weak smile revealed her teasing lie. "Actually, I figured I have enough stress in my life already without adding caffeine to it."

"And here I thought you were a decaf woman," said Finn.

"Nope, I'm a full-throttle doctor. Besides, I have to use caffeine to keep me awake when I'm dealing with your boring tummy aches."

"Maybe Oleg can hurt himself real bad and spice things up for you," responded Finn.

"If anyone is going to be needing a doctor, it's going to be you." Oleg was walking back to the center of the room as he delivered his threat back to Finn as he backhanded the air towards him. It brought a few smiles to the bridge.

"Are you worried?" asked Oleg to the Doc.

She stared at him. "Of course. Are you?"

"We Russians are not afraid of clouds," he responded with a smile.

Zeke ignored their good-natured banter and meandered over to the window. He gazed out for a few seconds then turned around to face everyone.

The room grew still.

"I wish I could tell you that everything will be fine. But as you all know, I don't sugarcoat things. The truth is, shortly before the creature arrives, we're going to shut the ship down and ride things out. We are out here alone. There is no rescue. So, it's up to us to keep our cool and tackle whatever problems arise. But we're all well trained, and I have the utmost confidence in each and every one of you."

He looked over at Finn. "Well, most of you."

Finn just shook his head as he smiled. "Thanks."

"But, look on the bright side, we're the ones who are going to have the first recorded encounter with an alien life form in the entire history of Earth. If it is any consolation, we'll be famous."

"If we make it back home," interjected Alina.

"Just think of the book and movie deals. It'll be great. So, remember that when you feel like running and screaming while you're bumping into each other in the dark. You don't want to look bad for posterity."

"Thanks for the pep talk," said Finn. "I'm really encouraged."

"Brought a tear to my eye," said Oleg.

"Glad to help." He took a step towards them. "When it gets here, I'm sure we will not be able to have any meaningful communication with it. We'll be literally flying blind until everything's turned back on. When we get to the Drake system, we can go into orbit and decide what to do. If the creature poses a distraction, then we'll adjust our mission parameters accordingly and get out of here. Personally, I'm expecting it to be curious about us just as we will be about it. Since it's intelligent, it'll be cautious. We will be, too. That's why I expect things to work out fine."

He turned around, faced empty space, and folded his arms. The Drake sun was a large star, easily visible. He spoke into the window, letting its concave form reflect his words back to them. "I'm looking forward to our encounter."

"Captain," said Janice. "There is a change in the status of the object."

Zeke dropped his arms as he turned around.

"It has increased its acceleration again. I do not understand how this is possible, but it has jumped across space and is very close."

"How long before intercept?"

"I cannot extrapolate accurately since its velocity is irregular."

"Give me an estimate."

"Minutes.

"Janice, begin the ship shut down immediately."

"Shutting systems down. I have begun…"

Everything went black.

Chapter 7
Helpless

Along with the blackness came weightlessness. Everyone except for the captain and Oleg had been sitting. So, the two found themselves slowly floating helplessly upwards.

"Everyone okay?" asked Zeke into the darkness.

They all responded in the affirmative.

"What the hell happened?" asked Alina.

"Don't know," said Zeke just as he managed to reach out and touch a wall. He knew where his mag boots and flashlight were, so, using the faint starlight from outside the window as a landmark, he aimed himself towards them and pushed off, but not too fast.

Oleg eventually reached the ceiling and gently launched himself towards the area of his equipment. There was a cabinet anchored to the ship so he could grab on to it if he could see it in the faint light.

Everyone else was still in their chairs, which all had weak magnets that kept them on the floor.

"Janice? System status?" barked Zeke as he floated downward.

Silence.

"Janice? System status."

Silence.

"Janice?"

Silence.

There was just enough light from the outside that they could see the faint silhouette of the captain against the starry background of the window as he floated towards his stash of supplies.

A light came on. It was Finn. He had been sitting the closest to his stuff and was able to retrieve a flashlight first. Harsh, angled shadows raced across the bridge's walls as he waved the light around at everyone. They were trying to retrieve their flashlights as well, and now with his light, they could easily see where to go. Within seconds, more shadows darted around the bridge, intersecting, then separating.

Zeke wasn't too far from his stash. He grabbed the corner of a small table that was secured to a wall and maneuvered himself into position.

"Mag boots, everyone."

One by one, they managed to awkwardly retrieve them. Within a minute, they all had them on.

Zeke scanned the room with his flashlight and then looked out the window. "Everyone okay?"

"Yeah," they said one by one.

"What the hell did that thing do to us?" asked Finn.

"I don't know."

They were looking around, checking with each other.

"Where is it?" Asked Oleg.

"I have no idea," answered Zeke as he peered out the huge window. "I don't see it out there."

"Turn off your flashlights. Maybe we can see it outside."

One by one, they switched them off.

Zeke moved closer to the window, the sound of his mag boot on the floor filled the room. He gazed outside for a bit, slowly looking left and right.

"Nothing."

He flipped his flashlight back on.

"I don't see it. But that doesn't mean it isn't there."

They all turned their lights back on.

"Finn?" said Zeke as he pointed his light at him.

"Yes, sir?"

"Check the engineering systems panel."

"Yes, sir." Finn headed towards a dark corner of the bridge and illumined it with his flashlight. The sound of the mag-boots connecting and disconnecting on the smooth flooring measured his steps.

"Oleg?"

"Sir."

"Check out Janice's status."

"Yes, sir." Oleg hurried to the A.I. Control Panel.

"Alina, the same with navigation."

"Aye, sir."

"Hahn, do a check of the other systems and see if anything's working."

"Yes, sir."

"Doc, I want you to stay here and assist them; however, you can."

"Will do."

"I'm going to take a quick look around the ship. I'll be back in a few minutes. And, I want everyone to have their comms handy. So, put them on."

Once again, they rummaged around their equipment, retrieved their comms, and attached them to their upper chests.

"The ship is dead, so the comms shouldn't work," said Finn.

Zeke touched a fingertip to the unit on his chest, "Finn, test, can you hear me."

"Nothing," responded Finn from across the bridge.

"Great. Well, let's keep them on just in case. I still have to check out the ship."

"Do you think that's a good idea?" asked Hahn? "Maybe we should just stick together for a while in case it shows up."

Zeke considered her words. "I need to find out the status of the ship. So, I'm going to take a quick look around. You all know what to do. Check all the systems and see if anything has power. I'll be back in a few minutes."

"Aye, Cap," responded Hahn and Oleg in unison.

Zeke disappeared through the doorway, pushing the shadows forward as he walked. Though he and everyone else had practiced moving around in zero gravity, it was still an awkward thing to do with mag boots. Instead of propelling himself by leaning forward slightly and pushing off with his feet, he had to lift each foot and consciously put it in place, one before another. It required using a different set of leg muscles, while occasionally bracing himself with his free hand, or whatever object or surface was nearby. It was slow going, but he was making progress quickly enough.

He finally arrived at the doc's office and went inside. Shadows darted across the room as he swung his flashlight back and forth. The only other light came from outside through the small portal. The distant stars were faint but visible. He turned off his flashlight and was instantly engulfed in blackness, but could still see a few stars that were framed within the small window. Though he had done the same thing on the bridge many times, here it was somehow disturbing.

With a flick of his light, he brought back the ghostly black shadows. He then checked the crews' quarters, storage, the shuttle bay, and the galley. The whole excursion took about five minutes. The entire ship was completely black, not a single light anywhere except for the one he was carrying. Whatever the creature did, it left them powerless.

It was time to get back to the bridge.

Along the way, he wondered where the creature was and what it had done to the Cascade. It had to be nearby. Maybe it was observing them from the outside, studying them. Or, he wondered, was it inside the ship? Not knowing poked at his mind. He pushed the thoughts away. Within 2 minutes, he was back on the bridge.

He looked around at the crew, who were all standing together. "What did you find out?"

Finn spoke first. "All the readouts are dead. I've never seen anything like it. It's as if all the energy in the entire ship just evaporated. As far as I can tell, all we are is a big hunk of metal hurtling through space."

"Anyone else?"

"It's the same all around, Cap," said Alina. "Everything's dead."

He illumined the other crew members.

"Yeah, everything's dead except our flashlights," said Oleg. "It doesn't make any sense."

"No, it doesn't," responded Zeke. "Maybe it has something to do with how they're constructed. They are very simple devices. The comms are not. So, maybe that's why."

His explanation was as good as any for now.

"What did you find?" asked Oleg.

"Same as you. It's dead everywhere."

He took a few steps closer to them.

"Finn, I checked engineering, but didn't see anything. That's your department, so I'd like you to go there and check on the quantum drive and the anti-matter containment. Report back here ASAP."

"Aye, Cap."

Finn abruptly turned and exited the bridge marking his departure with that same clunky walking necessitated by the mag boots.

"Oleg, are you sure the ship's batteries are completely dead? Maybe there's some juice coming into them from the Drake sun, by now."

"I checked them while you were gone. They were dead."

"I figured that, but we have a solar panel built onto the hull. There should be something. Even a trickle of energy should show up."

"I can check again." He walked over to the Solar Systems Panel.

"If the batteries are completely and totally drained," said Zeke, "as long as they weren't damaged, we can do an EVA and manually get the main panels extended to get some power."

"I agree," said Oleg. "But, we don't know if the circuitry is working between here and there."

The doc, Alina, and Hahn were staring at him.

"But," he said reassuringly, "I'm sure the panels can bring in power once we get them extended."

Zeke turned around once more and looked out the huge bridge window. It was a bad situation, and he was responsible for solving it.

"Any questions?" asked Zeke as he turned back around.

"No," said the doc. "But right now, we are sitting blind and helpless, heading towards the Drake sun at 70,000 kilometers per hour."

Zeke nodded slowly. "Yeah, not good. But we're far enough away that we don't have to worry about it for a few weeks."

He looked out the window. They *were* moving incredibly fast, but the staggering distances of space masked their speed.

The doc walked over to him, casting increasingly large shadows behind him as she approached.

Hahn asked. "Doc? How long do you think we have left of breathable air?"

"Well, it's a big ship, and there are only six of us. But off the top of my head, I'd say we have about a couple of weeks of breathable air. Then we can use auxiliary supplies. There are a ton of compressed O_2 tanks in storage. All we'd have to do is place them throughout the ship and turn on the valves. That would help until we are CO_2 saturated. But we should be good for a long time."

"Excellent."

"What about the cold?" asked Alina while looking at Zeke. "How long before the ship starts to freeze?

"The ship is very well insulated. So, we're good for now for several days.

"Got any estimate on how long before we're popsicles?" asked Hahn.

"Probably a couple weeks," responded Zeke. "But we can bundle up. So, for now, we're okay, and we've got at least that long to figure things out before it gets really bad."

He ran his free hand through his hair. "I wonder what the hell that cloud did to us."

"Excuse me, Cap." It was Oleg. He had walked over to them. "Yeah?"

"Still nothing from the solar panel batteries. It could be that it'll just take longer to register since we're pretty far away from the Drake System."

"Alright, what about the main ship's batteries? Can you go to auxiliary and check on them?"

"Aye, Cap." With that, Oleg slogged out of the bridge, leaving the sound of fading mag boots in his wake.

Finn had made his way to engineering, and like everything else in the ship, it was dead and black. He checked several subsystems and uselessly flipped several main circuit switches. Then, unlike the captain, he went to the quantum drive core and slid back a small door and looked in. Nothing but darkness. He jerked his neck back slightly on his shoulders and narrowed his eyes under his frown.

"That can't be," he said aloud. "We should be dead."

He lowered his flashlight and considered the enigma. A small circle of light partially lit up his pants, boots, and the floor. He then turned it off so he could peer in through the safety glass one more time in order to see the faintest of light. He gave his eyes some time to adjust. Still nothing.

"What the hell happened?"

He turned away from the glass and looked around and absorbed the empty and silent black.

He exhaled sharply before saying, "That's impossible."

With that, he flipped his flashlight on and headed back towards the bridge. As he left, he didn't notice that there was a slight shift in the light pattern of one of the shadows.

It moved into the hallway behind him and hovered in place as he disappeared.

The sound of Finn's footsteps accompanied the shadows darting ahead of him as he entered the Bridge.

They all were waiting.

He shook his head. "Dead. Absolutely dead." He took a few steps closer and exhaled sharply. "Everything is dead, even the quantum drive's core is dead."

"What?" exclaimed Zeke. "That's not possible."

"That's what I thought. It has no energy at all, and that's supposed to be impossible. You can't drain the core without breaking its subspace link. It derives its energy from piggybacking in subspace with antimatter. To break that link takes special equipment and a lot of expertise, so you don't blow yourself into oblivion. That is what makes no sense. The antimatter should have obliterated us if the core lost its energy, and the magnetic fields failed. But we're still here, and the core is dead. I can only surmise that the antimatter is gone, too. But I don't see how that's possible."

He paused and shook his head as he said in a different, more somber tone as he aimed his flashlight towards Zeke. "I have no idea what that creature did to us. But we're screwed. There is no way to get back home."

His description of the impossible brought a dreadful silence onto the bridge. Without the quantum drive, there was no way to create a subspace tunnel, which meant that even if they could survive out here, it would take decades to get back to Earth using their limited standard propulsion. And, without Janice's precise navigation calculations, they wouldn't know where to go. They were stranded.

Zeke asked in a slightly strained voice. "Is the whole core assembly missing?"

"No. Heck, I don't know. I couldn't see anything. And, even if I wanted to open it up to check, I couldn't do it without the tools in the cargo bay. It'd take hours. That thing is built so that no one can get into it easily and mess with it. But, there was no light in the viewing window, so I…" he stammered for words. "…I, I can only conclude that it's all just drained." He shook his head slightly as he said, "I just don't get it."

Finn's comments were interrupted by the approaching sound of footsteps. It was Oleg. They looked into the hallway and watched more strands of light slip into the bridge.

"Well?" asked Zeke.

"Auxiliary shows that the batteries are dead. But there's good news if you want to call it that. There's a trickle of electricity coming in from the reserve hull solar panel. It's next to nothing. But it's there."

"Why didn't you see it earlier?" asked Zeke.

"I think it just took more time to register in the low interstellar light, and since everything is completely dead, it had to build up enough juice to begin to register. We're pretty far away from the Drake sun."

"Well, we'll do better once get the main panels deployed," said Zeke.

"Yeah. They're incredibly efficient, and they should supply enough power to get the ship going again, even out here."

"Good. That's what we'll do."

Oleg looked around the room at the dejected crew. "What?"

Zeke rubbed his temple with his fingertips. "The quantum drive is completely dead."

Oleg stood still for a few seconds.

"Wait. That can't happen. Why aren't we dead from the antimatter explosion? The drive can't just lose all its energy. Isn't it supposed to last centuries?"

"Yeah, it is," said Finn. "But, I just got back from engineering. The drive is toast. No energy at all."

"Then that means the anti-matter has to be gone, too. That thing took our antimatter? That's... supposed to be impossible." Oleg scoffed out a disgruntled sigh and asked in a sharp tone. "What did it do? Eat it?" Then, after a few seconds, "This is bad."

"I heard that!" replied Finn.

Zeke, always the captain, jumped in. "All is not lost. We can do an EV and manually deploy the solar panels and get power to the ship."

"Wait a minute," interrupted Alina. "Why aren't we dead? I mean, the energy is all gone from the ship. We need energy to breathe and move. Why isn't the energy in our bodies gone, too?"

"I don't know," responded Zeke.

He turned to Finn. "I want you and Oleg to go outside the ship and deploy the solar panels by hand. There should be plenty of air in the suit tanks."

"Sure," said Oleg as he looked over at Finn.

"I love being volunteered," said Finn. "And, it doesn't bother me at all that there is a gigantic energy eating alien cloud out there. It'll be fine."

Zeke took a single step toward them all. "I know this is bad. But, without the solar panels, we'll die. So, let's do what we've been trained to do and solve one problem at a time."

"You got it," responded Oleg in a confident tone. "Look at the bright side. Maybe consuming all our energy killed it."

Zeke smiled back, but only briefly. "Great, that's a positive note. We killed the first alien that humanity has ever encountered. There go the movie deals."

He took a breath and lowered his flashlight to their feet.

"We all knew there would be risks when we signed up for this mission. Space is dangerous. But let's make sure that it doesn't kill us. So, first thing's first. It appears that the solar panels will work. Physically, everything seems okay, but we won't know for sure till we get power restored. Then we can get life-support and gravity back online. After that, we will get Janice working and go into a parking orbit around Drakus and stay alive until someone rescues us. So, all is not lost. Okay?"

No one said anything.

"Okay?"

They responded with half-hearted and disjoined affirmations.

"All right, good. Now, it appears that all of the systems that are connected directly to the ship have been drained of energy. But our flashlights, and our bodies, which are independent of the ship, still work. I suspect that when Finn and Oleg get to their EV suits, they'll be drained of energy as well because they are attached via their umbilicals. But like I said, they have plenty in the air tanks. So, we've got a workable plan."

He took a deep breath before continuing, but Alina interrupted him.

"And what about the creature?" She looked over at Finn and Oleg, then back to Zeke.

"We don't know where it is, and maybe it's waiting to sap our energy once we're going again."

Zeke acknowledged her comment with a slow wave of his hand. "One problem at a time. For now, we can only worry about what can take care of. We're going to get the ship running. But, since we don't know what the cloud thing is, or what happened to it, all we can do is work the problems we have right in front of us."

He took one noisy step forward and looked at Finn and Oleg. "Alright, you two, you know what to do."

"Aye, sir," said Oleg.

"But keep your eyes peeled. We don't know where the thing is and, well, you'll be exposed out there."

With that, Oleg walked over to Finn and hit him on the shoulder. "Ready?"

Finn flexed his jaw muscles. "No."

"Good."

Both of them headed off the bridge, their flashlights carving a visual path into the dark hallway.

"Anyone have any other ideas?" asked Zeke.

They looked around at each other.

"Nothing," said Hahn. "With everything being dead, we've got nothing to do until the systems are back up.

"Well then," he said. "We'll have to wait for them to get the panels deployed. So, that's it for now."

"I've got another flashlight in my quarters," said Alina. "I want to get it, just in case."

Zeke considered her comment for a moment. "I really don't think it's necessary. These flashlights are rated for months. And besides, we've got plenty in storage."

"Yeah, I know. But I also have to use the little girl's room."

"Oh yes, of course," he said. "That'll be fine. Hahn, you go with her."

"No," interrupted Alina. "I'd rather go by myself. I just need a little break."

Zeke weighed her request before nodding.

Finn and Oleg reached the EV room in no time. The first thing they did was to check the control panel on one of the suit's forearms. Nothing. The batteries in the supply cabinet were dead, too.

"Okay," said Oleg. "We'll just have to do this low-tech." He went to the back of EV suit and opened a flap. There was a valve with a small red knob. He turned it to the first notch and listened. A gentle hissing let him know the suit would have O2.

"Good, we've got air."

Finn did the same thing to his suit.

"How much air have you got?" asked Finn.

Oleg checked his readout valve's pressure. "Looks like enough for about six hours. You?"

"The same."

They continued to talk as they put on their suits.

"We're going to have to communicate with hand signals," said Finn.

"Yeah, no problem. We'll work it out."

"You worried?"

"Yeah. You?"

"Nerves of steel."

Oleg smiled.

They finished getting into their suits and then checked each other's equipment. Before they put on their helmets, they paused.

"You a praying man?" asked Finn.

"Yeah, are you?"

"No. But, since you are, can you offer one up for us?"

"In Russian or English?"

"I guess Russian will be fine, just do it after you put on your helmet."

"Posle tebya"

Finn raised his eyebrows as he looked at Oleg.

"After you."

"Thanks." Finn smiled and put on his helmet and snapped it in place. Oleg did the same. They lumbered over to the panel next to the inner door of the airlock, and, out of habit, Finn pressed it. Of course, nothing happened.

Oleg opened a panel and pulled out a hand crank. He shut it and located another door. He pressed it, and it popped open. Inside were two straps with carabineers. He latched one to each side of his suit and then into two hooks embedded in the wall. This would stabilize him in zero gravity and allow him to apply sufficient counterforce to open the door when he used the hand crank. After about two turns, the inner airlock door began to open. After another 20 turns, it was open enough for them to pass through. Procedure demanded that they leave the hand crank inside the ship. There was another in the airlock. So, Oleg unhooked himself and left the straps there. Approached the airlock compartment, opened up another panel, and retried identical carabiners, straps, and a hand crank. He strapped himself in and found the corresponding hole in which to place the hand crank.

He turned it vigorously, and the inner door began to close. After another 20 turns, they were sealed in. Then he unhooked the straps from the wall and walked over to the external door and found the corresponding hooks. He strapped himself into place and inserted the handle into the appropriate slot.

He clumsily turned to Finn and gave a thumbs up.

Finn returned the gesture.

Oleg began the slow process of opening the outer door. He was met with stiff resistance. But he turned harder until the handle started to move. With a quarter-turn more, it opened just a crack. Instantly there was the sound of rushing air, forcing itself into empty space. At first, it was loud, and they could feel the air move around their suits. But within seconds, it was all quiet. Oleg then cranked some more until the door to oblivion was fully open.

Alina had made her way to her compartment. After using the restroom, which was awkward in zero gravity, she started rummaging through some drawers looking for her other flashlight. After finding nothing, she glanced around the room. "Where the hell is it?" She tapped her flashlight into the palm of her hand and frowned. "Crap!"

The thought of reclining on a beach at a resort popped into her mind. It was a favorite memory to which occasionally retreated to help her relax and focus. She scoffed at its out-of-place appearance and sent it away. She walked over to her bed. Above it was a one-meter diameter window. With one boot locked on the floor, she lifted her other onto the bed. Then she leveraged the bed and broke free of the floor. She pulled herself close to the glass. The cold darkness outside was vast and unforgiving. And, to make things worse, it was occupied by something alien and powerful.

She lowered her light to the mound of sheets, muffling its brightness.

"Where are you?" she asked as she peered into the void.

A trickle of fear ran down her spine. She raised the light, twisted, and looked around the room cautiously. But, there was nothing. *Of course not*, she thought. *It's too big to be in here. It's outside.* She exhaled sharply and braced herself as turned back to the portal, but this time she inched a little closer to the glass. Was it out there?

She took a short breath before flipping off her light. Instant blackness enveloped her. She braced herself against the unexpected disorientation and focused on the stars outside to help give her a sense of location and balance.

She moved a little closer and touched her nose to the cold glass.

She could not see much of the ship, but she looked towards the stern. Then she turned her head and looked down the other side.

There was nothing.

Ahead was the Drake sun, but it wasn't visible from her window.

She clicked on the light, pushed herself away, and floated gently towards the floor until her boots clicked.

"Alright, Alina. Time to focus. Find that flashlight."

She put her head in both hands and ran her fingers through her hair as she exhaled. Then she turned towards the closet near the entrance.

"It's gotta be in there."

Outside the window was a barely discernable waft of dull light about a meter high and half a meter wide.

It passed through the walls as if they weren't there and followed her.

Finn and Oleg were making their way around the outside of the ship toward the Solar Panel Bay. It would be a slow, laborious task to extend them, but they could get it done with good old-fashioned muscle. There wasn't any danger of them drifting off in space as long as they kept their tethers attached. They had plenty of air, and if they needed, they could head back into the ship to get more. The hull had long railings along which their tethers could slide. Periodically they would move them beyond the next bracket, and they would have several more meters of free movement. This allowed them easy access to the entire outer hull of the ship.

Their visors were not powered, so they had to deal with the default setting, which was a little too dark. But they could see well enough. They moved slowly. There was no room for error in space.

Zeke was next to the bridge window, peering outward. He had positioned himself to its most far right side and was looking back towards the solar array area.

"Looking for Finn and Oleg?" asked Hahn.

"Yeah," he said. "But I don't see them. I guess they aren't out there yet, if at all."

Zeke kept watching.

He scanned the starscape for the cloud.

"I wonder where it is," he said to Hahn.

"I have no idea."

"Me either, and that worries me."

Alina was slowly rummaging through her closet.

The thing moved closer.

Then it dawned on her where the flashlight was, the drawer next to the bed. She turned around and pointed the light ahead of her. Wait. Did she see something? It was as though the one side of the bathroom door seemed slightly out of proportion. She paused a moment and looked at it carefully.

Nothing. It was normal.

"I'm starting to see things," she said aloud. "Great, and now I'm talking to myself, too."

She lowered the flashlight towards the floor and shook her head once as she took a deep breath. "Get it together, girl."

But, something didn't feel right. She looked around the room one more time and pointed the flashlight ahead of her as she scanned. There it was again. She stopped.

Yes, she saw it. There was a slight distortion of some sort. The bathroom door was definitely warped. Maybe it was the flashlight making things look wrong. Or, perhaps the ship has been damaged.

She pointed it in a different direction but kept her eye on the door. It seemed okay. She peered at the portal, her bed, the floor, then back to the bathroom. It all seemed normal.

"Forget this!" she said. "I'm outta here." With that, she turned and headed back to the bridge.

Chapter 8
First Casualty

Alina walked right into it.

Her flashlight went dark at the same instant, an intense nausea snarled her organs into a knot. She curled over and grabbed her stomach as she moaned. Then a stronger wave of sickness hit her. She cupped her hand over her mouth and forced herself to stand up and head to the bathroom. She took a single step and then...nothing.

She couldn't move.

Why not?

She tried to break free, but it was useless. She tried again. Nothing.

She stared into the complete, empty blackness, as she tried to figure out what was happening.

Was it paralysis?

Then she let her mind go to the impossible. *Is it the creature?*

She tried to inhale, but her chest would not move. She tried again.

No! She said to herself.

She tried again, but no breath came to relieve the creeping discomfort that had already begun to ache in her chest.

I'm suffocating! She thought to herself.

Again she tried to gasp for air, but could not.

She tried to scream, but there was only the still, black silence.

Then for no reason, memories suddenly began to flood her mind. They were of the earth, oceans, buildings, water, her childhood, back at home, her family, and more. They cascaded rapidly, uncontrollably.

It was too much for her. She recoiled.

Then they stopped.

She tried for another breath to quench the growing ache of suffocation, but it brought no relief.

What was happening? Why couldn't she move? Why couldn't she breathe?

The images started again. They were of the Cascade and the crew. Then she was eating, bathing, asleep. They continued.

Then she felt a woozy disorientation along with the increased feeling of suffocation.

She tried again to gasp for the unreachable air but could not find it.

There was only swirling vertigo. No up. No down. No sensation. Just black emptiness.

She felt her mind slipping, reeling from the disparate assault. Her body seemed detached, and the suffocation lessened as the loss of consciousness approached.

A bright light flashed into her eyes, but from inside of her mind, not from the outside. It forced her awake.

Then blackness again.

She struggled against the enraging fear and paralysis, against whatever it was that had captured her, and left her choking for air.

Then came pain. Great pain. Every nerve lit on fire.

She screamed in her mind, but it died in her throat.

She tried to cry. But she was met only with petrifying, suffocating immobility as thousands of images flooding across her mind in an uncontrolled overwhelming torrent.

It was hell.

The paralysis continued to imprison her. She was not her own. Her very soul was being raped by the terror of complete, helpless, agony.

Then, unexpectedly, a greater wave of pain pulsed into another level of searing fire. It was in her, moving, crawling, wreaking havoc as it passed through her organs, grating across every muscle, scraping through her mind, and ripping it open.

Then, unexpectedly, it all stopped.

She drifted near shocked, semi-consciousness until finally, her mind began to clear.

After a few seconds, she managed a gasping breath…and screamed.

Zeke was still looking out the window. Hahn was next to him. They watched the stars in the silence of a ghost ship.

"We're a bullet heading towards the Drake sun," she said.

"Don't worry. We'll figure…"

A distant sound interrupted them. It was muffled, but it was enough to stop Zeke in mid-sentence. Hahn was already staring out into the hallway.

"Did you hear that?" she asked.

"Yes. What was it?"

"It sounded like a scream," said the doc from closer to the door.

"Alina!" He bolted as fast as the mag boots would allow and headed down the hallway towards her quarters. The doc and Hahn were right behind him, clumsily lumbering in an awkward hurry.

It only took less than a minute to reach her quarters, but what they saw made no sense. She was suspended a few centimeters off the floor, hovering, motionless, spine arched backward with her face pointing towards the ceiling. In her hand was her dead flashlight.

Zeke got closer, and all of them shined their lights on her. She was engulfed in a scintillating distortion of space that looked like liquid glass.

"What the hell!" said Zeke.

"Her face!" exclaimed the doc.

Alina's eyes were wide open, staring upward, mouth agape. But, she was silent, motionless, floating inside this undulating, glass-like cocoon.

Hahn moved closer.

Zeke started to reach towards Alina.

"No, don't get too close," said the doc.

They all three moved around her, watching, hearing nothing, but seeing the slow rippling of space in which she floated.

"What is it?" asked Hahn.

No one knew.

"She's in pain," said the doc. "Look at her face."

It was contorted, frozen in a grimace of agony.

"We have to stop it!" she said as she stepped towards Alina and stuck her flashlight into the distortion. Instantly her flashlight went black, and it disappeared. Alina made no sound as her body relaxed in the room's weightlessness. Her mag boots slowly drew her to the floor and clanked with a soft connection causing her body to jerk limply.

The Doc grabbed her, and Alina's limp head bobbed forward.

Zeke looked at the doc then back to Alina. "Doc?"

She touched Alina's neck but found no pulse. "Give me your flashlight," she demanded.

He gave it up quickly.

The doc moved an eyelid back and checked her pupil. Then the other. Once again to the neck and then the wrist as she searched for a pulse. But, after a few seconds, she relaxed her shoulders. The doc looked at Zeke. "She's dead."

Finn and Oleg had finally reached the solar panel door. It read Solar Array Manual Deployment. They positioned themselves on opposite sides. Oleg pulled out two straps from his waistband with which he secured himself to the hull next to the door. Towards the bottom of the panel was a circle with the words "PRESS HERE." Oleg pressed, and it popped open. They both maneuvered themselves and took turns looking in to check the readout. It was showing a faint charge. Finn gave a thumbs-up as he looked at Oleg.

The Cascade had a solar panel embedded onto the surface of its hull. It was nothing more than a safeguard, a precautionary hold-over from earlier space travel. The engineers insisted on it, as well as the more extensive array that rested inside a large compartment. With the quantum drive, they weren't necessary. But, the policy of backup and redundancy had prevailed.

Once deployed, they could supply the ship with enough energy for most systems as well enough left over to charge the batteries.

The mass of the array was relatively small. It was the surface area of the panels that was important, and they were composed of a vast, foldable material. Therefore, they did not expect any difficulty hand-cranking the array out from the ship's hull and into space, since the gear ratio would make it possible, but not easy.

Oleg was first. He pushed on the handle forcing his body to move against the restraints. Once the leverage was ensured, he slowly began to crank.

The solar array design was simple. It consisted of a single, telescoping centerpiece that moved out from the ship's hull like an old-style mast with sails. As it emerged, it would pull expandable sheeting material away from the panel compartment that would then move into place along ribs that would also extend into position. It was a simple design, very efficient, and surprisingly large. The first section was designed to be deployable by human strength. Then, as the solar energy was generated, the whole assembly would reach a point where they would auto-deploy the rest of the way. Their final position would extent out a hundred meters.

In the bulky suits, movement wasn't easy, especially when using both arms to turn the crank. Not only did they have to fight the friction of the cranking, but they also had to fight their suits' rigidity while positioning themselves against the hull to which they were secured with straps. So, they fatigued quickly. Then there was the cold. Without power, the suit heaters did not work. But they were so well designed that they could be out there for a couple of hours before needing to return to the ship to warm up. Oleg and Finn would take turns every three or four minutes in order to catch their breath. They kept doing this back-and-forth until finally, after about 15 minutes, the initial section was about 10% deployed, and two panels, one on each side, were exposed.

Finn motioned that he wanted to look at the readout. Oleg, who was on the crank, stopped momentarily. It read 287 Watts at 7 amps. It wasn't much, but it was a good sign. He then adjusted his angle to get a look at the battery gauge. The primary backup battery showed .07%. He then motioned to Oleg to take a look. He did and returned a thumbs up. He unhooked the two straps securing him to the hull, which signaled it was Finn's turn. They had done this so many times by now that he just automatically moved into place, strapped himself in, and began cranking. They were on a regular routine.

About 20 meters away, there was a distortion in the starlight. Neither one of them saw it. But if they had been looking in the right direction, they might have noticed that a few stars were scintillating. And, if they had continued to watch, they might have noticed that their number was increasing.

By now, Zeke, Hahn, and the doc were carrying Alina's body to medical. The gravityless environment gave the corpse a lifelike appearance as they maneuvered it vertically down the hallway. Zeke was gently guiding it through the halls, trying to overcome its momentum and prevent it from bumping into walls. He lumbered forward, his mag boots noisily limiting his agility.

Leaving her in her quarters was pointless. Besides, the doc would perform an autopsy when they got the ship's systems back online. That is *if* they came back online. Maybe an autopsy might give them some clues as to what happened to her.

Hahn was leading the way. She kept her flashlight pointed forward. Doc was in the rear and had Zeke's light, her's being dead.

They kept moving, as they chased away the agitated fragments of darkness. Finally, Hahn said the obvious. "It's inside the ship."

Chapter 9
Rescue

Zeke and Hahn aimed their flashlights at the doc as she secured Alina's body to the cold metal table. They said nothing. Their crewmate was dead, and it was obvious that her death had not been an easy one. After the last strap had been tightened, the doc turned to Zeke and looked at him in silence. The awkward shadows caused by their flashlights could not hide her mournful expression.

"How soon can you perform an autopsy?" He asked.

She lumbered over to a drawer under some cabinets and pulled one open. Zeke pointed his light at it. Inside was a small examining flashlight which she retrieved. It flicked on. "After power is restored, not before."

Zeke exhaled and stared once again at Alina's face. The remnants of her painful ordeal were still clearly etched upon it.

"It must have been horrible," said Hahn.

"Yeah," said the doc gently as she returned to the table. "Who knows what it did to her. But it was bad."

The doc stroked Alina's hair gently.

Zeke watched as the doc expressed her mournful care.

The entire crew was Zeke's responsibility. Could he have done anything differently? Why did he let her go alone? He squeezed his flashlight and tightened the muscles in his jaw.

"This is my fault. I should've known better."

"You couldn't have known," responded Hahn as she took a step closer to him. The sound of her mag boots somehow seemed intrusive. "It was huge. No one thought it could shrink and get inside the ship. Not even Janice figured it out."

"I should've been more cautious. I'm the captain. Her death is on me."

"Hahn is right," said the doc. "It was massive outside the ship. You couldn't have known."

Zeke clenched his flashlight and lowered his head slightly as he stared at Alina's body. "It's my job to know. It's my job."

The doc and Hahn exchanged a look.

"Maybe we should get back to the bridge," said Hahn. "At least from there, we can see how they're doing with the panels."

Zeke kept staring at Alina. "The pain she experienced must've been incredible." He exhaled sharply as he shook his head again. "I should never have let her go alone." He drove his fingernails into the palm of his fist.

"Sir?"

He slowly turned to Hahn.

Her sympathetic look was a small comfort. "The bridge."

He turned back to Alina and waited a bit before speaking. "Yeah, you're right. We need to get back there."

He straightened up. "But I don't want anyone to be alone again. That's an order. Doc, wrap it up here as fast as you can. And, please, cover her face."

The doc's only acknowledgment was walking over to another drawer and pulling out a cloth. She then returned to Alina's body, laid it on her face, and tucked the edges under her head. In the shadowy room, the makeshift death shroud was an ominous reminder of the seriousness of their situation.

The doc looked at Zeke with a quiet, almost neutral expression, as he shined her small light on him. The self-punishing regret on his face was sharpened by its narrow beam.

"Let's go," he said.

The distortion hovered behind them about three meters away from Finn and Oleg. They were so engrossed in their work that they didn't notice anything. But, of course, they couldn't since their helmets permitted only a forward view.

Oleg checked the battery. It was at .09%.

Finn was on the handle. They were working in shorter intervals because they were getting exhausted quicker, but they were getting it done. He paused and began to unhook the strap as he looked at Oleg.

It was a twinkle of a star behind Oleg that caught Finn's attention. Then another. Was it something on his visor? He turned his head slightly to get a different angle. Yes, there it was again. It was the same star, but now it was several more. He examined them. It didn't make any sense.

The thought of the cloud entered his mind. He looked for it but saw nothing.

Maybe his heavy breathing had released too much moisture onto the inside of the visor. No, if that were the case, stars would blur where he looked. Besides, the pressure release valve was venting air into space. So, his moisture level shouldn't be a concern. He kept staring.

Maybe something is venting from the ship, he thought.

Oleg was looking back at him from behind his black, reflective visor. Finn tilted to his right to get a better look behind Oleg. This caused Oleg to begin a slow, laborious turn, to look behind him as well. He was restricted by the tether cable, which had secured him to the hull.

Once on the bridge, Zeke, the doc, and Hahn immediately headed to the window. They looked towards the right side of the ship along the cargo bay arm. It was clear that the panels had been partially deployed.

"There they are," said Hahn. She pointed in their direction. "They are just beyond the auxiliary thrust vent."

"Good," said Zeke. "It's working." He sighed and thumped his fist on the glass. "It's about time we had some good news."

"Are you seeing this?" Said the doc. "Take a look." She was staring out the window.

Both Zeke and Hahn looked. One of the two men was being jolted slightly by the length of the tether that jerked him back towards the hull. The other was moving towards him.

They watched.

"Oh no," said Hahn.

"Turn off your flashlights," ordered Zeke.

In the dark, they could see the awkward movements of one of them next to the other. Only one was moving. The other was drifting. Clearly, something was wrong.

Finn had seen the twinkling stars behind Oleg but didn't know what to make of it. It didn't match the description of the cloud, which, according to Janice, was huge and slightly luminous. Then, unexpectedly, something moved onto Oleg. He flinched against the straps, causing himself to bounce off the hull, only to be jerked at the end of the short tether. Finn was confused by Oleg's strange movement as well as the scintillating distortion that enveloped him. At first, he thought again about condensation in his visor, but he quickly dismissed that idea when he saw Oleg's stiff form still surrounded by the distortion.

"Oleg! Oleg!" said Finn into his powerless suit. Instinctively, he moved to get closer. That's when he noticed that Oleg appeared to be behind warped glass. It made no sense. But it was clear he was in trouble, so Finn reached for him to grab him by the arm. Instantly, he felt a searing pain and snapped his hand back.

The distortion disappeared.

Oleg remained stiff.

After the intense pain subsided enough for him to act, Finn carefully stretched out his arm, then withdrew it, testing for pain. There was none. The enveloping scintillation was gone, so he didn't think there was any more danger in grabbing Oleg again. He did and shook him. Oleg was unresponsive. He shook Oleg again, but there was still no sign of life inside.

"Oleg! Oleg!" Repeated Finn as he shook him.

Nothing.

Finn unfastened Oleg's harness from the hull and attached it to his own waist belt. He then transferred his tether to the rail and began his hurried return back to the airlock, pulling himself along, feeling the jerk of Oleg's body behind him, enduring its bumping into him as he pulled himself awkwardly along.

Zeke, the doc, and Hahn all moved as fast as their mag boots would allow. They were pushing off the walls as they rushed down the hallway to the airlock.

In the weightlessness of space, Finn did not have to worry about Oleg's weight, only his mass. It was awkward to control. Finn would move, and the tether would jerk Oleg towards him, and they'd collide. Then after a couple of seconds, he would reach hand over hand along the rails as he continued to move. The ungraceful jerking and colliding of their spacesuits slowed Finn down considerably. But he was getting the hang of moving more smoothly.

"Come on, buddy! Hang in there!"

Finn hurried, but he had to be smart. It was panicking in situations that killed. So, he focused on one thing, moving steadily to the airlock, hand over hand, trusting that the tether that tied Oleg to him would hold.

"Focus," he said. "Hand over hand. Don't make any mistakes."

It took a few minutes to traverse the length of the hull and get to the airlock. Once there, he slowed down and grabbed Oleg's suit with one free hand steadying him, while he held onto the rail with the other. He carefully detached his tether from the hull and slowly moved himself and Oleg inside the airlock compartment.

Zeke, the doc, and Hahn were jockeying for space to see through the airlock window.

After they were both in the airlock, he looked up and could see them all. He gave a quick wave of acknowledgment and put his hands together and rotated it in a circle, then pointed to the wall next to them.

Zeke had already found the hand crank and braced himself with the straps so that he could crank the inner door open after the outer door was closed. He gave a thumbs up. Finn transferred Oleg's strap to an eyelet, then secured himself in position so he could close the external door. It took him about two minutes, but after it was sealed, he gave the thumbs-up sign.

Zeke began cranking hard, and the air started rushing in. In half a minute, the pressure equalized, and the door finally was open enough for them to all move in.

Finn took off his helmet. By then, Zeke, Hahn, and the doc were removing Oleg's.

"That thing got him!" exclaimed Finn. "It had to be it."

The doc nudged herself between them and put her hand on his jugular. Finn gave way.

"He's got a pulse. It's weak and slow, but he has one. Let's get him out of the suit and into medical."

"Where's Alina?" asked Finn.

Zeke looked right at him. "I'll explain everything later, but for now, let's get Oleg to medical."

The doc and Hahn worked frantically as they twisted the gloves off of Oleg's suit and released the waistband lock. They pulled the top half over his head and then pulled down the bottom half from his legs.

"Okay, where's Alina?" asked Finn again. "Seriously, what's going on?"

Zeke stared right at him. "She's dead. We found her in her quarters. We're not sure what happened."

Finn froze in place and glared back at him with wide eyes. "What? Dead? What do you mean? What happened?"

The doc offered a quick explanation. "It looks like the thing got to her about twenty minutes ago."

Finn took a few seconds to process her words. "What the hell?" He looked at Oleg.

"Medical. Let's get him to medical," ordered the doc.

She and Hahn grabbed Oleg under each arm and easily managed to move him into the hallway.

"I'll help Finn out of his suit," said Zeke. "We'll meet you two there."

"Roger," said Hahn as they hurriedly and clumsily floated Oleg along between them.

"What's going on?" Asked Finn.

"We don't know what happened, but that thing, it had to be that cloud. It was in her room. We heard her scream. We got to her, and she was in the middle of this kind of distortion, this weird clear wave of…of… crap, I don't know how to describe it."

"I saw it," said Finn. "It was all around Oleg. I saw it. It did the same thing to him."

Zeke stopped and looked at him. "What?"

"Yeah, like I said. It was around Oleg. It looked like he was behind wavy glass."

Zeke received Finn's gloves and stowed them in the suit rack. "That's the same thing we saw in Alina's quarters. She was by herself, looking for another flashlight. We heard her scream, and when we got there, we saw it. It was all over her. She wasn't moving at all. It was like she was frozen. We could see her face. She must have been in incredible pain. Then the doc stuck her flashlight into it, into the cloud, or whatever the hell it was, and it disappeared. That was it. She was dead."

While Zeke was relating the events, Finn continued to get out of the suit, stopping momentarily here and there to process Zeke's words.

"It was the same with Oleg. But…" He stopped and stared at Zeke. "But Oleg's not dead."

"Yeah," said Zeke as he continued to help Finn. "I don't have any idea why."

Finally, after a few more seconds, Finn was free of the EV suit. He put on his mag boots, and then, with flashlights in hand, they were on their way to medical clomping along.

Finn was still trying to shake off the shock of Alina's death. "Tell me again what happened."

Zeke just turned to look at him as they continued their plodding journey down the hallway. He still blamed himself.

"She was alone in her quarters. It got her. It was encasing her in something. The doc put her flashlight into it, and it all stopped. Alina was dead. That's all we know."

"But if it got them both, why is he alive and Alina is not?" asked Finn.

"I know. It doesn't make sense. How long was he being attacked?"

"Not very long, maybe 20 or 30 seconds. I reached for his arm and, and I have never felt so much pain in my life. It was in my hand up to my elbow. It was incredible. I yanked my arm back, and the pain stopped. That's when it disappeared."

"Yeah, same thing when the doc put her flashlight into it when it was attacking Alina. It just disappeared. But, the doc didn't feel anything. I guess it had to be her flashlight that made it stop. And the flashlight went dead."

They were moving as quickly as they could toward medical.

"What's the status on the panels?" asked Zeke.

"The starter panels aren't deployed all the way. I'll have to go back out there later and finish."

"Maybe not. From what I saw, there might be enough of the panels exposed to feed the batteries enough to get them to automatically deploy the rest of the way when enough charge is built up."

They both stomped around a corner heading towards medical.

"Once the panels are deployed, then we have to work on getting the ship back to normal - if there is a normal to get back to."

"Normal?" Responded Finn. "Nothing is normal anymore. It's all chaos. Fubar!"

With that, they just kept walking, saying nothing. The sound of their banging mag boots was the only thing that gave away their approaching presence, except, of course, for the jolting shadows caused by their flashlights.

Chapter 10
Medical

By the time Zeke and Finn reached medical, the doc and Hahn had Oleg on the table. It was the same one on which Alina's body had been lying. They had placed her body in a body bag and moved it to the floor next to a wall. It was held in place with a couple small magnet.

"How is he?" asked Zeke as he looked over at the bag.

"I don't know. Without my instruments, an accurate diagnosis is impossible. His heartbeat and breathing are both steady but slow. His pupils dilate when exposed to light. His reflexes are still intact. So, that's good. Other than that, I can't tell you much."

"Is he in shock?" asked Finn.

"It's more than shock, maybe a coma, but I don't know for sure." She took half a breath and forced it out through her nose. Zeke shined his light on Oleg.

"I've never heard of anyone retaining an expression of pain while in a coma," said Zeke.

"Me either," replied the doc. "That is one of the things that is confusing. I, I just don't know what to tell you right now."

The doc took her flashlight and ran it up and down Oleg's body, but stopped at his chest and watched his breathing. She put her fingers on his neck again and checked his pulse. Then she looked at his pupils once more.

"Oleg?" she said gently. "What happened to you?" She grabbed him by the shoulders and shook him and waited for a reaction.

Nothing.

Zeke grabbed Oleg's hand firmly with both of his. "Hold on, man. Stay with us."

After a moment, he gently lowered it onto the table and turned to Hahn, the doc, and Finn. "All right, so we don't know what this creature is. But it's obviously dangerous. I want you to stay in groups of two, minimum. Doc, I want you and Hahn to stay here in medical and keep an eye on Oleg. Finn, you and I can go to the bridge. We should be able to see some power coming through from the panels by now. After they deploy, we should be able to get everything back online. Then, we will get Janice going too."

The doc pointed her flashlight at Zeke's chest so as not to blind him. It turned his countenance into a Frankensteinian appearance. "The sooner, the better," she said.

Hahn was rubbing her forehead with the tips of her fingers while breathing in shallow, quick breaths. Her eyes were closed.

"You okay?" asked the doc.

"Yes. It's just a lot to take in." She exhaled and straightened up. "I'm fine. Tired, but fine."

The doc looked over at Finn. He was stoic and hid his emotions behind an expressionless stare.

"No problem here, Doc. Just take care of him."

"You're beat, too."

"Yeah, but I'm fine."

The doc could see the fatigue in his eyes. It was, of course, understandable. "We're all tired." She turned her flashlight back to Oleg and furrowed her brow as she considered her patient.

Zeke continued. "Now, I don't have to tell you the obvious. Our situation is pretty bad. We already have one dead crewmember and another one in a coma, or whatever it is. So, first thing's first. We need the solar panels working. Then we get power going Janice back online. Then maybe we can figure out a defense strategy."

He focused on Finn.

"Ready?"

"Yeah."

He looked at the doc and Hahn. "You two okay here?"

"Yeah. We're not going anywhere," said Hahn as she looked down at Oleg.

"Just remember," said Zeke, "it seems to be affected by putting something into its field. So, remember that if it shows up."

They nodded.

"I don't like leaving you two here alone, but we have to split up for now." He looked over at Alina's body then back to them. "Let's focus and get things done, one thing at a time. We're going to figure a way out of this."

His confident tone might have been forced, but no one could tell. Either way, it was what they needed to hear. He turned around and started out the door. Finn looked at the women and nodded before following Zeke. Their muffled movements faded as they walked down the hallway.

It took a little more than a minute to get to the bridge. They went straight to the power control station and checked on the panel array. Sure enough, it was active. "We've got current. It's faint, but it's there," said Finn.

Zeke exhaled in relief. "Good. That's good news."

He moved to the left and checked the readout. Once verified, he said, "Let's see if any other systems are showing any activity."

They lumbered around the bridge, inspecting other panels and readouts. But, of course, there was nothing. The ship had been completely drained, and the only source of energy was from the solar panels, which had not yet fully deployed.

"Nothing," said Finn. "Everything's still dead." He shined his flashlight toward Zeke, then out towards the hall.

"Nervous?" asked Zeke.

"Damn right." He looked around briefly. "I don't want it to sneak up on me." He looked at Zeke. "Or you."

"Thanks for the afterthought." He checked the panel array again.

"There's nothing we can do right now," said Finn. "We can't force the panels to deploy. We gotta wait."

Zeke exhaled through his nostrils and aimed his flashlight at Finn's chest. "Yeah, you're right." He glanced around the bridge. "But I don't like waiting." He looked directly at Finn and changed his tone. "Boy, what I wouldn't give for a shot of whiskey."

"Whiskey? No thanks. I don't drink paint thinner. I'm a Tequila man."

Zeke let a slight chuckle break through his tough façade as he patted Finn on the shoulder. "Well, I'll still take my paint thinner over your toxic floor wax."

Finn smiled back. "Floor wax?"

Zeke was smiling. "When everything's up and running, how about you and I jimmy the food replicator and drink some paint thinner and floor wax?"

"I'm down for that anytime. But we don't have to jimmy anything. I have a stash."

Zeke shot some raised eyebrows at Finn. "Really?"

"Yeah. And, before you quote me some regulation, you started it."

"I won't say anything if you won't."

"Maybe we should be getting back to the girls," said Finn.

"Girls?" responded Zeke. "I don't think they would like you calling them that."

"Well, they're girls, aren't they?"

"Women, with names."

"Well, in that case, let's get back to the women-with-names."

Zeke smiled again. "You wanna have the women-with-names join us in that not-so-legal drink when this is all over?"

"Of course. If they found out we had some without them, we would never hear the end of it."

"True that," said Zeke as they headed towards medical. "What kind of tequila do you like?"

"The kind that hurts."

Outside the ship, the cloud was circling the Cascade the way a moon orbits a planet. It was slowly spiraling down the length of the vessel, passing by the cargo bay and communications array. Once it reached the stern, it headed back towards the bow. If anyone had been outside, they could easily have seen its movement against the starry sky.

"Any change?" asked Zeke.

"No change," responded the doc.

"He is still breathing, but his breaths are more shallow and slower. That's not good."

Zeke looked at Oleg's chest under the course flashlight beam. She was right. His breathing rate had changed.

She continued. "His pulse has slowed, too. And his pupils aren't responding very well to light when I check them." She shook her head. "It looks like he's dying."

She sighed yet again, frustrated with her inability to help him. "If medical only had power I could run some tests and maybe prescribe something. But, I can't do a damn thing, and it's frustrating as hell." She placed a hand on Oleg's shoulder as she looked at him with deep concern.

Medical was a sterile place. The metal table upon which Oleg was strapped, was in the middle of the room. It had wheels and was usually kept next to a wall that had some device attached to it that looked like a cross between an x-ray machine and a defibrillator. Of course, like everything else, there was a slight magnetic charge to the wheels that kept it anchored to the floor in zero gravity. It was also part of an elaborate diagnostic system. Its mundane basic metal slab appearance hid its many sensors. But, without power, it was just a table on wheels.

There was a door that led to the doc's office. Inside was a single desk with a large wall-mounted holo-panel next to an empty old-fashioned coffee pot on a shelf. And, of course, there was a window that peered out into the darkness.

"What gets me is why this thing is so small inside the ship and is so big outside?" Zeke had positioned himself so he could peer through the doc's office window. "Janice said that the cloud was luminescent. But, when we saw it on Alina, it was clear."

"Maybe it was something different," said Finn.

Zeke through a look at him. "I hope not. I hope it didn't bring company."

Finn shrugged his shoulders a little.

"Do you have any idea how big it was outside the ship when you saw it attack Oleg?"

Finn paused for a moment as he stared at retrieved memories. "The best I can tell you is that it was about the same size as Oleg. It was covering his whole suit. I didn't get the impression it was any larger than that. But I could be wrong. And, it was clear just like you said it was with Alina. But it was like a moving glass. It was weird."

"So, at least it is consistent," said the doc. She took her flashlight and set it down on the table next to Oleg, pointing it up to the ceiling. It stayed in place and provided a faint glow in the rest of the room. "You know, in all my exobiology classes and textbooks, nothing like this was ever even considered. They always assumed that life would take a biological form that would have adapted to a planet's gravity, air pressure, terrain, and such. But this is radically different than anything anyone dreamed of. I mean, think about it. It is a life form that lives in space that doesn't have flesh and blood, and it apparently eats antimatter."

Her words were both sobering and discouraging.

Finn added calmly, "Then that means conventional weapons probably won't affect it."

Zeke pressed his lips together before responding. "You're probably right." He looked over at Alina's body in the bag, then stiffened. "All right, once again. No one is to be alone. We eat together. When it's time to sleep, we'll do it in shifts, but not alone."

"Aye, Cap," said Hahn. "We understand." She placed her flashlight in midair, steadying it before letting go. It hovered, barely moving. She then twisted and flexed her back and stretched her arms behind her head. "Believe it or not, I miss gravity."

Oleg placed his flashlight vertically on the table next to the doc's. The vibration sent them both moving very slowly upward. "Good idea." He started stretching as well.

The slow movement of the drifting flashlights gave medical a surprisingly calm appearance.

"I think we need to keep our strength up," said the doc. "We might as well get to the mess hall and grab some food. The food processors are off-line, but there should still be plenty of packaged stuff to eat. How about Finn and I get to the galley and bring something back?"

"Good idea, Doc," said Zeke. "But, you need to be here with Oleg." He looked over at Finn and Hahn. "You two head to the mess hall and get enough food for us all."

"Sure thing," said Finn. He retrieved his flashlight and pointed it towards Hahn. "Ready?"

"Whenever you are." She reclaimed her flashlight, too.

"Good," said Zeke. "After you two get back, then we can head to the bridge and check things out.

"Aye, Cap."

Zeke nodded. "I'm guessing that the solar panels should start to self-deploy pretty soon. So, it's just a matter of time before power is restored."

The doc picked up her flashlight from just above the table. It was becoming her habit to point it at everyone she spoke to. "If you can get some fruit juice, too, that would be good. It would be good for all of us."

"I'm down for grub," said Finn as he exhaled sharply.

Hahn looked at him and shook her head. "Really?"

"What? I'm hungry."

She shook her head some more. "How can you eat at a time like this?"

He scoffed. "It's easy. Open mouth. Insert food. Chew. Swallow. Then do it again."

She rolled her eyes under a slight frown.

"My stomach doesn't know what's going on."

She exhaled. "Well, since its doctor's orders."

"Ladies first." He motioned for the door.

With that, Finn and Hahn started their trek to the galley. Soon they were out of audible range.

"I wanted to run something by you," said Zeke.

"Okay."

"It seems obvious that this creature is affected by something being put into its field while it's attacking us. When you put your flashlight into it while it was on Alina, it stopped. The same thing happened when Finn grabbed Oleg's arm. So, I don't know if that is our only defense. But maybe when we get power restored, you could see if there are some medical devices that you might use to interrupt it when it's attacking us. I mean, aren't there a lot of things in here that send out waves and signals? Maybe we could use something here and aim it at it instead of getting too close."

"I've been thinking along the same lines."

Zeke folded his arms. "Really?"

"Don't be surprised. Like you said, it's obvious that it doesn't like being disrupted. Medical deals with lots of different technologies. So, I was way ahead of you."

He raised his eyebrows slightly and nodded. "Good. Got anything in mind?"

"Yeah, a DBS. It stands for Deep Bone Scanner. It sends out a wave of high energy and reads what is bounced back."

"I like it."

"The only problem is it's dead. Everything in here is dead. We need power restored so I can charge it. Besides, I'd like to use it to check on Oleg."

"You need to check his bones?"

"It does a lot more than that."

"Okay, well, the power should be back on soon after the panels are extended."

She looked down at Oleg and sighed. "Or maybe the DBS will just piss it off."

"Let's hope not."

She cocked her hip to one side, something not easily done in zero gravity. "Maybe the reason he's not dead is because it wasn't finished with its attack when Finn interrupted it. We don't know how long Alina was being attacked, so I can only assume it was much longer for her. Maybe that's why she's dead, and he's not. Finn probably accidentally saved his life."

She broke the cadence of her own words as she looked into his eyes.

"Yeah?"

"You know we can't let it get back to Earth."

Zeke matched her serious tone. "Of course not. No matter what the outcome, it can't get back to Earth."

"No matter what?"

"No matter what."

"Good." She nodded and then lumbered around the table for a different view of Oleg in order to check his pulse again. She lifted up an eyelid and aimed her light.

She shook her head. "Not good."

He looked at his chest and counted breaths.

"He's getting worse." She looked at Zeke. "I know I'm rehashing this. But we need power. Soon."

"When the panels auto-deploy, we'll get it back. Then hopefully, you'll be able to help him." Zeke looked down at Oleg and gently touched his shoulder. "Hang in there."

Oleg's condition forced him to stare into the memories of today's events. He slumped his shoulders.

She saw it. "What are you thinking?"

He broke free. "This thing is like nothing we've ever encountered. It can move in and out of the ship and travel at incredible speed. It seems to be intelligent and, unfortunately, malevolent. So, after we get the power back, we can get Janice online. Then we can work on figuring out some way to fight it. Maybe she'll have some ideas."

"That is *if* you can get her back online," said the doc. "Maybe she's damaged."

"That's a possibility. But, all we can do is hope for the best. So far, it appears that only our energy is drained from the ship, and there are no signs of physical damage. So, let's keep our fingers crossed."

"But no quantum drive," said the doc. "We both know that without it we're stranded." She delivered the obviously depressing fact while still examining Oleg.

"One thing at a time," he said. "Maybe we'll just have to park our rears around Drakus and wait for rescue." He joined her in her brief scan.

"You know," she said as she faced Zeke. "I had a thought. Maybe it is lonely and is trying to communicate with us."

"You can't be serious."

After a few seconds, she added, "Actually, I think we're all going to die."

Chapter 11
The Galley

Finn and Hahn were rummaging through the cabinets and drawers. There was plenty of food that didn't require refrigeration. Since the storage units were well insulated, there was no immediate concern for spoiling. They found a plastic bag and began to fill it. Without power, nothing could be warmed up, so they got bread and lunchmeat out of a fridge along with some condiments. They grabbed a few large containers of apple juice. Finn hastily shoved some chips into the bag.

"They will get smashed," said Hahn.

"In zero gravity?"

"Yeah, when they get jostled."

He took them out and placed them in midair behind him. "I'll grab them on the way out."

While there were gathering supplies, they continued to periodically aim their flashlights around looking for the creature. When Finn would have his back to the room, Hahn would scan. Likewise, when she was rummaging, he was keeping an eye out. They wanted out of there and back with the others.

"Does this place give you the creeps in the dark?" asked Hahn?

"As a matter of fact, it does. Weird. I thought it was just me."

She handed Finn some more protein bars. He quickly put them in the bag as he looked around, jerking his flashlight from wall to wall.

They were too anxious and hurried to notice. But, near the main entrance to the galley, the creature hovered in front of a wall. It was about a meter across, stationary, and completely undetectable in the darkness. When they hurriedly flashed their lights around, it would occasionally be illumined, but they didn't notice because of their hurried and nervous pace.

"There," said Hahn after placing the last bottle of juice in the bag. "I think we have more than enough."

Finn nodded, but she didn't see him. He turned to grab the floating potato chips and place them in the bag. "Normally, I would say something like 'ladies first,' but given the circumstances, if you don't mind, I'll lead the way."

Hahn did not want to argue with his chivalry and meekly returned an appreciative, "Sure."

Both of them headed towards the door, cautiously moving their flashlights back and forth in front of them, sweeping away the darkness. But they still couldn't see the thing watching them as they hurried. Finn passed right by it as he plodded his way to the hallway. Once there, he swung his light around and checked both directions as he jostled the bag of grub in one hand. The long tunnel of darkness consumed his weak light. He turned his beam back into the galley onto Hahn, who was only two meters away.

She checked to the left and right and then headed for the door. But, something caught her eye. It was an oddity, a line that wasn't right.

Once again, Finn took his eyes off of her and glanced both ways down the dark halls.

Her flashlight blinked off.

Unexpectedly she felt intense disorientation. Then there was a mild ache in her back and stomach. Next, a torrent of agony scraped across every nerve in her body. Then images flooded her mind. She instinctively tried to scream but could not. She was frozen.

Finn had noticed that her light went out and had turned to check on her. There she was, motionless.

At first, he didn't know what was happening. *Why did her light go out, and why isn't she moving?*

Then he saw the undulating, glass-like cocoon engulfing her.

Finn lunged forward as he let go of the bag and aimed the flashlight at her. With his free hand, he reached out to grab her but recalled his painful encounter with it when he grabbed Oleg outside the ship. His instinct was to avoid contact, so he withdrew his arm, but his forward momentum was too great. He fell into the cloud and collided with Hahn and felt an incapacitating tsunami of agony that blasted every nerve into stinging fire. But, it only lasted for a second. The creature disappeared.

Their collision broke them free from the mag boots grip on the floor allowing both of them to tumble freely into the galley.

Hahn, hovering in semi-consciousness, let out a weak groan. Finn grunted and heaved short breaths into the air before the remnants of pain had dissipated enough for him to start to regain his composure. He shook his head once, then again.

They were still slowly tumbling. Their legs collided with a table and caused it to break free from its weak magnetic restraints, which sent it into some chairs. They were still spinning slightly from the impact. Finn managed to grab Hahn and, after waiting for full head over heels rotation, managed to stretch a leg down to the floor where his mag boot latched on. He slowly eased them to a stop at the same time the chairs collided with a wall. One chair latched onto it. The other moved upward towards the ceiling, where it clung upside down. The table made a clicking sound as it reattached itself to the floor, three meters away from its original position.

Finn maneuvered Hahn into position next to him. It was difficult to see her since there was only one flashlight, and it was tumbling through the air a few meters away. He didn't know when he had let go of it.

"Hahn?"

She didn't respond.

His light gently bounced against a wall and was drifting slowly back toward them. Finn let go of her and went for it.

"Hahn?" He asked as he shined the light into her face.

She squinted and turned away, shielding her eyes.

"Hahn?" He gently shook her.

She tried to push him away, "No," she said feebly.

"Hahn. It's me. Finn."

"No!" She pushed against him harder.

"It's me. Finn. It's okay."

As her senses came back, she moaned and squinted. Then after a few seconds, she looked into his eyes. They changed from awareness to horror.

She grabbed his shirt and pulled herself against his chest. He put his arms around her as she heaved out wails of anguish.

Chapter 12
Back to Medical

The doc was still monitoring Oleg and repeatedly checked his breathing and pulse. There was no change.

Zeke again looked out through her office window and into empty space, then back to her.

"The solar panel should deploy pretty soon." But, they weren't visible from medical.

"Then, we can power back, and you can help him."

She touched Oleg's hand again and spoke to him gently. "Don't worry, I'll figure this out one way or another."

She looked at Zeke. "But we need to hurry."

By now, Zeke was in the habit of scanning the medical area with his flashlight looking for the creature. But he didn't see anything. That was fine with him.

"How long do you think it will be after we get power from the solar panels that we can get gravity working?"

"I don't know. It all depends on the energy output. But the solar array is very efficient. Once Finn and Hahn get back, he and I can go to the bridge and monitor the systems from there. Life-support and gravity are our top priorities. It'll only take a few minutes."

She looked at him. "Why not get medical going first?"

"I know. I hear you. But, without life-support, it's all moot. It'll be the test. If it fails, we'd have to put all our effort into getting it running. Getting gravity going will be the real test since it's integrated through the entire ship. Then we can get power in here. After that, we'll get Janice going. But that will take longer."

The doc bent down to get a closer look at Oleg. She opened up his eyelid one more time and passed a flashlight by it. "He seems stable."

Zeke turned around and looked out into the hallway. He could hear the sounds of Finn and Hahn's approach. A soft faint, slow-growing shadow crept into the entrance of medical as they got closer.

Hahn was the first one to arrive. Finn was right behind her, pointing the way with the light as they entered. It was obvious from their expressions that something was very wrong.

"What the hell happened?" asked Zeke.

Neither Finn nor Hahn replied right away. They moved into the room. Finn tried to place the bag of food in midair, but it started to drift slowly away. Hahn lumbered over to the table where Oleg was, looked at him, but was staring at nothing.

"It was there in the galley," said Finn finally. "It attacked her."

Everyone was looking at Hahn. But she didn't say anything. Her back was moving rhythmically from deep breaths. She slowly rotated her head on her neck, then turned to them.

"It was horrible. It was pure pain. It was beyond anything I have ever experienced." She choked out the last word with a tremble. She brought her hands to her hair. They were shaking.

By now, the doc was next to her and had put the back of her hand on Hahn's forehead. Hahn flinched nervously. She was cold and sweaty.

"Finn? Did you get juice?"

"Yeah. Hell, I almost left it, but I didn't want to go back there again."

Zeke approached Finn. "What happened?"

"I felt it, too. When I saw it on her, I rushed to help and stumbled into it." He looked straight into Zeke's eyes. "I've never felt so much pain in my entire life. Nothing comes close. Nothing. It is unimaginable. It's hell. It's…it's … so… total. It is like nothing you've ever experienced. Nothing!"

Finn's deeply furrowed brows and anguished stare matched his desperate tone.

The doc was checking Hahn's pulse. "Look at me," she said. Hahn complied through dull eyes. The doc pointed the flashlight at them and spoke while checking. "You're sweating, and your skin is cold. You're in shock."

Hahn turned away. "Where is it?"

"We don't know," said Zeke.

"I was in the hallway waiting for her as she was coming out when it got her. I saw it around her. It was weird like, like liquid glass. She was suspended above the floor, frozen. I knew it was the creature, so I tried to help her, but I couldn't."

He looked at Hahn. "The pain was incredible."

She looked at him and wiped away tears.

"I felt it for only a moment," continued Finn. But you. You were in it for much longer. You're whole body."

Her face contorted with the memory.

The doc had maneuvered herself next to Finn and was checking his pulse. She moved her flashlight near his eyes. He was also sweating. "You're in a little shock, too. I want you both to drink some juice. But, you'll both be okay."

He glared hard at Zeke. "It was horrible. You don't want to experience it. You don't!"

Finn looked over at Hahn again, who was now staring into nothing. He furrowed his brows in an intense expression of sadness as he looked at her. She wiped away more pooling tears. Finn turned to Zeke.

"I tried to stop it. I did. I tried. I went to grab her, but I was moving too fast. I just stumbled into it. It was horrible. You have no idea how bad it was. And I only got a couple of seconds of it." He looked over at Hahn. "It was bad, real bad."

"Okay, Finn. I hear ya. Now take a breath and try and calm down."

Finn tried to shake off the memory of pain. "Yeah. You're right."

He took a deep breath, then another. "Okay." He inhaled again then let it out. "Yeah, I'm good. I'm good."

Hahn turned to face them. The sound of her boots drew their attention. "Finn's right. It was horrible, absolutely horrible." She spoke in a subdued, trembling voice. "I couldn't do anything. I couldn't move. I couldn't breathe. I couldn't even scream. It was, it was…unbearable, indescribable pain."

Her trembling voice faded away. Then she looked at Zeke. "It's evil. It's pure evil. It's going to kill us all. Do you hear me? We're all going to die."

The doc had returned to her. "Drink this." She handed her some juice.

Finn piped in. "She's right. We're going to die if we stay here. I say we bail. We can't stay. We have to get away. It's gonna kill us all. I don't care what it takes. We've got to leave. Now, not later. Now, no matter what. You hear me? We have to get away." Finn was starting to get louder and louder. "We have to do something. We can't let it…"

"Finn!" said the doc. She moved in front of him and grabbed him by both shoulders.

He stopped and stared at her, blinking hard. His breathing was quick. A frantic expression crawled across his face.

"Do you two want some sedatives?" asked the doc.

Finn stared at her with a half frown. "No. No… I'm okay. I'm cool." He took a deep breath. "I'm good."

Obviously, they didn't believe him.

"Hahn?"

"Hell, no!" said Hahn sharply. "I need to be alert, not sedated."

Her expression changed from anguish to anger. "I don't want anything in my system that can dull my senses. I need to be absolutely awake because I am not letting that happen again. If anything, I'll take a stimulant."

She looked at Zeke hard. "Finn is right. We're going to die if we stay here. We gotta figure something out. We've gotta leave."

Zeke glanced back at Finn, who was nodding. "I heard that!"

Hahn ran both hands through her hair. "I couldn't even see it. I mean, we were looking for it, and it just came out of nowhere."

She squinted a little bit and looked down as she remembered. "Wait. There *was* something. Right before I was attacked, I thought I saw something. It was near the door. It was just, I don't know, it was like a distortion or something." She looked up at Zeke. "That was it. That had to be it. I saw it, but barely. I didn't know what I was seeing. I didn't know what was there."

"Describe it," said Zeke.

She returned to her downward gaze as she reflected on the image, searching for words. "It was clear. The only thing that gave it away is that it made the corner where the door met the wall look a little distorted. That's the only way I can describe it. It was as though what I was looking at was just twisted a little. I don't know how else to describe it."

"That helps," Hahn. "It's similar to what we saw when it was attacking Alina. It was like what Finn said, liquid glass moving around Oleg, too. It must bend light somehow. But you said it was hardly detectable in the galley. So, that tells me it can change its appearance and that it isn't visible in the dark. So, we're going to have to keep our eyes peeled." He looked back at Finn.

"Is that what you saw, a kind of a shimmering aura around her when it was attacking her?"

Finn was rubbing his temples, but he didn't answer. They waited.

"Finn?"

91

He lowered his hands and took a deep breath as he let it out slowly. "We are all going to die horrible deaths."

It took a while for both Finn and Hahn to settle down. They were understandably edgy and jumpy. Little sounds caused them to lose focus and look around nervously. Hanh repeatedly scanned medical with a small flashlight the doc gave her.

Finn, who hadn't been as badly affected, was able to settle down more quickly. But, he was far from over it. He, too, examined the room, looking out the doorway, and glancing over at Hahn every now and then.

Zeke stared at the doc as he raised his eyebrows.

"They'll be okay," she said. "But it'll take a while for them to fully recover. Right now, they're dealing with the after-effects of adrenaline and trauma. Just think of fight or flight." Of course, she was talking loudly enough for both of them to hear.

"I'm not calming down," retorted Hahn. "You can take your fight or flight crap and shove it!"

The doc raised her eyebrows in a direct stare at her.

Hahn closed her eyes for a moment, took a calming breath, and raised an open hand towards the doc. "Sorry."

"It's okay. I understand."

"You have no idea how bad it was," said Finn. "Unimaginable pain. Pure hell! I didn't know I could hurt that much."

The doc's instinct was to heal, and, in this case, changing the topic was her way of easing their suffering, though it wasn't much of a change.

"I don't know if I'm right or not, but I think the creature is showing up about every 30 or 45 minutes or so."

Zeke looked at her. He thought it through and then replied. "Yeah, that seems about right."

"Then that would mean its due to hit again in about a half-hour," she said as she realized she wasn't helping Finn and Hahn calm down at all.

"Hell no," said Hahn. "I'll eject myself into space before I go through that again."

"I second that," added Finn without hesitation.

"Alright, alright," said Zeke as he patted the air. "I know it was bad. But for now, we all need to focus. We need to get to the bridge. I don't like the idea of moving Oleg, but we need to keep an eye on him. It'll be easy to move him."

Hahn was once again absentmindedly running her hands through her hair. Finn's head was down, staring at the floor.

"Are you two good to go?" Zeke knew they weren't.

Finn swallowed, exhaled hard, and straightened up. "Yeah, I'm good to go. I'm good." He looked over at Hahn.

"I have to be," she said in a hollow voice. "But, if it shows up, I'm running, and I suggest you all do the same."

"All right. We'll keep that in mind. But for now, we've got things to do. And, if what the doc says about the creature is correct, then we can expect another attack in 20 or so. But, who knows."

Hahn's body language stiffened.

Zeke continued. "Based on what Finn said about interrupting the attack on Oleg outside the ship and what happened in the galley, I think that we can disrupt it by putting something into its field, maybe a glove or something. That way, we won't be risking our flashlights."

"Yeah," said the doc. "We need 'em."

Finn chimed in. "There has to be something in the cargo bay. Maybe I can whip up some rods with electrical... crap, forget that. We don't have power." He sighed. "But there are probably some batteries someplace that are still good. Hell, maybe we can find some sticks to throw at it while we use harsh language."

"We're going to find a way, Finn. We get the power back online, get Janice running, and figure out how to defend ourselves. We're already learning stuff about it. So, for now, we stay in groups, and if it attacks, we just throw something at it."

Finn straightened up and leveled his eyes on Zeke. "I hear you, and that's good. But I have to say something. It's going to sound weird."

Zeke focused on him.

"When I was in contact with the cloud, even though it was only for a second, I saw something, something strange. I don't know how to explain it. At first, I thought it was my imagination, but I've been thinking about it." He paused for a deep breath. "Even though there was incredible pain, I was still aware of what was happening. And, the room...it...well, it flashed like a strobe, really fast."

"It was the flashlight," said Hahn. "It was spinning in the air, remember?"

"Yeah, I know. But what I saw was faster than that. When it stopped, so did the flash. Actually, I don't mean it stopped. It slowed down. It was different. I don't know what to make of it."

He paused again as he searched for a way to explain. "It was as though...as though time was altered. I don't think what I saw was the flashlight spinning. I don't know how I know, but it was something different."

He broke free from his thoughts and looked at Hahn. She glared back at him.

She raised her right hand slightly for emphasis. "I'm only gonna say this because Finn brought it up. But it was the same for me. I thought I was just messed up from the pain, but, like he said, it felt as though time was out of sync." She stopped and looked at Zeke and the doc. "I don't know how to explain it, and maybe I'm way off, but like Finn said, there's just this feeling that time was, it was… different." She frowned as she listened to her own words. "I know it doesn't make sense, but I'm only saying it cuz' he said it first."

Finn latched on to the phrase. He was nodding. "Yeah, it was like time was different."

He was almost smiling as he looked at the doc. Then after a few seconds, the smile faded. "Does that make any sense, or are we both psychotic?"

The doc considered her words carefully. "Psychotic? No. But, it is possible that since you were in such trauma that your brains played tricks on you. Then again, since we don't know what this creature is capable of, maybe it has some weird relationship to time. That's possible because Janice said that there was a temporal aspect to the signals. So, who knows. On the other hand, and no offense meant, maybe it was your mind playing tricks on you. The brain is pretty powerful and can react in some pretty strange ways under high stress."

Hahn just stared at the doc, stiffly. "Both of us?"

"Yeah." She continued. "Both of you if you experience the same thing. But, like I said, we don't know really what is going on with the creature. So we can't rule anything out. But one thing is for sure. It's dangerous."

"That's more like it, Doc," said Hahn. "And we've got to find a way to kill it."

"Amen to that!" said Finn.

"Not so fast," said Zeke. "Okay, so Janice said there was a time signature in some of the pulses that it sent back. And that weird crap about getting a signal back one second before sending it. So, yeah, maybe you two are on to something. So, I don't think you're crazy. But that raises a lot of possibilities as far as what it can do and how it might affect us and the ship. That's why we have to get Janice back online and run this by her."

Hahn nodded as she took a step closer to Zeke. "Let's get Janice back online and figure a way to either get the hell out of here or kill that damn thing!"

"And what about studying it?" retorted Zeke.

"Studying it? No way." Hahn looked at Zeke as if examining something broken. "Look, I know you think I'm not being objective. And you're right. You wouldn't either if you went through what I did. But, hey. The scientist in me says that maybe it's possible that it relates to time differently than we do, and because of that, we need to study it. After all, it is an alien life form." She paused, closed her eyes for a couple seconds, and added, "But on the other hand. It has wreaked havoc with our ship, killed Alina, and has attacked Oleg and me. So, maybe we just need to find a way to fight it and get the hell out of here."

Her tone was strained as she tried to balance rationality with the memory of an agonizing encounter. "But, I agree with you, Cap. We need to get Janice running. Maybe, she can figure a way to deal with it. Heck, maybe we can use this time thing to our advantage."

"Interesting thought," said Zeke. "Got any ideas on that?"

"No. I'm just saying that maybe she can figure something out." Her voice trailed off as she closed her eyes for a couple seconds. "Look, I'm getting tired, and I'm sick of this."

"That's normal," interjected the doc. "You're body is recovering. I can give you something to help you stay alert and maybe even calm you down as well."

She looked at her and shrugged her shoulders. "Yeah, sure."

The doc walked over to a cabinet and pulled out a bottle that was floating slightly above the shelf. She lumbered back over to Hahn and handed her a pill. "You can chew it. It'll help you focus and counter the fatigue."

"Thanks," said Hahn as she popped it into her mouth.

"Can I have one, too?" asked Finn?

The doc smiled, took another pill from the bottle, and floated it to Finn. He retrieved it and ate it right away.

Zeke held out his hand, and the doc sent one more floating towards him. "All right then," said Zeke. "Let's get to the bridge. We have to get power restored and get Janice running. Then maybe we can come up with a plan. Let's get to it."

He popped the pill into his mouth.

Chapter 13
Power

Getting Oleg to the bridge was easy in zero gravity. But, securing him to the holo-table wasn't. It didn't have straps. So, the doc brought some standard Velcro and jury-rigged a way to keep him secure. He was quiet and motionless, and if it weren't for the doc's periodic checkups, they could easily have forgotten about him.

Hahn was munching on some of the supplies retrieved from the galley. Finn had a bottle of juice in his hand. He was next to Zeke as they were both checking the solar panel readout.

"It's gotta be soon," said Zeke.

The doc walked up to him. "Here." She offered him some juice. "You need something in your system."

Zeke obediently complied, took it, and sucked it down. Once done, he handed the empty back to the Doc.

Hahn was keeping guard by carefully scanning the bridge with her flashlight. She slowly inspected every surface for any distortion. It had been about 45 minutes since the last attack, so she was on edge. But, with the meds the doc had given her, she felt calm and alert.

No one knew what to expect. If it attacked, their plan was to put something into its field. The doc and Zeke had filled them in on their theory. It was their only option. So, they had assembled some odds and ends, a dead flashlight, some loose equipment from a cabinet. They were ready as best they could be.

"There!" Finn shouted while staring at the solar panel control board. He pointed at the green light that had just flickered on. It was followed by a monitor that flashed 'Solar Panel Array Controls.' He turned to Zeke. "The secondary power system just kicked in. It means that the panels are deploying."

Zeke looked out the window, and sure enough, he could see them slowly extending. He exhaled and banged his fist hard on the window. "Finally!"

Hahn and the doc joined Zeke and gazed outward. It was a sight for sore eyes.

Zeke turned to Finn, who was still at the solar panel controls. "How long before they're finished?

Without taking his eyes off the monitor, he said, "From what I see, at the rate the electricity is coming in, I would say they will be at 100% deployment in about twenty minutes. Then, it's just a matter of deciding which systems we want to turn on first. Those solar panels are really efficient, even this far from the Drake sun. So, we should have enough juice to turn most everything on."

"Good," said Zeke. "Once they are deployed, we will get life-support working. Then gravity. Afterward, we need medical running. After that, Finn, you and I can work on getting Janice back online."

Zeke looked around the room. "Good. The thing hasn't shown up, at least not here in the bridge. So for now, let's keep focused."

"Aye, Cap," said Finn without turning around. "Maybe it's checking out the ship to learn our weaknesses."

"Thanks for that disturbing thought," said the doc.

"Yeah, I guess it is," responded Finn, still inspecting the readout. "Sorry."

Zeke took a deep breath and scratched his head with his fingertips. "Well," he said, "wherever it is, at least it's not here."

"Amen to that," said Hahn. "It can have the whole ship as long as it leaves me alone." Of course, her statement didn't really make sense. But, no one minded.

"Maybe I was wrong about the timing," said the doc. "It's overdue."

"Or maybe it's changing its tactic," responded Zeke.

Except for Finn, they all would periodically scan the bridge. Occasionally a crisscross of flashlights would cause a shadow to come alive, and someone would flinch and stare at it. But, somehow, they managed not to get too jumpy among the disjointed, dark shadows that gave the bridge an eerie feel.

That is why they didn't see it. They were looking in the wrong place.

Just outside the ship, it slowly approached the viewing window and stopped about twenty meters away.

The crew was waiting for the panels to deploy fully and get power back. The doc was hovering near Oleg and would periodically check his pulse and breathing. Hahn kept scanning the room. Finn focused on the panels' progress.

"Any change?" asked Zeke to the doc.

"No. He's stable. At least I don't think he's getting worse. When we get power back, I can tell you more."

Hahn had carefully checked the bridge for the hundredth time. The remnant of the pain was still very fresh, and it's stinging memory motivated her to stay alert. She flexed her shoulder blades and rotated her neck on her shoulders. The tension was taking its toll, and she knew it. So, she decided to go to the window and peer out. At least she could do two things at once, look for the creature outside and enjoy the beauty of space. She meandered over.

Her flashlight led the way. Of course, there were random beams of light coming from the others behind her as they went about their business. But for now, she tried to isolate herself from them if only for a few moments. She flipped off her flashlight and stared out toward the Drake sun.

Like the rest of the crew, she was drawn to space. She'd always loved the stars and found their random arrangement on the vast black canvas to be comforting as well as beautiful.

Did the Drake sun just twinkle? She looked at it. Yes, it did. She focused and looked at another point of light next to it. It flickered as well. She gasped then stood back. "It's out there!" she shouted.

Everyone stopped and turned their flashlights toward Hahn at the window. The sudden barrage of light cast her shadow on the glass and obliterated the stars outside.

"Turn off your flashlights!" She said as she backed away.

One by one, they clicked off until they were engulfed in darkness, dimly lit only by the few monitors that had come to life.

"I saw some stars twinkle. It has to be the creature."

Zeke moved just a bit closer. He focused on the Drake sun. Then, after a few seconds, it dimmed and then brightened. "Yes, it's out there."

"Where?" asked Finn.

"Look at the Drake sun."

There was no need to approach the window. A few meters would make no difference in interstellar space. Besides, it was easily recognizable. Sure enough, it twinkled and faded before brightening again. So did another star. And then, another and another. Their number was increasing as it approached.

"It's coming!" said Zeke.

Everyone turned their lights back on and backed away from the window. They stopped next to the holo-table where Oleg was lying and watched. But they couldn't see anything.

"Turn your flashlights off. We can't see it outside with them on."

Only the doc turned hers off.

"Off!" demanded Zeke.

The rest complied.

In the dimness, their eyes quickly adjusted. They could see the stars twinkling, and as they watched, the diameter of those engulfed in its presence was growing.

They were all fixated, pressed back against the holo-table. Hahn groaned as she moved around to the other side. The doc glanced down at Oleg. His breathing had increased.

Should they flee? Should they scatter into the ship? Or, would that only delay an inevitable attack? It could exist anywhere, everywhere. They were trapped. Running was useless.

The Solar Panel display brightened slightly which enabled them to see the slow increase in the diameter of the twinkling stars that gradually filled the viewing window. It was either very close or very large, or both. Hahn took another step back and retreated towards the hallway entrance, ready to run. She was hyper-focused on the creature, taking short breaths, forcing back the panic. The doc was instinctively trying to guard helpless Oleg.

Then, the focal point of the stars shifted. It was like an optical illusion. It didn't make sense. They were seeing the stars, but somehow, they appeared to be just a few meters away.

"Are you seeing this?" asked Zeke. "Do the stars appear to be inside the bridge?"

"Yeah," said Finn, in a sharp voice.

"Same here," said the doc.

"Me too," said Hahn from behind them.

"It's inside the ship."

They all instinctively moved back even more as they watched what appeared to be a giant wall of liquid glass pass through the huge window and into the bridge. Hahn flipped on her light first. Everyone else followed. But what they saw didn't make sense. Their light beams hit the creature but seemed to slow down as they passed through it until finally emerging and lighting up the frame of the window behind.

Zeke took his flashlight and aimed it towards the top of the alien from left to right in a slow movement. To his and everyone else's amazement, they could see the light slow inside the creature in a corresponding fashion with the movement of his flashlight.

Only it was many seconds delayed before the light eventually passed through and lit up part of the ceiling at which he was initially aiming.

The doc glanced over at Oleg. He was breathing more rapidly. She reached over and felt his wrist. His pulse was elevated. But she kept that to herself, for now.

It did not advance. It stayed where it was, just inside the ship, filling the entire area of the window. They watched as the stars slowly shifted back and forth, rippling inside of it. But, to their surprise, the Drake sun was no longer twinkling or undulating. It was clear, steady, and enlarged.

"Do you guys see that?" asked Finn. "The Drake sun isn't twinkling or moving, but everything else is."

After a few seconds, Zeke nodded and said, "Yeah," followed by the doc's and Hahn's acknowledgment.

Unexpectedly, there was a beam of light that emanated from around the Drake sun and moved towards a small spec of light.

"Is that Drakus?" asked Finn.

"I think so," responded Zeke.

Then light emanated from the Drake sun and flashed outward in every direction, lighting up the bridge, but only for a moment.

They took a step back. Then another pulse of light radiated outward, lighting the bridge up again. After that, it went back to its normal glass-like undulation. They waited.

Finally, Hahn asked quietly, "What was that? Why those two pulses of light?"

"I have no idea," responded Zeke in an equally subdued tone. He looked over at the doc. "Any ideas?"

"None."

"Finn?"

"Really?"

They watched the creature as it stayed in place, slowly undulating, causing the stars which were actually behind it to appear twinkling inside the bridge while the Drake sun remained steady.

"It knows where we're headed," said Finn.

Zeke spoke to the crew. "I'm going to launch my flashlight into it and see what happens." He lifted it and pointed the beam towards the creature. He held it in his hand as if he was ready to launch a paper airplane.

"Do you really think that is a good idea?" asked Finn. He was calmer now. "I mean, you don't want to piss it off."

"Got any other ideas?"

Finn said nothing.

With a slow and steady movement, Zeke sent the flashlight floating through the bridge towards the creature. It wobbled slightly. They could see the beam captured inside of it the same as before until it finally seemed to pass through onto the window behind it and was reflected back through the alien to them. The whole cycle seemed to take about 10 seconds.

Finally, the flashlight passed the barely perceptible boundary of the creature. But nothing happened. The creature stayed. Then, it stopped moving. The light went out.

Hahn took a step back. She tilted her head forward slightly and looked at the creature through the top of her eyes. She clenched her flashlight. "So much for your theory about disrupting it."

Finn looked over at Zeke.

The flashlight was clearly visible, slightly undulating in the creature's field. Then they watched as it disappeared and then it reappeared, but it was pointing back at them - and turned on. The beam was pointing back towards them. Then, in a slow movement, it left the creature's field and returned towards Zeke, but without any wobble at all.

As the floating flashlight got closer, its brightness grew more intense, brighter than its highest setting. They all began to squint.

Zeke shielded his eyes as did the rest of the crew. Then, suddenly, the flashlight went back to its normal intensity, and they could once again open their eyes. When it was close enough, Zeke grabbed it, turned it around, and aimed it back at the creature. But it was gone. The stars were no longer inside the ship.

At first, they stayed where they were. Hahn automatically started looking around, checking for an ambush. Her light bounced off various parts of the bridge sending faint shadows once again, jumping around at odd angles. Zeke approached the window. Finn joined Hahn in her inspection of the bridge.

Nothing. It seemed to be gone.

The doc turned her attention to Oleg and checked his pulse. She put the beam of light on his chest, and she counted his breathing. He was back to normal.

"Cap?" Her words broke the cautious silence.

"Yeah?" he said, still keeping his eyes forward.

"When the creature was here, Oleg's pulse and breathing were increased. When it left, they went back to normal. There has to be a connection."

He turned to face her. "Okay." Then, he turned back to the window.

The stars beyond were unvarying solid points, no scintillation.

"I think it's gone," he said. The concave shape of the window reflected his voice clearly back to them.

Finn once again joined Hahn in scanning the bridge with his flashlight. Zeke finally relaxed, as little as that was, and walked over to the doc. He put his hand on Oleg's shoulder.

"Keep a close eye on him. When we get medical going, you can run some tests."

She nodded.

"I don't know about the rest of you," said Finn. "But that was bizarre."

"I hear that!" said Hahn eagerly as she pointed her light towards the door.

"Okay," said Zeke. "I guess that was our visit. Hopefully, it won't be back for another hour or so." He pointed his flashlight over at the solar panel readout and started walking towards it as he said, "We need to get the power restored."

Finn met him there. "The current is strong."

"Look," said the doc. She was staring at a wall of readouts that were flickering on. "We've got power."

It was obvious that the solar panels were feeding into the bridge instrument panels. Monitors came to life, one after another.

Zeke walked back to the window and peered towards the solar panels. "They're almost fully deployed." He hurried over to the control systems on the bridge. Finn was already checking them. Finally, after a couple minutes, he said, "Everything seems to be okay. I was expecting some systems to have been damaged, but when I do a quick check on them, they're all fine. I didn't expect that, but I'll take it."

He turned to Zeke. "With your permission, I'll get life-support back online."

"Of course."

They all watched as Finn directed some energy from the solar panels to life-support. Then he walked to the Life Support Control Panel and waited. Finally, the words "Life Support Systems: Begin Check" appeared in white against the black screen. He paused for a few seconds before eventually extending his finger and pressed the words. Instantly "Life Support Systems: Check In Process," appeared in green letters that pulsed slightly.

"It'll take about 30 seconds for this check to be completed," he said aloud, without turning around. "The whole thing is pretty simple. A monkey could turn on life-support with proper training, which is why I can do it."

They recognized his feeble attempt at humor, but no one acknowledged it.

Finally, the words "Life Support Systems: Verified" appeared on the screen. Underneath them, the word "Initialize?" materialized in that slow pulsing green.

He let his breath release as he relaxed, turned around to scan the bridge once more for the creature, and then said, "All right, it all looks good. So here goes." He turned back, and with a single press of his finger, he touched the screen and then took a step away. Lights flashed on in the bridge.

At first, everyone squinted. It was Hahn who first spoke, "Thank you!"

Zeke walked over to where Finn was and put a hand on his shoulder. With his other, he leaned on the console. Finn was scrutinizing the life support monitor, waiting for the final message to appear. Then after five seconds, the words "Life Support Activation Complete" flashed onto the screen.

"Excellent," he said with a grin as he looked around at everybody. They were all squinting and smiling. But his celebratory attitude was instantly interrupted when he looked at Oleg still lying on the table. His comatose body was starkly visible in the restored light.

"All right, let's get gravity back online," said Zeke as he flicked off his flashlight, followed by the others. "I'm tired of shuffling around in these grav boots."

"I heard that!" Finn walked over to the solar panel control, and with a few swipes and presses, the Gravity Control System Panel lit up. He walked over to it, followed by Zeke and Hahn. The doc stayed next to Oleg.

After about 30 anxious seconds, the words 'Gravity Control Systems: Begin Check' appeared on the screen. He stared at it for a few moments. "It seems okay. No apparent damage." He glanced around at everyone before pressing the words. Instantly 'Gravity

Control System: Check Is In Process' appeared in letters that pulsed slowly.

After about 30 more seconds, the panel displayed 'Gravity Control System: Verified' with the words 'Initialize: Yes No' in that same slow pulsing green.

Finn turned around. "It looks like the system is good to go. But I suggest you grab onto something. It's going to feel a little weird."

Everybody grabbed something near them.

"Okay, here goes." He pressed 'Yes.' Then, within a few seconds, everyone felt a gentle downward pull upon their bodies that gradually grew stronger. The system was designed to come to full strength over 15 seconds.

They heard a few muffled sounds coming from inside a cabinet. It was various objects that had hit bottom after being reclaimed by gravity. Something in one of their bags slid down against something else, making a slight rubbing sound.

Their weight increased.

It was a strange sensation. They had become accustomed to weightlessness and the ease of motion that accompanied it. But, with gravity back online, their bodies once again became thick and cumbersome.

"Well," said the doc. "I feel like I just gained 200 pounds."

"Make that three for me," said Finn.

Zeke cracked half a smile. It was a stark contrast to the dire situation in which they found themselves. But, the good news was much needed. "Good job."

"Great work!" said Hahn.

Zeke continued his directions. "Finn, can you get full power here on the bridge and then medical? And after that, get power to as much as the ship as you can."

"Shouldn't be a problem, Cap. But do you mind if I get out of these boots first?"

"Make it fast," said Zeke as he looked over at Oleg.

Finn reached down and unlatched a buckle, then another. He kicked them off and tossed them into a corner out of the way. He flexed his toes inside his socks and walked over to his stash, and within seconds, he had his shoes on. Everyone else followed suit. It felt good to be free from the rigidity of the boots.

Finn walked over to the Power Grid Monitor and pressed on the word "Index." A menu slid out to the right. He drew his finger down the list and pressed "Bridge." Immediately the words "Power On" appeared, and he touched it. A few other panels flickered on as did the light on the holo-table, which, unfortunately, once again brought their attention back to Oleg's condition.

Finn walked over to another panel with the words "Ship wide System Power Grid." The word "Schematic" was underneath it. He touched it, and the layout of the Cascade appeared. He then tapped the medical bay. It read 'Medical Power Off' and 'Medical Power On.' He pressed 'Medical Power On' and a green boundary around medical lit up. He turned to the doc.

"You've got power."

"Good," she responded. Without hesitation, she turned to Hahn. "Now, if you don't mind, would you go with me to medical and help me retrieve a gurney? We can be back in a couple minutes and get Oleg back there."

"Sure thing."

"Remember," said Zeke. "Stay together."

With that, they headed out.

"The Ship's COM systems should be up," said Zeke to the women as the left. "If you see anything at all out of the ordinary, you let us know. We'll come running. But Finn and I will be here trying to get Janice online."

"Roger that," said Hahn with a raised hand as she kept walking out into the hallway.

"All right, Finn, time for Janice. Got any idea how long it will take?"

"Well, to be honest, my guesstimate is less than a half-hour. But then again, the geniuses back on Earth pretty much built in a fail-safe system of starting her, so it shouldn't be a problem. It will be a matter of activating certain lower functions, powering the processing systems, then memory, and CPU Rack initialization. But I won't be rushing it. If it's anything like the other systems we just turned on, everything should be fine."

"Good," said Zeke. "I'll assist you."

When Hahn and the doc reached medical, the first thing they did was look over at Alina's body, which was still resting on the floor.

"I can set up a makeshift morgue in that room," said the doc as she pointed to a door labeled Storage. "But, not right now." She went in and unhooked a gurney hanging up on a wall and carried it out into the main area. It was very light. She laid it on the floor, straddled it, and with each hand on the sides, flipped a couple of levers, and then jerked up. The gurney latched in place about 6 inches high. She then stepped to one side and put her foot on a metal lever and pulled the entire frame to full height.

"Good," she said.

Hahn was staying clear of the doc, vigilantly scanning the room. The memory of the excruciating ordeal with the creature still haunted her, which is why she was holding onto her flashlight, even though it was off.

"You don't need to carry that anymore," said the doc.

Hahn spoke in a mocking tone. "A flashlight worked before, so I'll keep it close. It's is my only weapon against that thing. I'll shove it down its throat if I can."

She looked at the doc and scoffed. "I'm pathetic, aren't I?"

"No, you're not. I get it."

Hahn just stared at her through a corner of her eye and thought, *No, you don't. You have no idea.*

"Let's get back to the bridge and get Oleg," she said, purposely dismissing Hahn's obviously tense body language.

Hahn walked over to her.

The doc maneuvered herself to one end and started pushing it out into the hallway. Hahn followed closely, wide-eyed, glancing left, right, and behind as they went. They hustled toward the bridge.

From within medical, on the wall farthest from the entrance, there was a slight distortion. It wasn't large. But, it moved and floated above the ground near the doc's office door.

Soon after the sound of the doc and Hahn's footsteps had faded away, it moved across the room towards Alina's body. When it got there, it hovered in front of it. Then, after a few seconds, the faint light that it was emitting slowly began to morph into a swarm of hundreds of sparkles that began to swirl within its undefined boundary. They moved and flowed from one part of the creature to another before intermingling with other lights and then moving on to another area of the creature. It was as though each light itself was alive and was interacting and communicating with the others in its ill-defined form that amounted to a breach in space.

After a while, the lights began to slow down until they all stopped their rhythmic dance. But they did not disappear. They stayed where they were within the creature as it descended and engulfed Alina's body.

Chapter 14
Sound

The doc and Hahn made the trip back to the bridge in no time. Once there, Zeke and Finn moved Oleg from the holo-table onto the gurney. In gravity, he was substantially heavier, but they easily managed. The women hurried back to medical with him in tow. Being confined in a narrow passageway with the creature being loose didn't help their already frayed nerves. So, when they entered medical, they naturally looked around, making sure it wasn't there. Then they both checked on the body bag, which was still resting on the floor.

Feeling sufficiently safe, they maneuvered the gurney parallel to the table. The doc locked the wheels, then went over to a drawer and retrieved a sheet. She shook it loose from its folds as she returned to the gurney and, with a sweeping motion, laid it on the table. She spread it out along the table's length and looked at Hahn.

"I'm going to pull Oleg onto his right side. You tuck the sheet underneath him. Then I will lay him back down on the sheet, and we can then pull him onto the table.

"Got it," said Hahn. She tucked her ever-present flashlight into her pants pocket.

They worked quickly and efficiently. In less than half a minute, they were ready to transfer him.

"On three," said the doc.

"Okay."

"One, two, three."

With a single motion, they transferred Oleg. The doc then tilted him on his side again as they remove the sheet.

"Could you move the gurney over into the storage room?" asked the doc as she handed the crumpled sheet to Hahn.

She didn't nod or speak. She just delivered the gurney to storage and then immediately came back. By then, the doc had picked up an instrument off a shelf that was now activated by the restored power. She was slowly waving the device over his head.

Hahn immediately returned to scanning the area. She really didn't expect it to show up, at least not for a while, but the painful memory of her encounter kept her at a constant vigil.

Medical was brightly lit. It had that examination-room look and smelled clean and sterile. Cryptic instruments were on tables and counters. On one of the walls was a large video panel at eye level. The word "Diagnostics" shined brightly.

Hahn looked over at Oleg. He was lying on the table, which, as she examined it, appeared to be well designed. Several lights and a panel of some sort had come to life on one side. There were section breaks that allowed its shape to change from flat to reclined. She reached over and pressed on its slightly padded surface. It was firm but comfortable.

She then looked around the room again for the creature. But this time, she focused on any visual disturbances. She saw none.

The doc went over to a set of drawers that were built into a wall and unsnapped one of several devices that were locked into their cradles. She pressed a button. It lit up. She walked over to Oleg.

Hahn watched as she slowly scanned his entire body. The image of Oleg's physique appeared on the diagnostics panel showing his bones, organs, and circulatory system. A list of medical terms with numbers next to them appeared on the display. When she finished, the doc put the instrument down and walked over to the panel for a closer look. Hahn glanced around once more before joining her.

"According to this, he's asleep." She spoke the words slowly as if she was talking to herself. She shifted her weight to one hip and folded her arms.

"Next," she said. The screen moved from right to left, showing more information.

"Next."

For a few seconds, both of them were distracted by the intricate visuals on the display, so when they heard the unexpected noise, it caused them both to jump.

"What the hell was that?" asked Hahn, staring anxiously around the room.

The doc said nothing.

"You heard that? Right?" asked Hahn again.

"Yeah, I heard it."

They both looked everywhere, trying to see any distortions. There was no sign of the creature. Everything seemed normal.

After a few seconds, the doc said, "Maybe Finn turned something else back on, and it made a noise." The doctor looked at Hahn, who was visibly shaken and nervously looking around the room.

"Where did it sound like it was coming from?" asked Hahn.

"From over there." The doc nodded to the wall where Alina's body was.

"Yeah, same here."

They waited in dead silence. Neither moved.

"What's on the other side of that wall?" asked Hahn.

"I think it's a storage area off of cargo."

Hahn once again looked around the room. "I have no idea what that was," she said. "But, I hope it wasn't the alien."

"I'm sure it was nothing. This ship has been through a lot. It was cooling off, and now it's heating up again. So, I guess it would be normal to hear some strange noises."

Hahn looked at the doc, "So, our ship is creaking?" Her doubtful tone was unmistakable.

The doc chuckled once. "It's better than being haunted."

"If that was an attempt to be funny, it didn't work." Hahn's response was firm, almost rude. She straightened up and looked around the room again.

"I know this isn't easy. You've been through a lot. I'm stressed, too."

"Hell yeah, I'm stressed." She stared directly into the doc's eyes. "I would rather die than go through that pain again."

"It was that bad?"

Hahn pressed her lips together and inhaled deeply. She leaned forward slightly and said slowly, "It was worse than you can possibly imagine."

The doc stood motionless and absorbed the intensity of Hahn's words.

"I'm sorry," she responded.

Hahn just looked around again. "So, what about Oleg?"

She looked back at the panel. "It doesn't make sense. I thought he was in a coma. But the readings are a bit confusing. They suggest that he should be conscious. But he's not."

Hahn gazed at him and frowned. "Well, maybe he is conscious. Maybe he's fully aware and can't move."

"Yeah, that's what I was wondering. But I didn't want to suggest it. It'd be pretty horrible being fully aware and trapped in your own body. But, on the other hand, there are some other readings that kind of contradict that idea, though I'm not sure what to make of them." She pointed to a set of readings on the display. "It is almost like he's both asleep and awake at the same time."

Hahn just frowned some more and tilted her head to one side. "Well, that makes sense since everything else doesn't."

The doc swiped in the air from left to right, and the initial image of Oleg's body reappeared. She touched the head, and it expanded on the screen. "Cerebral activity." She said. The image of Oleg's brain lit up as it showed various areas of stimulation. The doc pointed at the parietal lobe.

"It looks like he is in pain according to that area of the brain. But it also looks like he's dreaming." She then put her fingertips on her chin and tapped. Then after a few more seconds, she pulled a menu from the right of the screen and swiped down. She touched the words "Heuristic diagnostics." Immediately a list of technical terms appeared with some more numbers and new symbols. It was all well beyond Hahn's expertise.

"It doesn't make sense," said the doc as she folded her arms again. "Who knows what that creature did to him. His brain is all out of sync." She turned around and went over to some more drawers on the wall. She pulled one open and retrieved a packaged needle and swab. She then opened a cabinet, and a small vial of something fell out. She skillfully caught it.

"Nice catch."

"Thanks. Things got jostled a bit in zero gravity."

She returned the vial and began to rummage through a cabinet above and found a small container of liquid. She turned back to Hahn, who was now standing by Oleg's side, half watching the doc, half perusing the room.

"If he is conscious of everything, is in pain, and he can't move, it would be a nightmare." She looked at Hahn. "Exactly. So, I'm going to give him a sedative that should put him to sleep. That is if he's awake somehow."

She opened the package, took the swab, and wiped the inner bend of his elbow. She then opened the needle package and stuck it into the upturned vial. She withdrew some liquid and tapped on it. Then after finding a vein, injected Oleg. She wiped the puncture wound with another swab before walking over to a silver trash bin and dumping everything in it.

"You still use needles?" asked Hahn.

"I know. It's old fashioned, but the hypo-spray isn't as precise as I'd like. And besides, I want it in pure liquid form, not the vaporized form."

116

She then headed back to the display panel. After about a minute, she slumped her shoulders and turned to Hahn. She was clearly frowning. "The sedative doesn't seem to be working." She looked back at Oleg. "I hope he's not conscious."

Zeke and the Finn were reading through the instructions on the A.I. Control Panel on how to get Janice back online. It would take a few steps, but it seemed surprisingly simple considering how astonishingly complicated she was. The process consisted of activating one system at a time, in a specific order, waiting for the system to self-check, then proceeding to the next. With power restored to the bridge, the A.I. Control Panel would take them through the process step-by-step.

"This doesn't look too difficult," said Finn. He had been going through the instructions for a few minutes.

"I know you can do it. I just hope she's okay when she comes back online."

Finn didn't respond. He was reading some instructions, frowning. He turned back a page, read for a few seconds, then went forward again. "Back on Earth, I was briefed through this procedure, but to be honest, we didn't spend much time on it. Janice is so integrated into the ship with so many backup systems that the possibility of her not being operational wasn't taken seriously. They figured that if Janice wasn't running, it was because the entire ship was destroyed. I'm sure no one even considered the possibility of total power loss due to an alien encounter."

"We'll have them include that in their updated manual when we get back."

"Good idea," said Finn slowly as he concentrated on the instructions.

Zeke looked carefully around the bridge for the creature. They were alone.

Finn leaned forward and looked at the panel more closely before straightening up again. "At least the eggheads back home knew what they were doing. We need to begin the boot-up process, just like she was being turned on for the first time. It should be fine. I *hope* it'll be fine. If not, we're screwed."

"Space is unpredictable," said Zeke. "They couldn't have thought of every contingency. And it doesn't matter anyway. They're there. We're here. So, I just choose to believe that she will be fine. Everything else came online okay. Why shouldn't she?"

Finn just turned and gave Zeke a glance out of the corner of his eye then returned to his work. "I hope you're right."

After another few seconds of reading, Finn chimed in with one more comment. "One good thing is that those know-it-alls back on Earth made it easy enough that a monkey could do it."

"Well?" said Zeke as he made a hand motion encompassing both of them. "That's why *we're* here."

Finn chuckled.

The doc was checking on Oleg. She'd pulled out some more medical instruments and was poking and prodding. Hahn watched but spent most of her time looking around the room with a seemingly permanent semi-scowl etched on her face. Occasionally, she would take a deep soothing breath, crack her neck, stretch, and continue scanning.

The doc, of course, was quite aware of Hahn's nervousness. "How do you feel about me giving you a quick exam?"

Hahn cocked her head. "Really?"

The doc smiled. "I can do it while you're standing there."

"Maybe later."

She then turned her attention back to examining Oleg and glanced over at the diagnostic panel.

"Well, that's weird," she said as she slowly straightened up. She was holding a multi-pronged instrument.

"What?"

"Best I can tell, he's fully conscious. At least that's what the readings *say*, but I don't know if they are accurate."

She tapped her forefinger on the instrument while she thought it over. The doc was on a mission. She went over and opened up a drawer and pulled out another piece of medical tech. It looked like a small display about 15 cm x 15 cm, with no buttons or knobs. She moved back over to Oleg and hovered it over his forehead, then double-tapped on the screen. Hahn could see a small hologram appear over it, but she didn't know what it was from her angle. It didn't matter. Her main concern was guard duty. After about a minute, the doc tapped her fingernail on the back of the gadget, and it turned off.

"So? What's up? Got anything figured out?"

The doc slowly turned to face her. "Yeah, I do. I don't know what the problem is."

Hahn scoffed.

"Well, his frontal lobe function is quite active. And, I don't see any damage at all to the motor cortex. It just doesn't make any sense. Everything looks okay, more or less. He seems to be conscious. In fact, he seems to be either thinking or seeing something or experiencing something."

She paused for a moment as she let her own words settle in.

"Anything would be better than what I experienced," offered Hahn.

The doc didn't say anything. She was lost in thought.

"Well, is there a way we can communicate with him?" said Hahn. "Maybe we could slap him in the face and see if he reacts?"

The doc looked at her sideways.

Hahn shrugged her shoulders.

The doc reached down and, with her thumb, opened one of his eyelids. His eye was moving rapidly.

"REM?" she said aloud to herself.

"What?"

"That's new. I checked his eyes a few minutes ago, and they weren't moving."

Hahn took a few seconds out of her continuous scanning to watch the doc who was in her own little world, talking to herself, thinking everything through.

"Rapid eye movement occurs when someone is asleep and dreaming. He is either dreaming or…" She faded off.

"Or what?"

The doc turned and faced Hahn. Her brow was furrowed. "Or something totally new is happening to him. After all, we don't know anything about this creature. We don't know what it did to him. So, Oleg is either dreaming, thinking, locked in his own world apart from his body, conscious or unconscious, something else. But part of me leans toward the idea that he's experiencing something."

Hahn stared hard at the doc. "Experiencing what?"

"I don't know, but I don't think it's good."

Chapter 15
Caution

"Yes!" Finn fist-pumped the air.

Zeke had been standing by the window, staring out into the stars, but moved closer to get a better look.

"Green! Green is good!"

He was smiling hugely as he looked at Zeke. "It means that her systems check out." Then after a therapeutic exhale, "I wasn't worried at all," he said in a sarcastic tone.

The captain scanned the bridge. "How long before she's up?"

"Not long," he replied in a trailing voice.

There wasn't much Zeke could do except stay out of Finn's way. The last thing he wanted was to slow him down. So, he thought about their situation, considering different options and possibilities. Besides, Finn was quite capable of getting Janice back online by himself, providing there wasn't any unforeseen problem. So, Zeke stood guard and divided his time between checking around the room, looking for the creature, and contemplating their situation. He walked over to the window.

The Drake sun was clearly visible, brighter, and larger than any other stars. It was directly ahead of them. In a few weeks, they would arrive. But, would they be alive, and if so, what would they find there? One thing was for sure. Because the quantum drive was dead, a lot of what they came to do would not be possible. They were limping along, entirely on their own.

He looked over at Finn again. "How's it going?"

"Fine."

Without the quantum drive, there was no hyperspace tunneling for a return trip to Earth and no subspace communication.

Alina was dead, Oleg was in a coma, and Janice was offline. It was bad. But, the solar panels were working and would keep the ship fully charged. They would have to go into a parking orbit around Drakus, the fourth planet, while they waited for rescue. But doing that without Janice would be very difficult. Hopefully, she would be back online soon. They needed her desperately. She *had* to work.

He turned to Finn, who was tracing his finger on the panel reading some directions. Should he go over and assist? Nah, it was best to stay out of his way.

So, Zeke scanned the bridge again for the creature and then turned back to gaze out into the darkness. He had spent many years in its depths. He had always been fascinated by the interstellar cosmos.

"Things are going fine," said Finn to Zeke, interrupting his musing. "I don't get it. We lost all our energy, and yet every system seems to be okay. Weird. But, as far as I can tell, I should have Janice up and running real soon. But, I'm definitely not gonna rush it."

While Finn had been talking, Zeke joined him at the panel. He offered a supervisory glance.

"Well, take your time. Do it right."

"It's hard *not* to do it right. If it works, I really can't take any credit. Like I said, monkeys."

Hahn was habitually looking around medical. Anything out of the ordinary was upsetting, especially after hearing that noise, which they could not explain. If Hahn even *thought* she saw something, she would jerk around and examine it hard before returning back to a semi-normal scan.

The doc walked over to the table and held Oleg's right hand in hers. She sighed and then pressed her lips together in her frustration. "With all these instruments and advanced technology, I can't figure out what's wrong with him."

Hahn didn't reply.

"Could you go over to that drawer and get me a hypodermic needle?" The doc pointed as she spoke.

Of course, she could do it quicker, and Hahn knew that.

"These instruments are really good, but sometimes it just helps to see a person's blood under a microscope. I'm a little old-fashioned that way."

Hahn walked over and retrieved the item.

"Could you grab me an alcohol swab also, in the same drawer?"

Hahn gave her a look that said, 'Why didn't you have me get it before?' But once again, she quickly retrieved the object and handed it to the doc with a slow presentation of her hand.

"Thanks," she said with a half-smile.

Hahn started to look around again. "I know what I'm gonna do when that thing comes back."

"What?"

"Run!"

"It didn't attack us on the bridge."

"So? We don't know why. Like I said, if it appears, you can count on me getting out of here."

The doc ignored Hahn's ultimatum as she began to prepare another vein on Oleg's arm. She tossed the swab into the trash. Then with the practiced skill of the thousand stabs, she pierced the vein. Oleg showed no reaction.

"Good." Finn was talking to himself loud enough for Zeke to hear. "Another subsystem came on just fine." He walked over to a panel and tapped a button underneath it. A keyboard emerged. He typed in, 'Janice; Test; 1234567890; Test; Janice.' He folded his arms and waited. Within a few seconds, the word 'VERIFIED' manifested. Finn nodded, reached for the display, and tapped on the word three times. It disappeared and was replaced by 'Initiate A.I. Lower Systems Protocol: Yes No.'

By now, Zeke was behind him, watching. Finn turned halfway around and looked at him over his shoulder. "Here we go." He then tapped on 'Yes' and stood back. "This is gonna take about a minute. There is an automatic self-diagnostic system that has to run first, and then we'll know if we can move forward after that. But, so far, so good."

Zeke nodded and rechecked the bridge. He didn't see anything. But, of course, he wondered if it was watching them.

"You know something?" said Zeke. "When the alien was here, and the stars were inside the room, it didn't attack us. I can't stop thinking about it. Why didn't it attack us?"

"Maybe it was studying us, trying to figure out our weaknesses."

Zeke pressed his lips together and exhaled. "No, I don't think so. It's intelligent and..." he paused as he considered what he was about to say. "What if it wants to communicate with us?"

Finn looked at Zeke. "When did you start taking your stupid pills again?"

"No, I'm serious. Think about it. It can move anywhere in the ship it wants to, outside or inside, doesn't matter. Maybe it wasn't intending to kill. Maybe it's so different that, that it hurts us when it encounters us."

Finn was staring at the captain with a discernible frown.

"It could've attacked us all. But it didn't. It sent the flashlight back. It has to mean that it wants to communicate with us."

Finn looked back at the screen, waiting for the check to complete. Then he turned his attention back to Zeke. "You have your theories, and I have mine. As far as I'm concerned, we can't trust it. Yeah, I know it's alien life and all that, and maybe we ought to try and study it. But it's already killed Alina and Oleg is in a coma. It hurt Han real bad, and I don't mind saying it got me, too. It's drained all our power, and now we're stranded. This thing is dangerous. We need to protect ourselves from it, not sit down and have tea with it."

Zeke just looked at Finn and crossed his arms. "Maybe you're right. But whatever we do, we need to move carefully."

"Now you're finally making sense," said Finn as he continued to stare at the screen. The diagnostic was not yet complete. "How are the ladies doing?" He asked.

"I'll find out." Zeke walked over to a display and tapped on "Open Communications." A window expanded on the screen with a list of areas on the ship. Normally, he would just ask Janice to convey a message to somebody. But for now, this would have to do.

"Are the comms working?" asked Finn.

"You know, in all the excitement of getting everything turned back on, we didn't check to see if they were."

"Yeah, we *have* been a little distracted." Finn turned his attention back to the communications display, found medical, and tapped on it.

"How are you ladies doing?"

He heard an indistinguishable sound that was accompanied by foul language. Then, after a few seconds, Hahn responded. "Can you give us a friggin' warning before you start talking out of nowhere? You scared the crap out of us!"

125

Zeke's face was wrapped in a smile as he imagined both of the ladies flinching. "Sorry about that." His insincerity was obvious in his tone.

"Yeah, right!" He heard the doc saying sarcastically.

"Any news on Oleg?"

"No, he's the same. I drew some blood, and I'm running some tests. But I'll say this. So far, the readings don't make sense. I think he might very well be conscious and just unable to move. But I don't know for sure. And I also tried to give him an injection to put him to sleep, just in case he was somehow awake. But there was no change in his brain activity. So I just don't know what to make of it."

"Well, what does your gut tell you?"

"My gut says he's all screwed up," replied the doc clearly. The short definitive answer carried the subtle tone that said she wanted to be left alone to do her job.

"All right, just keep me informed."

"One more thing," said Hahn. "A little while ago, both of us heard a noise. It caught us off guard. But I was wondering if it could be the ship cooling and heating, and maybe some creaking."

"What did it sound like?"

"Well," said Hahn. "It was kind of like a faint scraping or creaking. Maybe like something brushing up against something else. It only lasted a second. But it was loud enough to get our attention" She looked at the doc.

"Yeah, that pretty much sums it up."

"I don't know what to tell you," said Zeke, "Without hearing it myself, I wouldn't know where to begin to try and figure it out. Like you said, maybe it has something to do with the ship heating up. Right now, that is good an explanation as any."

He looked at Finn and raised his eyebrows.

"Yeah, its got to be the ship reheating," said Finn loudly. "I wouldn't worry about it." He threw an I-don't-know-what-it-is look back at Zeke.

"It has to be the ship getting back to normal," said Zeke. But, he had never heard any sound that would fit the description they gave. And, he'd never heard of the Cascade making noises from cooling and warming up. But, then again, it was a few years old, and who knows what the creature did to it. So, maybe it was possible.

"That's what we were thinking," said the doc.

Zeke looked at Finn and nodded his head upward once as if asking for Finn to add more. Finn shook his head and went back to work.

"Just keep your eyes open for that thing. For all we know, it could be something caused by the creature." He instantly regretting his words.

"That's just great," said Hahn. "First, it's the ship creaking, and now it's the monster."

"Sorry. But considering everything that's happened, we can't take anything for granted. So, keep your eyes peeled. And if you hear that sound again, let us know, and we'll come and check it out."

"Great," said the doctor. "Men to the rescue."

Zeke chuckled slightly. "Well, if it makes you feel any better, you can come and rescue us here if it shows up. Just listen for two men screaming like babies. Oh, and on your way, could you stop by the galley and bring us some sandwiches?"

He waited for the responding insults to rain down on him from the speakers.

"We are not can it dignify that." It was Hahn.

Zeke looked over at Finn, who was shaking his head and said, "You know, sometimes I worry about you."

"Me, too," said the doc over the speakers.

"And you'd be right to worry," said Zeke. "But hey, look at the bright side, we're alive and kicking."

"For now," said Finn.

Zeke looked at him. "You're not helping. I'm just trying to relieve the tension a little. Besides, the ladies need it, too."

"You know we can still hear you?" said Hahn.

The doc came back online over those same hidden speakers in the bridge. "How's it coming along with Janice?"

"Great!" said Finn. "So far, so good. I expect her to be up and running in no time."

"Glad to hear it. If you two men need any help, just let us know, and we'll come and rescue you."

Zeke smiled. "Sure thing, just remember those sandwiches." He was surprised by his own willingness to tease them, giving the dark situation. As soon as he realized that, it killed his good mood.

"Do you like digging a hole for yourself?" asked Finn.

"Only in interstellar space." He tried to smile, but it didn't manifest. The seriousness of their situation had come ebbing back.

"Wait!" said Hahn. "There, there it is again. We just heard that sound again."

"Hahn?" said Zeke into the air. "You okay?"

Nothing.

"Hahn? Doc?"

Hahn's scream filled the bridge.

Finn bolted out of the bridge first with Zeke right behind him. It would take about 20 seconds at a good run to get there. They covered it in less as they raced through the ship.

Chapter 16
Bright Light

The creature was hovering over Alina's body, elongated, mimicking her proportions. Small undulating lights that sparkled moved in indistinguishable patterns within its vague boundary. It almost looked like space with stars in it, but it was different and had a strange depth that seemed to proceed further than the wall which was behind it.

They all watched in silence, waiting to see what would happen. Hahn, who had promised to flee at its next appearance, stayed. She was furthest away from it, wide-eyed and taking rapid, shallow breaths.

Zeke and Finn were closest. The doc was by the table with Oleg

"It just appeared out of nowhere," said the doc. "It's been shimmering like that the whole time."

"Has it moved?" asked Zeke.

"No."

They all stood transfixed by the alien image before them. It wasn't acknowledging their presence, at least as far as they could tell. Then what appeared to be a wave slowly pulsed from one end of it to the other. As it passed, it seemed to dim the lights' intensity within the creature, but they returned in strength just a little brighter after it passed.

Everyone had moved back toward the table that held Oleg.

Its ill-defined boundaries seemed to change slightly, but overall, it remained the same size. Then, as it continued to undulate, it slowly descended upon Alina's body.

Both Zeke and Finn stepped sideways as they moved around the table in retreat.

Within it, a single wave moved from one end of Alina's body to the other, then it started again from her head. With each cycle, the speed slowly increased, as did the intensity of the lights within it. There was no sound. There only that wave and the hundreds of sparkling lights within the creature's amorphous shape.

"What the hell is it doing?" asked Finn in a whisper.

Nobody said anything.

Zeke took a step towards it.

"Stay away from it," said the doc in a stern and muffled tone.

He took another small step.

No change.

"Zeke!"

Another step, then another. The creature's visual display slowed to a stop. Zeke waited. Was it aware of his presence? He took one step back. Within a few seconds, the creature started its display again. Zeke looked around at the others. Then he turned his attention back to it and took one more step towards it. And once again, the visual spectacle stopped. Zeke then took another step back, and the creature continued.

He slowly backtracked and joined the others. "What do you make of that?"

"What I make of it is that you're an idiot!" said the doc.

"Look, it didn't attack us on the bridge."

"So?"

"So, I figured it might not be trying to hurt us."

"And you're willing to risk your life over that?"

"I don't think it was much of a risk. I wonder what would happen if I got even closer."

She grabbed him by the shoulder and gave him a hard look.

He got the message.

"Doc!" said Hahn. "Oleg!"

They all looked at him. His eyes were open, but his face was contorted. The doc bent over him and looked into his eyes. "Oleg?"

She glanced at the creature that was still engulfing Alina's body before returning her gaze to him and placing her hands on either side of his head. She gently shook him and spoke with a soft intensity. "Oleg! Oleg!"

There was no response.

"He looks like he's in pain," she said.

Hahn clenched her fists and glared over at the creature, half in anger, half in fear. "It's hurting him." She unsheathed her flashlight from her pocked ready to throw it at the creature. "Do something!"

The doc slowly moved over to a set of drawers on a wall next to her office door. She pulled one open, grabbed a mysterious medical device before returning to Oleg. She pointed it at his left temple then looked at the display screen. She furrowed her brow, "What the....?"

"What?" asked Zeke.

She looked at Zeke, puzzled. "It doesn't make sense. The instruments say one thing, but what we see is another. And, I don't get this, but the readings seem to change. There really should be one constant reading here. But it changes. It's like there are two brains in the same place." Her words trailed off as she said them.

"What do you mean?" Zeke spoke to her in a subdued voice while keeping an eye on the creature.

She didn't say anything.

"Doc?"

"The readings are off. It's like everything is happening in his brain all at once." She looked back to Oleg. "But..." she paused. "There is another... no wait." She paused again and glared at Zeke. "This can't be right." She lowered the instrument and looked into Oleg's tortured eyes. "He must be in hell."

Oleg was slowing opening and closing his mouth, but he made no sound. He was pressing his head back against the table, almost lifting his shoulders off of it. His brow was furrowed, and his eyes were wide open. He gripped the edges of the table and slowly strained against them."

"Can't you do anything?" asked Hahn desperately.

"I wouldn't know where to begin. I might hurt him trying to help."

"You can't hurt him any more than what he's going through now," responded Zeke.

"Look," said Finn nodding towards the creature.

The pulsing was now quite rapid, about three times per second.

"The light," said Hahn. "Why isn't it casting any shadows?" They all glanced at her briefly, not understanding what she was saying. "Look. It's pulsing light, but there are no shadows anywhere. The light isn't shining on us or this room, only in the creature."

Zeke, the doc, and Finn all looked around.

"You're right," said Finn. "It's emitting light, but there are no shadows from it. It's as though the laws of physics don't work around this thing."

The doc looked back to Oleg. She raised her eyebrows, sympathetic to his pain, but aggravated that she couldn't do anything to help them. "Screw it."

She returned quickly to the same set of drawers, but this time opened up a large one near the floor and pulled out a device. It resembled an awkward combination of a camera attached to a rectangular display screen that had handles on either side. She returned to where Oleg was.

"This is a Deep Bone Scanner. It sends out an energy field." She slid the power switch on top of the DBS. It lit up. "I have no idea if this will work since it is designed for very close range, but let's see if it does anything to this bastard."

"Wait!" said Zeke. "I'll do it!"

"No!" she retorted. "I'm sick of this!" She was on the other side of the table from Zeke. He began to move towards her, but she ignored him and stepped forward, stopping just short of where Zeke had been before. She raised the instrument, pointed, and with her thumb, pressed a button on the handle.

Immediately the pulsing in the creature stopped. She lowered it and took a step back.

They waited.

Its light show did not return. Instead, it slowly began to morph into a dull, grey. Then, it seemed to disengage from Alina's body. It elongated to about a meter high and half a meter wide. Then, it moved towards them just a bit and stopped.

They all stepped back.

It moved towards the doc. She stepped back further. The creature stopped.

It hovered in front of them. All they could see was a grey hole in space without any discernible depth to it.

Zeke, who was now closest to Oleg, looked down at him. His eyes were closed once again, and he no longer appeared to be in pain.

The creature pulsed in size by a few centimeters then shrank back. After about a second, it again grew by a few more centimeters before shrinking back again, each time getting a little taller. This repeated for about half a minute until it was about two meters high and one wide as it hovered before them. Its edges were slowly undulating, blurring the boundary between it and the room. Then, once again, it moved towards them, but only a little. They all took a step backward. It stopped.

The doc began to raise the DBS once again. At about halfway, she hesitated. What would using it again do? Would it make the creature angry? Would it attack them? She lowered it.

They watched as its edges slowly swelled, then retreated only to do it again and increase in size. There were no visible edges, just a vague penumbra of light and dark that surrounded a grey hole in space.

The doc checked on Oleg again. He had returned to his apparent coma.

Within the hazy boundary of the creature, the grey began to fade and was slowly being replaced by the increasing darkness. Then, a few faint dots of light appeared. One of the lights grew in size until it clearly dominated the others, which were morphing into circles of differing sizes. One had a ring around it. Another had horizontal stripes. One was rust-colored, and another was bluish.

Transfixed, the crew watched the otherworldly display.

"Wait," said Zeke. "That's the Drake system. That is the Drake sun with the planets around it."

Immediately Hahn shouted, "Look!" She pointed at Alina's body, that is, at the body bag. But, it was empty, flat. "Where's her body?"

All they could see was the empty plastic sack.

Their shock was interrupted by another of the creature's small movements towards them. They retreated an equal distance darting their eyes back and forth between it and the empty body bag, still trying to process the disparate and confusing events.

Alina's body was gone. The creature was displaying the Drake system, and it had made small advances towards them.

"Doc?" said Zeke, breaking the silence.

"Yeah?"

"Get ready to use that scanner if it comes at us again."

"Okay," she muttered as she firmly gripped the instrument.

They had all moved back and were near Oleg's feet. The doc, always the one concerned for the health of others, put a hand on his foot before returning it to the DBS.

The creature did not advance. Instead, it hovered and continued its vertically elongated morphing shape with its edges pulsing slowly. Within it, the Drake solar system was perfectly steady. They watched. Then, a line formed from outside of the creature, from inside the room, and arced into the stellar display, moved towards the sun and intersected the fourth planet.

It was their flight path.

Stunned and speechless, they all stared silently, motionless.

It hovered above the floor, continuing to pulse slowly, and retained its overall shape as the Drake system stayed steadily visible within its boundaries. The display repeated the single light that arced from outside the creature, into its form, around the Drake sun, and intersected the fourth planet.

Then the creature moved towards them a few more centimeters.

The doc raised the bone scanner and pressed the button. Immediately its internal depiction of the Drake system disappeared, replaced by a gray hue.

She let go of the button.

It hovered in the same place, undulating, morphing, and then once again, the Drake system appeared with that same flight path. The doc lowered the bone scanner.

It moved towards them again, but more slowly.

They backed away the same distance it approached. The doc raised the scanner. It continued forward slightly. She pressed the button once more. The Drake system disappeared, and the same gray hue replaced it. But the creature kept moving forward. She kept the button down as she backed up. They all backed up. But the creature kept approaching. Then, in an instant, it jumped forward and engulfed the doctor. Everyone instinctively bolted away from her.

The doc was frozen, caught in a painful expression, slightly hunched over. The DBS was engulfed in its glassy form.

After a few moments, Zeke lunged towards the table and grabbed an instrument the doc had placed there earlier. He intended to shove into the creature's field. But, before he could, it emitted a powerful, intense white light that forced them to shield their eyes and turn away. Zeke struggled to see what was happening, but it was too much. He could barely open his eyes, but only if he kept his hands over them. Finn had hunched his head down between his shoulders, his back to the creature's brilliant display. He covered his eyes with his forearm. Hahn had likewise turned away, covering her eyes with both hands.

Then without warning, the incredibly intense light disappeared. The doctor fell to the ground.

Chapter 17
Footsteps

It took a few seconds for their eyes to begin to readjust. Zeke, Finn, and Hahn all blinked through the remnants of eye strain as they tried to search for the creature.

"Where is it?" asked Hahn nervously. She covered her eyes slightly as she checked medical.

"I think it's gone," said Finn. His voice, too, was strained by the discomfort.

"Doc!" said Zeke.

She was lying limp on the floor. They rushed to her side.

Zeke bent down, put his fingertips on her jugular, and paused. "There's a pulse."

Finn tried to straighten out her crumpled form as he slid the DBS away.

"Check on Oleg," said Zeke.

Finn quickly moved over to the table. Oleg's eyes were open, staring at the ceiling. "He's awake!"

Zeke sprung up quickly, got to the table, and leaned over him. "Oleg?" There was no response. "Oleg?"

He slowly moved his eyes and looked directly into Zeke's. Then, with short breaths, he tried to form a word. Zeke brought his ear close and listened, but couldn't make it out. He glanced down at the doc. Hahn was by her side.

"I'm here, buddy. I'm here. Talk to me."

He pressed his lips together and whispered one word. "Pain." Then he closed his eyes.

"No," said Zeke in pleading voice. "Stay with me. Stay with me." He put his fingertips on his jugular once again. The pulse was still there.

Oleg's lips moved again, and Zeke once more drew close and put his ear to Oleg's mouth, but nothing came out. He pulled back to look. Oleg's lips were moving.

"It looks like he is forming a 'p,'" said Finn.

Then Oleg let out a long breath, and his chest stopped moving

Zeke checked him again. "No pulse."

"Oleg!" he shouted.

Nothing.

He looked at Finn. "Get the defibrillator!"

Finn and Hahn looked around the room frantically. But, they didn't know what to look for or even where to look. Where did the doc keep it? They both scrambled through cabinets and drawers as fast as they could, but it was useless.

"We can't find it!" said Finn.

Zeke jumped up on the table and straddled Oleg's abdomen. He then clasped his hands together and started pushing down on Oleg's chest, counting. "One, two, three, four, five, six, seven, eight, nine, ten." By then, Finn was with him. "Check his pulse," said Zeke as he stopped.

Finn checked his neck artery. After a few seconds, he said, "nothing."

Zeke began the compressions again. Five seconds, 10 seconds, 15, 20 seconds of pumping. He stopped. Finn automatically checked for a pulse again, looked up at Zeke, and shook his head.

Zeke continued. Another 20 seconds of compressions. He stopped. Finn checked for the pulse once more. He looked at Zeke shook his head. "He's gone."

Zeke slammed his fist on the hard table. "No!" For a few moments, he stayed in his awkward position until he clumsily got off the table.

"This can't be happening!" Zeke said loud and clear. He paused for a moment and processed Oleg's death. He looked at the doc and bent down to check on her. She was still breathing. He checked her pulse. It seemed strong.

"It's picking us off, one by one," said Zeke.

"We've got to kill it!" said Finn as he looked at Oleg and then over at Alina's empty body bag. "We have to kill it. We have to find a way to destroy this thing before it kills us all!" He looked at the doc on the floor.

Zeke formed a fist and pressed his knuckles onto the floor next to the doc. After a few seconds, he stood up. An expression of determination accompanied his words. "Alright, it's just the three of us now. So, we have to get our crap together."

He took a forced breath and pressed his eyelids closed. Then another before glaring at Finn. "No more. We have to fight it."

He ran his fingers through his hair as he closed his eyes and swallowed hard. "Let's get the doc on that gurney," he said as he nodded to the one over by a wall. "We'll take her with us to the bridge. The attack on her wasn't a very long, so maybe, just maybe she'll come out of it. But for now, we need to get Janice back online. Then we can start figuring out a strategy and maybe find a way to help the doc."

"Yeah, and she can help us figure out how to kill it," said Finn as he returned a cold stare into Zeke's eyes.

Zeke looked over at Hahn. She was rubbing her forehead with her fingers, eyes closed.

"Hahn?"

She didn't respond.

"Hahn!"

She looked at him.

"Are you okay? Are you up for this?"

She dropped her hand to her side and took a breath. Her tenseness and forced movements were obvious, as was her reply. "Yeah." Then after a few seconds, she added, "I'm up for killing it."

"I heard that," said Finn in a strong tone.

"But for now, let's rely on our training and work one problem at a time. This creature is changing its method. Who knows how long before it attacks again. So, for now, we all stick together."

"Yeah, sounds good," said Finn. He looked over at Hahn. She nodded.

"Hahn, can you get the gurney?" He spoke while nodding at it by the wall. She finally complied, but not before approaching Finn and hitting him in the shoulder. "Let's kill it."

"Finn?" said Zeke as he bent down to the doc.

Together they lifted her onto the gurney and strapped her in place. Then Hahn checked the carotid artery. "Her pulse seems strong."

Finn held her hand and stared at her expressionless face as he drew close. "Hang in there, doc."

Zeke got Finn's attention by looking at him. "Let's get Janice back online and figure out how to kill this thing."

"Agreed," it shouldn't take…"

There was a faint noise that came from outside in the hallway.

"What was that?" asked Hahn as she backed away from the door.

They were all three looking out of medical. They listened, but there was nothing more. After a moment, Zeke said, "Hahn, is that what you heard earlier?"

She didn't respond.

"Hahn!"

Hahn's fear-ridden face jerked towards Zeke.

"Was that what you heard before?"

"No. It's different. It was a scraping sound before. That was metallic." She was breathing in quick, shallow breaths, showing a deeply furrowed brow.

Zeke walked over to the door and stuck his head out in the hallway. "I don't see anything."

He went back into the room near Hahn. Her eyes were locked on his.

"It's okay. It's nothing," he said reassuringly. "It's the ship warming up, making some sounds."

"It's not nothing!" she snapped. "It's never nothing. You saw what that thing can do! It's evil. It's going to kill us!"

Zeke grabbed her by the shoulders. "Hahn!" He shook her. "Get it together! That's an order!"

She looked at him and shrugged herself loose and took a step back. "Get it together? Sure, I'll do that as soon as we kill it!" She then looked past them out into the hallway. "You heard that. We all heard it. It didn't sound like some sound the ship would make. What the hell is going on?"

She stepped closer to Finn, staring out into the hallway.

"Why don't you take a look?" She asked.

Finn stared back at her and trying to muster some courage, said, "Okay,"

He took a deliberate breath and then walked over to the door and stuck his head into the hallway. After looking in both directions, he turned back to face them both. "Nothing." He stepped back into the room.

"We all heard it," said Hahn. She looked at Finn hard. "You're the engineer. Have you ever heard a sound like that before on the ship?"

"No. I haven't. Maybe it was the ship. Maybe something's wrong with the ship. I don't know."

"It's the creature," said Hahn. "It's doing something."

"We don't know that," said Zeke. "The ship has been through a lot, and so," he paused. "...and so, we just don't know what it was. Let's not make this into something it isn't."

Hahn stepped forward and looked at Zeke almost with a defiant glare. "You saw Oleg's face. He was in agony, and I know why - because he *was* in agony. It's like being in hell. The pain is

141

total. It is absolutely horrible, and I *never* want to experience that again. I'd rather die first." She paused and forced herself to calm down. "And now there's another sound. Something's not right." Her voice was still shaking, gradually rising in pitch. "Maybe we should kill the doc right now and put her out of her misery."

"Stow that, Hahn!" He grabbed her by the shoulders again and shook her firmly. "We're going to beat this thing. You saw what the bone scanner did to it. It can be affected. We're going to get Janice back up and figure this out. So, until then, stay focused. That's an order."

She shook herself free. "Yeah, sure. Whatever you say."

Zeke turned to Finn. "There's nothing more we can do for her right now. So, let's get her to the bridge and get Janice powered up."

Finn nodded. "Agreed."

He looked over at Hahn. "You going to be okay?"

"Hell, no!"

"Good, then let's go."

With that, Hahn bent down and retrieved the DBS from the floor while Zeke and Finn moved next to the doc on the gurney, one at the head, the other at her feet. They all turned towards the doorway.

But, there was another metallic sound. With it, came a fear that robbed them all of movement. There it was again. Then another. It sounded like a shuffling, a clicking…and it was getting louder.

They stood quietly, fixated on the doorway.

A drop of sweat rolled down Finn's temple. He swallowed. Hahn gripped the DBS.

Zeke took a half step towards the door but froze when he heard the sound yet again. It was definitely louder, definitely closer. Then another sound and but it was muffled. Zeke moved back towards the table. Hahn raised a shaking DBS towards the hall. Her eyes were wide open, shoulders tense.

There was no way out of the room. They were trapped. The only exit was towards the noise that brought with its approach a paralyzing fear. It wasn't the ship. It was something else. Had the creature found a way to move through the hallways? No, that was ridiculous. But, they all heard it. They all froze in fear at the approaching sound.

Hahn glanced down at the DBS, hands trembling, fumbling as she tried to figure out how to turn it on.

"It sounds like mag-boots," said Zeke.

The sound was getting closer. The muffled sound of footsteps grew louder, then slowed.

It was close.

Alina took a step into the room. "What's going on?" she said with a confused frown. "When did the lights and gravity come back on?"

Chapter 18
Confusion

Alina squinted in the harsh light of medical as she stared at her three stunned friends. She took a step inside. They moved back, intently focused on the impossibility before them. It made absolutely no sense.

"What the hell happened to the doc and Oleg? Are they okay?" Alina started to move further into the room.

All three of them retreated.

"What's going on? What's wrong with them?" Her voice was strained. She looked groggy and was squinting under her partial frown.

"Stay there. That's an order," said Zeke automatically.

Alina complied. She looked at them and then back to the doc and Oleg again.

"Would you mind telling me what the hell is going on? What's wrong with them? When did the power come back on?"

No one said anything.

"Why aren't you answering me?" asked Alina. "Say something." She took another step forward. And again, the group took a corresponding step backward.

She stopped once more.

They all stood there, staring at her, trying to absorb what they were seeing.

Alina shook her head once and rubbed her forehead. Then, she approached them again.

Zeke put his hand up, palm facing her.

She stopped.

"What's wrong?"

They said nothing.

"Cap? What's going on?" She looked around. "Talk to me! Why won't you answer?"

The impossible was standing before them. Was it really Alina, or was this some trick the creature had manifested?

"When did gravity and the lights come back on?" she asked.

Zeke could see she was wearing the mag boots. But they had taken them off when they put her in the body bag.

She took another step towards them. Hahn retreated again, but this time both Zeke and Finn stood their ground.

"Alina?" Said Zeke cautiously.

"Yeah? What? What's happening?" She rubbed her temples with both hands and blinked hard.

"You're dead," blurted Finn. "You're dead. You can't be real." He was staring at her with a stern, hard look.

She jerked her head back on her shoulders. "What are you talking about?" She moved further into the room.

"Don't come any closer!" said Hahn. "It's gotta be the creature," she said to Zeke. "Don't trust it!"

"What are you talking about? Come on, what's happening?"

She looked around the room. "The lights are on." She looked down at her mag boots. "Gravity is working. I don't get it. This doesn't make any sense. I was in my quarters and then…" She strained to remember. "Then the power was on, and I was in the hallway."

She returned her gaze back to the doc.

"What happened to her?" asked Alina.

They were still assessing, still coping with Alina's presence. She looked at Oleg.

Silence.

"Damn it! Talk to me! Tell me what is going on!" She took several steps closer to them as she spoke. Her flashlight was tucked in her pants pocket.

Zeke stayed where he was. "What's the last thing you remember?" he asked.

"I'm telling you it's a trick," said Hahn. "It's the creature, pretending to be Alina."

"Maybe," said Zeke. "But then, where's her body?"

Alina, confused, looked at him and rummaged through her incomplete memories. "The hallway," she said with a frown as she stared blankly at the floor. I was suddenly standing out there in the hallway." She looked at Zeke and frowned. "But I was in my quarters." She looked at them as she cocked her head slightly. "It doesn't make sense. I was in my quarters, then in the hallway, and now the lights and gravity are on."

She blinked hard twice and shook her head. "I don't feel good."

Hahn and Finn looked at each other then back to Alina.

"How did I get in the hallway? I don't remember how I go there. But, I heard you all talking, so I came in." She rubbed her forehead with her fingertips. "It's weird. I feel weird." As she spoke, she looked aimlessly past them, struggling to understand.

"Pain. I'm not sure, but I think I remember pain." She squinted and furrowed her brow at the reemerging memories. She ran both hands through her hair and clinched it in her fists. "Yeah, pain. I remember pain."

Her face was twisted in confusion. "Was that real?"

"Yes," said Zeke. He took another step towards her.

"Careful," said Hahn.

Alina tried to handle the memories that were flooding back. She pressed her eyes closed and tilted her head down as she tried to make sense of everything.

She opened them. "It was horrible." She let her arms fall to her sides as she stared blankly passed them. "I've never felt anything like it. The pain was so bad. And, and I couldn't move. I was suffocating." She scanned each memory carefully. "But, it feels like a dream, as though it wasn't real." Then she stared at Finn. "I remember something, but it…it is like it wasn't really me."

Zeke took a single step towards her, examining her words and movements.

"I remember that someone was there. I remember a presence. It was in me, but it wasn't me. It was alive. It hurt. The pain, the pain. I felt pain."

She shuddered and then shook herself free. "Or did I? In a cracking voice, she looked to Hahn and said, "Did I die?" She mumbled slightly. "Tell me. Tell me what happened."

Zeke looked at Finn and then to Hahn before turning back to Alina.

"You said you felt pain?"

"I did? Yes. I did. I felt pain. A lot of pain."

She ran her hands through her hair again, then rubbed her forehead with her fingertips. "I don't understand." Her voice trailed off. Her hands fell to her side as she tilted her head back. "But it feels like something that wasn't me."

"Alina?" asked Zeke.

She closed her eyes as her head dropped forward and wobbled. She began to fall.

Zeke bolted and swept her up in his arms. Then, just as he caught her, she started to come to and managed to look into his eyes.

"It's all right. You fainted," he said softly.

She was able to get her left arm free and once again put it to her forehead. Then after a few seconds, she said, "I'm okay. I'm okay."

Zeke gently put her feet down. He stayed close.

"I don't know why I fainted. I guess this is all too much for me right now. Yeah, it's too much. Everything, the pain, lights, gravity, Oleg, and the doc. And, those weird, distant images. Weird. And you are all acting so strangely. I guess… I guess it was too much." Her words trailed off as her fatigue robbed her of strength.

Zeke reached out and gently placed his hand on her shoulder. Alina immediately responded by smiling and placing her hand on his. She looked at Finn and Hahn and back to Zeke. Then, after a deep breath, she calmly pushed out the words, "Please, tell me what happened."

Zeke moved his hand to her elbow and then slowly guided her further into the room. She willingly complied as they approached the table. Hahn stayed where she was and maintained both her distance and mild scowl.

"Is it really you?" he asked.

She stared back at him. "Of course, it's me." She looked at the doc and Oleg. "Okay, I, I'm really confused. Why you are asking me these questions."

"Alina," said Finn. "I'm going to it give it to you straight." He looked at Zeke as though asking permission. He nodded.

Finn looked straight into Alina's eyes. "Now, this is not going to make sense, because, well, because it *doesn't* make sense. But, you were dead. The creature did something to you. It attacked you, and when it stopped, you were dead. It all happened in your quarters."

Alina tilted her head slightly and narrowed her eyes as she examined Zeke and Hahn for any signs of deception. They had fixed and somber expressions. "You guys are serious, aren't you?" Her voice was closer to normal.

Zeke nodded slowly.

"That can't be possible. I wasn't dead.... Wait, I was. No..." She shook her head as she squinted. "I was in my quarters. There was this pain. And then all of a sudden, there was blackness. I remember empty blackness. Then, I was in the hallway, and the lights and gravity were on. I heard you all talking, so I came here. But... but, weren't you all on the bridge?"

Her voice retreated back to a strained timbre. Zeke moved over and again put his hand on her shoulder. She looked up into his eyes.

"It's true," he said.

"No, no. It can't be." Her voice retained the remnants of trembling.

"Alina," said Zeke. "When the creature intercepted the ship, we lost power. Everything was drained instantly. You remember that?"

"Yeah," she said softly. "That's clear."

"You went to your quarters to get another flashlight. We heard you scream. When we got to you, the creature was all around you, shimmering, doing something to you. When it let you go, you... you were dead."

Alina kept staring at him, examining his face. She took a deep breath and let it out through pressed lips.

Zeke continued. "Finn and Oleg then went outside the ship to get the solar panels deployed manually so we could get power. That's when the creature attacked Oleg. Finn managed to get him back inside. And..." He paused, then looked over at his body. "He just died a few minutes ago."

She looked at him. "Oleg is dead?"

"Yeah."

Alina looked at the Doc on the gurney. "And the doc is dead, too?"

"No. It attacked her, and she's unconscious. We were going to head to the bridge when you came in. And, I must say, you scared the crap out of us."

Hahn was checking the doc by placing her fingers on her neck. "She's still with us."

Alina moved over towards Oleg's body on the table. Finn and Hahn stayed where they were. She touched his hand and rubbed his skin with her thumb. She slid her fingers and pressed his wrist.

After a few seconds, she slumped her shoulders. "Oleg." A tear fell on his sleeve.

She turned to Zeke, then she went over to the doc lying on the gurney. "Will she die, too?" She asked tenderly.

"We don't know," said Zeke.

Alina took the doc's hand in both of hers and let her fingertips feel the pulse in her wrist. She exhaled and looked back over at Oleg's body. Tears ran down her cheeks. She sniffled.

Zeke approached her again and gently put his hand on her shoulder. "I'm sorry, Alina. I know this must be very difficult for you."

She didn't respond. More silent tears. She wiped them with the back of her hand.

Zeke continued. "Needless to say, the doc's situation is bad. We don't know what to do with her or how to help her. But, since we managed to get power restored, we were working on getting Janice back online. The doc and Hahn were in here checking on Oleg. But the creature showed up. It got the doc."

He paused and examined her to see how she was doing. He decided to continue. She was still holding the doc's hand, staring at her face.

"They already had you in a body bag. You were over there." He nodded towards the wall at the empty bag on the floor.

She glanced at Zeke and followed his nod at the flattened, empty sack.

"The creature was in the room hovering over you, over your body. It was shimmering. It was doing something to you. The doc had some bone scanner instrument that she aimed at it, and the creature didn't like it. That's when it attacked her."

He looked over at the doc. "We think she's in a coma. But we don't know for sure. It was the same with Oleg before he died." Instantly he regretted saying the last sentence.

Once again, she wiped her tears with the back of her hand.

"I know its a lot to take in."

After a few seconds, she relaxed her shoulders in quiet resignation. "Okay, if that's what you say happened, then that's what happened. I'll just have to accept it."

Finn moved his head back on his shoulders. "You seem to be handling this pretty well."

Alina straightened up. "It's pretty simple. You're all telling the truth. I can see that. The last thing I remember was being in my quarters in the dark. You were all on the bridge. Then there was pain, but that part seems vague. Then, all of a sudden, the lights and gravity were on, and you were in here. So, as far as I'm concerned, it all adds up to you telling the truth. I lost some time. And, I...I was dead." She stared off the distance as she said the last statement and paused as if trying to remember. Then she looked at Zeke. "I'm not sure why I can accept this so quickly. It's so strange, but it seems true."

"Strange is right," interjected Zeke.

Alina continued. "Yet, somehow, it makes sense." Her words trailed off.

"What do you mean?"

She again stared into nothing, frowning while she forced her memories loose. "I remember death."

"What?" asked Finn.

She stared at him. "I don't know how to explain it. But I was somewhere. I don't remember where, but at the same time, somehow, I do. It was blackness, emptiness, but there was something far off, getting closer...and then I was here." She broke herself free from the strained and odd recollection. "You must all think I'm crazy."

"Not at all," said Zeke. "Who knows what that thing is capable of or what you experienced. Maybe it's all your imagination, or maybe it's not."

She focused on Zeke, frowned, and shook her head, then spoke in a measured pace. "No. It wasn't my imagination."

Alina took a breath, and her countenance changed to a more relaxed composure. "But I don't know, for sure." Her words had trailed off again as she tried to remember. "So, what do we do now?"

"We'll give you some more details later," said Zeke. "But we have to get to the bridge and get Janice back online.

Zeke turned to Hahn and, with raised eyebrows, said, "How are you doing?"

She scoffed, shook her head, but didn't say anything.

"Hahn?" Said Alina softly.

Hahn still did not respond. Her eyes were narrow, untrusting.

Finn jumped in. "You have to excuse her. The creature got her, and me, too. And yeah, I get it. It was horrible pain. But she had the worst of it. It was really bad. She's still jumpy."

Hahn stared at Finn with a slight glare. "Yeah, I guess you could say I'm jumpy." She looked at Alina. "And let's just say I'm being cautious."

Alina took a small breath and, in a clear, steady voice, said, "Okay. I understand." She looked back to Oleg and the doc. "Here we are, one dead, one in a coma, and one resurrected." She looked at Zeke. "So what are we going to do now?"

Zeke chuckled once. "Yeah, it's you. Only Alina would be so logical so quickly. Welcome back."

She nodded with a forced breath and slight frown.

"Well, since we're all accepting the impossible surprisingly well, I think we need to get back on track and get to the bridge."

"How do we know this isn't a trick?" Interrupted Hahn.

"It isn't a trick. It's me. I don't know how to convince you that it really is me, but it is. I was in my quarters right after the power failure, and now I'm here. I don't know what to tell you. But it's me." She blinked away the remnants of tears from her eyes.

Hahn's demeanor didn't change. "Maybe, maybe not."

Alina took a step toward her, and Hahn took a half step backward.

"Remember when you and I first arrived on the ship? We went and got something to eat in the galley. You told me about your sister and how she didn't like the idea of you going into space. You told me that it's what you loved to do. Then, you accidentally knocked over a glass of water. Remember? You were reaching for a fork and spilled the water."

Hahn's expression relaxed a little.

"Since you woke up from hypersleep, you and I haven't had much time to spend talking, but we did manage to have a few conversations about our families back home. You told me about your last get-together down by some lake with your sister and her husband and kids. You said you cooked steaks and threw rocks into the water."

Hahn relinquished just a little bit of her scowl. "Yeah, I remember," she said cautiously.

Alina continued. "If what Zeke said about the creature is true, then it's obviously dangerous. But could it have known about the stuff that happened when we were back on Earth?"

Hahn's shoulders seemed to fall back into their natural position. "Alina?"

"Yes."

Hahn took a cautious step toward her. Then she looked at Zeke. "For now, I'll go with it. But, if this is a trick, it's a damn good one." She looked back at her. "It seems impossible, and I'm not entirely convinced, so you'll have to excuse me if I don't get all emotional and hug you."

Alina smiled. "Okay, we'll save that for later. But, it's good to be here with you all, except that I don't remember being gone. Well, I do a little." She then looked at the doc on the gurney.

Finn walked over to Alina and put his hand on her shoulder. "It's good to have you back. I don't know how it's possible. But I'm glad you're back."

She looked up at him and smiled as she put her hand on his. "Thanks."

Finn, of course, being an engineer, liked to deal with hard facts. To him, this was far easier to accept than it was for Hahn. He could not deny that Alina, or what appeared to be Alina, was standing in front of him. And, given that they had just encountered an entirely new creature that apparently had some strange relationship with time, acceptance wasn't that hard for him.

"Do you mind if I give you a welcome back hug?" He asked.

"I'd like that."

He opened his arms, and she willingly fell into his embrace. After a moment, he gently moved her back by her shoulders and looked into her eyes.

"I don't know what the hell is going on. But I'm glad you're here."

He looked at Zeke. "It looks like we have a new norm where anything's possible."

"You got that right," he responded.

Finn was right. There was a new reality where the ship's energy can be sapped in a second, where a quantum drive can lose all of its fuel, where anti-matter could apparently disappear without obliterating them, and where death and resurrection were apparent realities. The facts were there, and their understanding of space had been drastically altered.

"Okay," said Zeke looking to Alina. "If the doc were conscious, I'd have her do a check-up on you. But that's not happening. So, let's get to the bridge and revive Janice and take it from there."

He glanced over at the doc. Her breathing was labored, but she was clearly alive. Hahn, a little more relaxed, noticed Zeke's stare. She approached from the other side of the gurney and gently grabbed her hand. She looked at him, then Finn, and Alina. The hours of tension that were taking their toll on everyone, especially Hahn. Though she tried to remain stoic, she could not stop the tears from welling up in her eyes. She blinked them away.

Finn could tell she was stressed. He gently patted her arm. Hahn did not acknowledge it, but she didn't reject it either. She smoothed her hair back over her head with both hands. Then through wet narrow eyes, she glared at Zeke. "Yeah, let's get to the damn bridge, get Janice working, and then let's figure out how to kill this bastard."

Zeke nodded slowly and then looked at Oleg's body before turning to Finn. "You and Hahn get to the bridge and get Janice going. I'll stay here with Alina and check on the doc some more. Then we will join you there with the doc."

He turned to Alina. "No one is to move about the ship alone. We go in groups of two or more."

"Understand?"

"I understand."

He nodded. "Good."

"What are you going to do with Oleg's body?" asked Finn.

"For now, nothing. It's fine where it is."

Finn nodded and motioned to Hahn. They head out of medical. But, of course, they were cautiously checking every corner as they went. The remnant memory of Alina's ghostly entrance from the hallway caused them to slow down a bit as they entered. They checked both directions before heading on their way.

Alina glanced over to the body bag that lay empty on the floor.

"That is where your body was when that thing was, like hovering over you," he said.

She looked back at him inquisitively.

"Sorry. I didn't mean to be insensitive," he said apologetically.

"You weren't." She turned to face him. "I know you already explained it once, but tell me what happened again."

"Sure. Finn and I were on the bridge, trying to get Janice back online. We heard Hahn scream and ran in here. The creature was hovering near your body, kind of over you, and it was shimmering. It was there for a while, and then it descended on you. It was pulsing with some weird light show. The doc aimed the DBS at it."

"The what?"

"Deep Bone Scanner. She said it sends out a high energy pulse that is used in examining inside the body of a patient. So, the doc aimed it at the creature and turned it on. It reacted. It turned grey and tried to get closer to us, but we backed away. It stopped moving. Oh, and it grew to about two meters tall and about one wide. Then inside of it, it displayed the Drake solar system with our flight path laid out around the sun to Drakus. It knows where we are going."

Alina's face was a mixture of intrigue and surprise. Her apparent resurrection had not dulled her sharp mind, which by now, had cleared. "Do you think it was trying to communicate with you?"

Zeke's eyebrows shot up. "I was wondering that, too. It's a possibility. But it's killing us, and we've got to fight it. So, who knows what's going on. And that reminds me. A few hours ago, it appeared on the bridge."

"What?" His comment jerked her to attention.

"Yeah, it appeared to us inside the ship, on the bridge. It filled the whole window and just stayed there. It happened right before we got our lights back on. It was able to make the stars look like they were inside the ship. I took my flashlight and slowly tossed it in the air towards it. When it got into the creature, the light went out, and then it turned it around and sent it back with the light on. I don't know what to make of it. Now, part of me thinks it wants to communicate. But, the other part wants to kill it."

Alina stared at him, considering his words. She frowned as she thought about it and looked at the body bag and then to the doc and Oleg's body. "So, it brought me back to life, as weird as that sounds. But yet it killed Oleg and attacked the doc. Right?"

"Yep."

"Then, why would it show you the Drake system?"

Zeke just shrugged his shoulders. "No idea."

Alina was brilliant. She had great insights when it came to problem-solving. But, her words were a surprise when she spoke again. "I don't think it means to be hostile."

Zeke's eyes bugged. "Seriously?"

"Well, if it was hostile and was trying to kill us, then why didn't it just take each one of us out quickly? And why bring me back? If it's showing the Drake system, that means it knows where we are going. It is trying to communicate. Maybe it's trying to learn about us. After all, to it, we are alien creatures invading its domain."

"That's a possibility. But whatever its intentions are, it's extremely dangerous."

Alina nodded her head. "Yeah, I get that. But, maybe that's not its intent. After all, we are as different to it as it is to us. Who knows, maybe radar kills it. Maybe subspace frequencies annoy it. Or maybe it's the simple motion of our ship through space that alters space-time is what got its attention. It could be anything. And since it pursued us and communicated with us mathematically, and showed you the Drake system, then I can only conclude that it's interested in us. Of course, *we're* just trying to survive but, maybe it's trying to figure us out and doesn't understand how dangerous it is to us."

"Alright, I'll bite. Then why did it attack the doc?"

"Well," she looked past Zeke for a moment before returning her eyes to his. "You said that she aimed the bone scanner at it.

Maybe it didn't like it. Maybe it was just defending itself. Or maybe it thought the doc was trying to talk to it. Who knows."

Zeke considered her words. Could she be right? They had been in such an intense survival mode that they were assuming it was hostile. But, maybe Alina saw something he'd overlooked. At least, her theory had some merit.

"I don't think Finn and Hahn will agree with you. They both experienced how painful it was, and to be perfectly honest, I think it's compromised their objectivity."

She let out a slow breath. "I understand. But then again, maybe my brain is all mixed up. After all, I was dead, right?" She smiled slightly.

"You seem as sharp as ever," responded Zeke, returning a smile. "Maybe you're right. Maybe not. But we need to consider all the possibilities so we can best figure out what's going on."

He looked over at the doc on the gurney. "Let's get her up to the bridge so we can keep an eye on her. After we get Janice running again, *if* we get Janice running again, we'll have her do some tests on her."

With that, they got into position to move the doc. Zeke went to her head, Alina, to her feet on the gurney. They carefully guided her around the center table and out the hallway door.

They didn't look back into medical. But, after they left, a distortion manifested in the wall under the portal in the doc's office, and through it, the creature entered. It slowly moved near the floor and stopped near Oleg's body.

Chapter 19
Janice

Alina and Zeke were heading towards the bridge with the doc in tow.

"You know," said Zeke. "That creature is unlike anything anyone back on Earth even dreamed of. And yet, it is real, it drained the ship's energy, disabled the quantum drive, and I am talking to you like you were never dead." He shook his head. "If we told them what was happening out here, they'd think we were sick with space psychosis."

"It's like what Finn said, a new norm."

"When I was doing my video log back to Earth, I was complaining about how boring things were. Now, I would give almost anything to have boring all over again."

Alina smiled, "Yeah, I think boring would be good."

As they entered the bridge, Finn and Hahn greeted them with a quick look and a nod. Zeke nodded back to signal that everything was okay.

Finn went back to restoring Janice.

"How is she?" asked Hahn.

"The same," he Zeke. "Also, I caught Alina up to speed a little more."

"Good," said Finn without turning around. "Let's just hope the doc doesn't end the same way as Oleg."

He and Alina moved the gurney next to the holo-table, and then after checking her one more time, they joined Finn.

"How's it coming with Janice?" he asked.

"So far, so good." He looked at Alina with a long stare.

Alina stared back and, after a few seconds, raised her eyebrows as if to say, "Yes?"

"Sorry, this whole coming-back-to-life thing is weird. I know it's you, but wow. Wait till they hear about this back home. They'll think we've suffered from deep space psychosis."

Alina looked at Zeke and smiled. "Yeah, we thought the same thing."

"I think they already knew that about you, Finn." It was Hahn.

"A joke? Really? Not bad, but I didn't think you were in a joking mood."

"I'm not. I'm serious."

"Ouch," responded Finn with a raised tone as he turned back to the A.I. Display Screen. "And I thought we were getting along so well."

"How long before Janice is back online?" asked Zeke.

"If all goes well, she should be up and running any minute."

Hahn, of course, was still slightly suspicious of Alina but was trying to be cordial. She nodded appropriately and smiled at her from the place on the bridge she had positioned herself so she could watch for the creature.

"Like I said before," said Finn to Zeke, "the eggheads back on Earth made this pretty foolproof. So far, there have been no problems, and I'm about to begin the final step."

He had been staring at a screen while talking, watching numbers slowly count up, 84%, 85%, 86%, etc.

"When it hits 100 then all I have to do is enter the final security code for the reboot."

...91%, 92%, 93%, 94%, 95%, 96%, 97%, 98%, 99%, 100%.

The panel displayed, "Enter A.I. Initiation Security Code."

"There it is. After this, she should come back to life."

Zeke turned and faced the panel and said, "Alpha 153, Omega 8, Janice 1224."

The screen went blank. Zeke stepped back, and so did Finn.

"How long does it take?" asked Alina.

"A few seconds."

Two lights on the panel flashed green three times. Then it illuminated with a gray hue that slowly faded to black. After about four seconds, the words 'A.I. Boot Sequence' appeared in the center. The same two green lights flashed on again three times each. The screen went blank for just a bit, and then the company's logo appeared. It rotated on its axis and expanded to fill the whole screen before dissolving into nothing.

Then, after about five more seconds, the words 'A.I. Reboot Successful' blinked off and on at one-second intervals. Underneath, numbers counted down, 10, 9, 8, 7, 6, 5, 4, 3, 2, 1, 0. The words, 'A.I. Online' appeared.

"I am glad to be back," said Janice.

"Yes!" Said Finn. "Welcome back. You're a sight for sore eyes."

"How long have I been offline?"

"Isn't your chronometer working?" asked Zeke.

"Yes, it is, and it says I've been offline for two minutes and thirty-three seconds. But, my sensors show that we have traveled a distance far greater than three minutes would allow. Since you and Zeke both have increased stubble, it is obvious that I've been offline for several hours. I can only assume that the arrival of the creature had a significant effect on the ship and myself."

"That is an understatement," said Zeke. "After the creature hit us, we lost power everywhere."

"I see. I will then calculate a more precise time frame based on stellar measurements.

"In the meantime," said Zeke. "We're glad you're back. A lot's happened."

Janice spoke again. "The quantum drive is not working, and the solar panels have been extended. You are using the panels for energy, thus enabling me to be back online. I do not detect the creature anywhere. Yet, its arrival obviously drained the entire ship of its power. I must say, the quantum drive's inoperability due to the missing anti-matter is a fascinating enigma. If it had been present, we would all have been destroyed when the quantum drive lost power. The creature must have inter-dimensional characteristics that might allow it to handle the anti-matter. This might also explain its temporal aspects. Fascinating. Nevertheless, our situation is serious, and we are presently stranded. Do you care to fill me in on what happened while I was offline?

Zeke smiled while looking at Finn. "She's back."

"Was the power-loss instantaneous or gradual?" she asked.

"As far as we can tell," said Zeke, "it was instantaneous."

"From what I know about the laws of physics, that is impossible. Nevertheless, it has happened. Perhaps we can discover how that occurred at a further date. Also, subspace communications and tunneling are unavailable due to the quantum drive's energy depletion. We cannot communicate with Earth."

Zeke spoke. "You got that right. Our situation is pretty bad. When it hit us, everything went dead. There was no power in the entire ship. Well, not entirely. We theorized that anything that had batteries that were not directly connected to the ship retained their charge. But anything attached to the ship's power grid was drained. So, obviously, with the quantum drive down, the only source of power we could get was from the solar panels. In the meantime, we were using flashlights to get around. But we needed power, so Finn and Oleg went outside the ship and had to manually deploy the panels. Once they got to a sufficient level of exposure, they were able to self-deploy."

Zeke paused for a moment and regrouped his thoughts.

"But before they did that, Alina went into her quarters by herself and was attacked by the creature. Somehow it was able to reduce its size and enter a room. She screamed, and we ran to her. We saw it, the creature. It appeared as a shimmering cloud that engulfed her. She was in a lot of pain. The doc stuck her flashlight into the creature's field, or cloud, or whatever it was, which apparently disrupted it, and then it stopped and left."

"How big was the creature?"

"I don't know, big enough to engulf Alina, but it did not fill the room."

"So, it can alter its size," said Janice stating the obvious.

"It can do a lot more than that," said Zeke. He paused again, but this time for a few more seconds. He looked over at Alina briefly. "But, we'll get to that. After the creature disappeared, Alina was dead."

Zeke paused to let the information sink into Janice's circuits. But he knew she would process it in microseconds. Not only that, it would be a good test of her systems to see how she reacted to such an apparent incongruity since he had just said that Alina was killed, but there she was in the room.

"She was killed?"

"Affirmative. She was killed."

"Then how is it possible for her to be standing behind you?"

"All we can tell you is that the doc and Hahn were in medical with Oleg, who was on the med table. Alina's body was in a body bag on the floor. The creature appeared and scared the hell out of them. Finn and I came running and found it hovering over her body. Then it engulfed her. But it was different than when it killed Alina. It pulsed and had a wave of lights that seemed to flow through it. Then afterward, it moved away from her and showed us the Drake solar system with our flight path clearly laid out to Drakus. The doc aimed a Deep Bone Scanner at it, and apparently, it didn't like it. It attacked her, and now the doc is in a coma of some kind. We have her here and not in medical because we did not want to leave her unguarded."

He paused, took a breath, and added. "Anyway, shortly after it attacked the doc, we realized that Alina's body was gone. Then seconds later, she just walked into medical. We were cautious at first, but it really does appear to be her. There, now you're caught up."

"Since Alina is standing before me and since I can tell from your biometrics that you are telling the truth, I must conclude that the creature brought her back to life, unless, captain, there is a secret technology you've not told me about."

Zeke kind of jerked his head back a little. "If that was an attempt at humor, you've got to work on it. But, no, it wasn't us."

"Wait," interrupted Hahn. "Can you tell if it really is Alina and not some trick?" She looked Alina half apologetically.

"From what I can tell from her biometrics, it really is Alina. Her locator chip is operational, as are all of yours. Of course, we could run further tests in medical if you desire."

Alina shifted her stance a bit as she looked at Hahn and said to Janice. "I'm okay with tests if it'll make you feel better. Besides, maybe we'll learn something valuable about the creature."

"Well, if Janice says it's really you, then it's really you." Her tone wasn't entirely sincere, but it was good enough. She smiled and nodded. "Welcome back."

Alina smiled and nodded in return.

Zeke continued. "When Oleg and Finn were outside the ship getting the panels going manually, it attacked Oleg." Zeke's tone changed to a more somber timber. "He died about 20 minutes ago right before Alina showed up."

Zeke frowned and shook his head once. "But, of course, you know this, right? I mean, are your sensors working properly?"

"Yes, they are, and I am aware of Oleg's death and the doctor's coma. But please continue."

"Tell her about the light and when it appeared on the bridge," said Hahn.

"Yeah, thanks. When it attacked the doc, it emitted this incredibly intense light. It didn't last very long, but when it was over, the creature was gone, and the doc was unconscious. We haven't been able to revive her." He looked over at her. "We were hoping you could help us."

Zeke turned to Finn and then to the two women before looking back to the panel, which had become the de facto non-face of Janice.

"One more thing. It appeared on the bridge a few hours ago, but it didn't attack us. It showed us the Drake system and Drakus. It knows where we're headed. It was just there. It had this weird effect where it could make the stars look like they were inside the bridge. It just stayed there, watching us. So, I tossed my flashlight into it to see what would happen. It turned the flashlight around and sent it back. But, the light got so bright we could hardly see. Then the flashlight went back to normal, and it was gone."

Without pause, Janice jumped in matter-of-factly. "It does not appear that the ship's systems have been structurally damaged. Aside from the incongruity of Alina's apparent resurrection, the quantum drive's energy depletion, and the disappearance of the anti-matter, everything else is consistent with the normal parameters of operation, both biological and mechanical. Is there anything more you wish to tell me?"

Through all of the explanation, Janice's compassionless tone concerning the doc and Oleg was obvious to everyone. Her unemotional approach seemed almost rude and disrespectful. But, after all, she was only a machine, a very smart machine.

"It's evil," said Hahn. "It killed Oleg and put the doc in a coma. She's just like Oleg was before he died. And the pain it caused me was horrible. It was incredibly bad. I can't even begin to describe it. It had complete control over me." Hahn's voice was rising in intensity the more she spoke. "We have to find a way to kill it."

"When were you attacked?" asked Janice.

"Zeke forgot to mention that part. I was in the galley with Finn getting some food. We were leaving, and that's when it got me.

Finn reached out to help me and stuck his hand into it to grab me, then it disappeared. And, all I can say is that it was the worst pain I've ever felt. It was terrifyingly bad, and I'd rather die than go through that again." Her voice was rising in pitch and fervor the more she spoke.

"I am sorry that you and Alina suffered such pain. You have my sympathy."

Of course, they knew that Janice's sympathy amounted to electrical programming switches producing a response.

"Thanks," said Hahn insincerely.

"I want to add my two cents," said Finn. "When my hand came in contact with it, it was the worst pain I've ever felt in my life. It was only for a moment, but it was hell." He looked over again at Hahn while still speaking to Janice. "I can't imagine what she went through."

"Thank you for sharing your experience with me," said Janice. "I am sorry that you experienced such great discomfort."

Finn looked at Hahn and shook his head. He mouth the word 'discomfort' accompanied by raised eyebrows.

"With the quantum drive not working," said Janice, "we are stranded 22 light-years from home. We are on our own."

"That's what we figured," said Zeke. "We're stuck here."

Janice offered some quick calculations. "We are 209 trillion kilometers from Earth. With gravity assist around the Drake sun and then using all our chemical propulsion reserves, the Cascade can attain a speed of approximately 348,000 km/h. It would then take 68,000 years to return to Earth."

They already knew their dire predicament, but the sobering reality of her calculations were nails being driven into their coffins. After a few disheartened seconds, Zeke finally spoke up.

"Do you have any recommendations?"

"I recommend that we go into a parking orbit around Drakus. Undoubtedly after our lack of communication, as well as our failure to return to Earth, the Company will most probably consider our mission a loss. Since the company has significant investments in the development of the Drake system's resources and since other usable planetary systems are much further away, it is logical to assume that they will send another ship to continue exploration and development. Then, provided they do not have the same encounter that we have had with the entity, you can be rescued. I would then remain in orbit and continue to feed information back to Earth if and when a means of communication can be re-established."

Again Janice's calm presentation of facts seemed to rob the situation of its seriousness. It was one thing to deliver information. It was another to experience that dreadful expectation of being marooned so far from home.

"Janice?"

"Yes, Finn?"

"Before its initial attack on the Cascade, you were able to trace the creature's location. Can you still do that?"

"Yes, if it displays the same energy signatures as before. However, I do not detect it at this time."

Zeke frowned and exhaled through his nose. "Do you have any theories about what this thing is or what we can do?"

"The creature is unlike any on Earth. I have searched my database for information on theoretical xenomorphs and found nothing of use. The only other field of research that deals with nonbiological lifeforms are the domains of theology and the paranormal. But, I do not know if they are relevant here. Nevertheless, we can conclude that the entity is intelligent since it understands mathematics. Its communication through prime numbers and its display of the Drake system to you in medical and the bridge, tells me that it has intent. However, I do not know what that intent is. Its rationality suggests that it might have a moral system, though it could be radically different than our own. It has killed two people, but brought one of them back to life, and put another in a coma. This could be interpreted in three ways. First, the entity could be malicious and intends to harm. Second, it is not malicious and does not intend to harm, but has accidentally done so."

"If this is what it's like when it's not mad," said Zeke interrupting Janice, "I'd hate to see it when it is. By the way, how is Doc doing? Can you figure anything out with her here?"

"She is stable and appears to be in a coma. But further examination would require that you return her to medical where I could instruct you on what to do."

"I would like to add something," said Alina. "I know you said it's a possibility that the creature is not intending to be harmful, and I agree. It is a possibility. I think showing the Drake system to them in medical, and the Bridge is evidence of that. So, we need to seriously consider that option and possibly try to communicate with it. But of course, we need to maintain extreme caution."

Hahn scoffed loudly.

"Agreed, Alina," said Janice. "But, I would like to continue to the third option. We must consider that it is in pain. Like any creature that is suffering, it can strike out. Perhaps the very presence of the Cascade in its space causes it pain. Maybe its attack on the ship was a means of defense. But then again, it might only be experiencing pain when it is interacting with biological organisms. After all, it is nonbiological and completely different. Consider Hahn's reaction to the pain she suffered. She wants to fight it. Perhaps the creature is fighting against the Cascade and its inhabitants due to some form of pain induced by its presence. Of course, I do not know. I am only theorizing since its behavior can be interpreted that way."

"But," said Alina. "We know that it is intelligent. And, it showed us the Drake system with our flight path to Drakus. If it is in pain, why would it do that?"

168

"Since it is a creature that I am not familiar with, I cannot explain its behavior. Perhaps, like humans, it can experience pain but still operate at a rational level. I was merely offering a possibility to consider."

Alina interrupted the flow of the conversation. "I've got a question. How does it know were going to the fourth planet, Drakus? We could be going anywhere."

"Logic," said Janice. "We can assume that it is familiar to some degree with our ship, with its gravity, the air, and the biological makeup of its crew. Now, if we assume that it is familiar with the planetary system to which we're headed, then it would be able to deduce which planet we would be visiting. It is only Drakus that fits within the physical boundaries with which the equipment in the cargo hold can operate."

"Then, that would imply that it can understand the purpose of the equipment," said Alina.

"Perhaps. But consider the idea of something as basic as the wheels on the vehicles. They would not work on the gas giant, nor on the planets that are extremely hot. The last planet is frozen and consists of methane and ammonia. Logically, the creature could examine varying items in the cargo hold and deduce where we're headed."

"Okay," continued Alina, "obviously, it is intelligent, and given that it showed the Drake system and our path there, I think it means it wants to communicate with us."

Zeke nodded. "I agree with Alina. Janice, since it responded properly to the prime number tests, I can't help but wonder if it might not be logical in other areas, too. So, I think Alina is right. I think that it is trying to communicate with us. It is an option to consider, though I have no idea how that would work."

Janice continued in conversation. "Philosophers and theologians have debated the topic of the universal application of the laws of logic for centuries and how they are obtained by different sentient beings; namely, humans. I am a highly sophisticated computer with extremely complex programming. I can only operate within the laws of logic, those same laws that you can access even though you are biological. We are different in our essence, yet we both obtain and utilize those same universal laws. We apply them to situations, mathematics, morals, etc. Since the creature is intelligent and appears to understand complex mathematics, then it also uses those same laws. But, perhaps like you, it can break them and not act logically. Nevertheless, I suspect that it will possess similar, if not identical, logical processes as ourselves, at least in some areas. Therefore, I conclude that it is theoretically possible to communicate with it. Mathematics and logic would have to be our common language."

Alina was nodding confidently. But Finn's eyebrows had slowly raised during Janice's explanation. He blinked slowly and shook his head.

"Laws of logic?" asked Finn.

Alina turned to him. "Basically, in classical logic, there are three primary laws. The first is the law of identity. This means that something is what it is and is not what it is not. The second is the law of non-contradiction. This means that a statement cannot be both true and false at the same time and in the same sense. The third is the law of excluded middle, which affirms that statements are either true or false. Then there are others such as the law proper inference. This means that if A equals B, and B equals C, then A equals C. There are others that are more complex, but they are the basic ones. But as I said, philosophers have been debating the abstract nature, their ubiquity, and how we obtain them, for centuries."

Finn frowned slightly, nodded, and slowly said. "Thanks for clearing that up." He looked towards Hahn and shrugged his shoulders a little. She smiled and shook her head at him. It was the first real smile she'd shown in hours. "Its basic philosophy," she said with a smirk. "It was one of my minors."

Finn just stared back blankly. "Well, I like fixing things."

Alina took a half step forward. "We have to find a way to communicate with it using logic and math. We were able to send energy pulses in mathematical patterns before, and it responded properly. So, we have to do the same thing again."

"Agreed," responded Janice.

"Are you able to access the same sensors that you used in the energy pulses earlier?" asked Alina.

"Yes, I can. They are operational and do not appear to be damaged."

"Then," she continued, "We could use them. Maybe we could develop a language based on math?"

"I propose a multistep process. The first is to let it know that we are trying to communicate with it. I suggest that we begin with pulses that progress in complexity. I will send primary numbers sets, the same as before, up to, and including 101. Since it has previously responded to those patterns, then I expect it to respond again, most probably in the same way. However, in order to facilitate more accurate communication, I suggest that we set up three sensors on the bridge and send the patterns from here. The three sensors will triangulate a specific location."

"Wait," said Finn. "Are you crazy? You want it to come here? You were just talking about how dangerous that thing is, and now you want to bring it here on the ship and what, share a cup of tea?"

Alina jumped in. "It showed you the Drake system in medical. It wasn't hostile then, was it?"

"Yes, it was!" Blurted Hahn. "It attacked the doc and put her in a coma."

"But that was only after she aimed the DBS at it. What I meant was, when it was showing you the Drake system, what was it doing? Attacking or just sitting there?"

Janice interrupted the developing dispute. "Its actions due to the DBS could be construed as an act of defense, which you said had an effect upon it. So, we cannot determine if its actions against the doctor were aggressive or defensive. But for now, I am interested in its display of our trajectory to the Drake system. It is showing you what you already know. I conclude that it is attempting to communicate with you."

"It's hostile," said Hahn in a terse voice. "Trust me on that!" She forced herself to calm down before continuing. "And why do you want to bring it to the bridge?"

"You said it appeared in a much smaller form. Then this means that the bridge is a logical place for our attempt at communication. It is a central hub where you can assess any changes in its status and the status of the ship, thus allowing a quicker and more capable response should one be needed. This room is large enough to accommodate the sensors, as well as all of you. The holo-table will provide a means of projection. And, considering that it has free reign of the ship and can do what it wants to you whenever it chooses, why not attempt to communicate with it here where you might be less subject to surprise attacks?"

Finn seemed to relax a bit at Janice's reasoning. "I still don't like it."

"What sensors are you planning on using?" asked Zeke.

"In the cargo bay, there are 12 Argus Wave Sensors. Three of them can be modified to emit energy pulses appropriate for our use. I can instruct Finn on how to do that."

Finn folded his arms and shook his head at the prospect of being roped into helping the creature appear. "And how do we know using the sensors won't send it into a rage?"

"We do not," said Janice. "But the evidence suggests it wants to communicate with us. Also, the sensors operate differently than the DBS. So, I do not expect hostility, though it is still a possibility. If it shows up here on the bridge, I will use the holo-table to display various images where I can use pulses to assign a numerical value to each one. Then, I will send a signal that corresponds to an image and see if it responds. I hope that it will be able to produce images as well since, as you have reported, it generated an image of the Drake system. If this occurs, we have communication."

"But," added Alina, "how do we know it can recognize what an image is or even if it can see them at all?"

"That is a good question, Alina. Do you see an object the same as I do? Sight for you occurs in your brain. For me, it is in my circuits. But your brain and my circuits are very different. Yet, we both recognize the same thing and can communicate very well regarding that object. Perhaps the creature cannot see images the way we do, or maybe it can. We would need to find out. But, since it apparently is aware of the structure of the ship and the location of individuals within it, then it must have some sort of visual sensory capability. Therefore, I think it is reasonable to conclude that it can perceive the images that I project."

"And if this doesn't work, do you have any backup plans?" asked Finn. "Like, maybe using some form of the bone scanner as a weapon?"

"I do not believe that will be necessary. Let's hope that communication succeeds. If it does not and if the creature continues its hostilities, then it will be necessary to develop some sort of defense against it. I have already analyzed the DBS and see a potential use as a weapon based on its design."

"Now, we're talking," said Finn.

"I second, that," added Hahn eagerly.

"How sophisticated do you think you can get with it doing this image, pulse thing?" asked Zeke.

"I can get very complex. But whether or not it can adapt and learn is unknown."

"Well," said Zeke as he looked around the room at the others, "we can either try and communicate with it, or we can fight it. I'm for a parley."

"There is another option," continued Janice. "We could do nothing. But I do not recommend that. It is obviously both dangerous and curious about us. If it continues its actions, it could accidentally or deliberately kill you all and most probably shut me down again. Since we cannot travel back to Earth, our best option is to seek to develop a means of communication with the creature where we can, hopefully, avoid future harmful encounters. We can then place the Cascade in a parking orbit around Drakus and wait for another expedition to arrive."

Alina cleared her throat, loudly. They all turned around. "If it can extrapolate our trajectory into the Drake system, can it also extrapolate our path back to Earth?"

"Possibly, but not likely," responded Janice.

"Well, that's great. That's just fantastic," said Finn in a raw voice. "There is no way we can let it get back to Earth. Could you imagine what it could do there?"

Hahn jumped in, "I vote for developing a weapon. It's too dangerous, and we can't take any chances." Her tone was firm.

"All right," interjected Zeke. "Let's not get ahead of ourselves. Remember, the earth is 22 light-years away. I don't see how it could find out where we came from. After all, we are way out here. What do you think, Janice?"

"While you were in hypersleep, I made several course adjustments due to five previously unmapped comets and a large asteroid. Though they were minor corrections, I am confident that the creature cannot locate Earth."

"I don't know if that's supposed to make me feel any better," responded Finn sarcastically. "But, it doesn't."

"Just for the record," said Hahn. "I think trying to communicate with it is a bad idea. It could be playing with us and trying to get more information to use it against us. I don't trust it. It's deadly. You shouldn't trust it either."

"And it can bring people back to life," responded Alina.

"Yeah, but why? Is it a cruel game? Maybe it is lonely and wants lab rats to torture."

"Or," said Janice, "It is learning about us and will modify its behavior accordingly."

Janice's last statement ended the second repartee between Hahn and Alina.

"All right," said Zeke with a wave of his hand. "I think trying to communicate with it is our best option. Janice, since you proposed putting three sensors on the bridge, then let's do that. It's as good a place as any."

He turned to Finn. "Can you work with her and get it set up?"

"Aye, Cap," said Finn in a tone of disapproval.

"Good."

"Janice? How long do you think you will take to complete the modifications?"

"About two hours."

"Then, Hahn, you assist Finn. Alina, you and I will take the doc back to medical and see if we can run tests under Janice's direction. Who knows, maybe we can help her."

Alina nodded. "Okay."

Hahn stressed her disapproval by looking away.

"We all have a job to do. So, let's get to it. And once again, no one is to be alone."

Chapter 20
Consciousness

Finn and Hahn had no problem modifying the Argus Sensors per Janice's instructions. It wasn't pretty, but when they were finished, there were three sensors on the bridge in an equilateral triangle, three meters apart. From each of them, two sets of cables snaked across the floor and out to the primary power grid access in the hallway. Because of the modifications to the sensors, Janice did not need a hardwired connection. She could control them remotely.

Right about the time they were finishing up, Zeke and Alina came back into the bridge.

"Where's the doc?" asked Hahn.

"We ran some tests on her with Janice supervising. She had us administer some meds. It took a while, but she's improving."

"That's great," said Finn. "But, you left her in medical alone? What about your orders?"

"Yeah, I didn't like the idea. Janice will explain," he said as he rubbed his eyes between his forefinger and thumb.

"Medical is designed with monitoring and diagnostic equipment that is better than anything here on the bridge. After analyzing her condition, I have determined that there is nothing wrong with her body. The problem rests in her brain. It has experienced a trauma that appears to be caused by some form of neural overload. I had Zeke and Alina start an IV attached to several medicines. I can monitor her brain activity and will work in concert with the other diagnostic equipment attached to her. I am then able to remotely infuse various medicines into her system to induce healing. This can only be done there. Additionally, if there is a change in her condition or the creature manifests in medical, I will alert you, and you can get there quickly. Finally, I do not know exactly how long it will take for the doc to recover and, given the fact that we need to begin communication with the creature, it is best if everyone is here."

"What did you do with Oleg's body?" asked Hahn in a slightly suspicious tone.

"We moved it into the same body bag that Alina was in." Zeke yawned after he spoke, then looked at her apologetically.

She just offered a half-smile and a nod. "It's okay."

Hahn and Finn looked at each other out of the corner of their eyes. It was obvious that neither one liked the doc being alone. But, medical *was* the best place for her to be.

Janice continued. "I also had them do some tests on Oleg's body. The results were informative. I discovered that the problem was also with his brain, and the cause of his death was a neural overload. It is the same as with the doc but to a much greater degree. It was as though all his neurons were firing out of control. The area of the brain that registers pain had been very active. But for some reason, though the doctor was affected similarly, the effect upon her is not as bad. I am optimistic about the doctor's recovery."

"Well," said Hahn. "I don't like here being alone."

Zeke looked at her through tired eyes. "Me, either."

"Technically, she's not alone," said Janice. "I am with her."

"Ah, right," said Hahn halfheartedly. She stretched and yawned. "If you say so."

Zeke again rubbed his eyes between his forefinger and thumb. "Babysitting isn't what we need to do right now. Trust me, I don't like the idea of leaving her there." He yawned. "But, that's what's best for her now, and besides, we've got to all be here when we try and talk to it."

He tried to resist another yawn, but it manifested strongly.

He was not the only one fighting fatigue. The constant tension and lack of sleep were taking their toll on everyone. While Finn was prepping the sensors, he barked at Hahn for not moving fast enough. Hahn was already on edge, and she snapped back. Alina was the only one who seemed to be doing okay, sleep-wise. Was it a byproduct of being raised from the dead? They were all struggling, but they did what they had to do as they continued to push through their exhaustion.

Finally, the sensors were ready.

"Alright, everyone," said Zeke. "We need to take a break. We're all tired. So, let's be back here in two hours. I know it isn't much time, but we need the rest. So, try to sleep if you can." He forced back another yawn. It triggered one in Finn.

"Janice, if there is a change in the doc's condition, notify me."

"Yes, Captain."

"Of course, watch for the creature and warn us if it manifests."

"Yes, Captain."

"Also, wake us up in two hours."

"Yes, Captain."

"What if it attacks us in our sleep?" asked Hahn.

"We need sleep," said Zeke. "We'll be no good if we can't function. So, we've got to risk it. Besides, Janice can warn us if it shows up again."

Rest wasn't likely, given the creature's sporadic presence and their desperate situation. But, they knew they needed to take a break before the next phase of their journey began. They split up into two groups and went to the crews' quarters. Zeke went with Alina, and Finn went with Hahn. Both men insisted that the women get their own beds while they slept in some chairs. Their chivalry was not challenged.

Surprisingly, everyone fell asleep within five minutes.

The creature appeared outside the ship, near the solar array. It was not luminous, nor did it distort the light from the stars. It was simply staying there, undetected. After about a half-hour it slowly drifted to the bridge window where it remained for a long while. Afterward, it returned to the solar panels and hovered near them.

The crew continued to sleep.

"Wake up," said Janice.

It took only a few seconds for them to regain consciousness.

"Captain, there is a problem."

"What is it?" Zeke pressed his eyes closed as he rubbed his forehead, trying to gather his thoughts. He yawned hard.

"The solar panels have stopped producing energy, and we are presently on battery power."

That jerked him to attention. "Instruct everyone to go to the bridge immediately.

"Yes, Captain."

Within two minutes, they were all assembled.

"What's the doc's status?" asked Zeke into the air.

"I have been monitoring her closely. She is improving. I expect her to regain consciousness within the next few hours."

Zeke's nodded. "That's great."

"Great news," said Finn.

"Amen to that!" Alina.

Hahn smiled.

"Okay, Janice. Fill us in."

"The solar panel stopped producing energy. So, I woke you up immediately."

"How long were we asleep?" asked Hahn.

"Approximately three and a half hours."

"I asked you to wake us up after two hours," responded Zeke with a definite tone of irritation.

"Yes, Captain, you did. But if I may remind you, per company directives, when the doctor is incapacitated, then I act in her stead. Therefore, I have the authority to override your orders should I deem it necessary for the health and safety of the crew. I have been closely monitoring all of your vitals, and you are all in need of rest. Given that we are in a dangerous situation, your lack of sleep can significantly impair your judgment and performance. Furthermore, since we are about to implement a plan of potential communication with the creature, I decided that given the importance of such an attempt, the extra sleep would statistically reduce your potential of error, by 43%. Therefore, I chose to extend your rest time."

Zeke exhaled hard and ran his hand through his hair. It was no use arguing with her. She was right. And besides, he was thankful for the extra sleep. Besides, if the creature showed up and they somehow established communication, the slightest misunderstanding could be catastrophic. He let it go.

"Okay, so the solar panels. What's wrong with them?"

"The creature has appeared between the solar array and the Drake sun. It is blocking the sunlight."

"I knew it," said Hahn. "It is screwing around with us. We've got to do something." She looked at the captain. "Are you finally convinced that it's hostile?" She then turned to Alina. "So much for your theory that it might not be aggressive and wants to talk. We are in a battle for our lives, and this thing is now trying to destroy our only source of energy. We have to fight back."

"Fighting may become necessary," interrupted Zeke. "But, for now, we move forward cautiously. We do not know why it is blocking the sunlight.

"Caution, my ass!" Hahn was clenching her fists, straining to speak calmly. "I say we figure out how to kill it."

"We don't even know if it *can* be killed," interrupted Finn.

"It's alive, it can be killed," retorted Hahn. "Think about it, we know it doesn't like the bone scanner, so maybe Janice can figure out how to use it as a weapon. Maybe we can make a big pulse cannon of some sort and blow it into oblivion."

"Hold on," said Zeke. "Hahn, I understand your concerns, and they're duly noted. But we need to move slowly."

"Cap!, I don't..."

"Stow it," ordered Zeke.

Hahn stopped, folded her arms, and stared back at Zeke through narrow eyes.

He ignored her suppressed defiance. "We still don't know why it's blocking the sunlight." He paused for a few seconds and thought about the possibilities.

"Janice, how long will the batteries last, given the present energy usage of the ship?"

"Seven hours. But, we can extend that significantly by shutting off various systems throughout the ship."

"Janice, do you have any theories on why it's blocking the panels?"

"I can propose several, but without more information, they would have little..."

She stopped in midsentence and then said, "Please wait."

After two seconds, "Please wait."

They all lingered in a quiet but tense expectation. Finally, she broke the silence.

"The creature is using the panels to communicate with us. I do not know how it is doing it, but it is allowing sunlight to reach the panels in short prime number bursts. Thus far, it has produced the prime numbers 2, 3, 5, 7, and 11."

She paused again. "Please wait."

After about 30 long and uncomfortable seconds. "It has repeated the prime number sequence of 2, 3, 5, 7, and 11."

"Please wait."

After another 30 seconds. "It is now repeating the same sequence. It is trying to communicate with us."

Alina was the first to speak. "That's good," she said as she looked at Hahn. "It wants to talk."

She returned a hard gaze. "Look, I know I'm Ms. negative here, but you do not know its intention. It could be a deception. It could be toying with us. So, let's not go into this half-cocked. We can't trust it!"

"You're right. We must proceed with caution," said Zeke. "Hahn, I'm sure you'll speak up if any of us gets too cozy with this thing."

"Sarcasm aside, Cap, you bet I will."

He nodded. "I was serious."

Hahn responded by relaxing just a bit.

"All right, everybody, this is it. Once we start, we could be in for quite a ride." He looked around the room. "So, is everyone ready?"

"No," responded Finn. "But, that hasn't stopped me from doing something stupid before."

Zeke flexed his jaw slightly as he eyed Finn.

"Yes, sir," said Alina.

"Ready," said Hahn reluctantly.

"Janice, please begin."

Each of them looked at the triangle of sensors and waited. Nothing happened. No lights came on, and there was no sound.

"They should be working," said Finn. "But don't expect to see or hear anything. They are sensors that don't operate in our range of seeing and hearing."

"Are they working, Janice?" asked Zeke.

"Yes, Captain," responded Janice in her normal matter-of-fact tone. "I am sending out prime number sequences through them."

"All right then. Let's see what happens."

"I hope we're not pissing it off," said Finn.

The cap faced him. "Really?"

Finn shrugged his shoulders slightly.

They all focused on the three sensors. Would the creature appear? If it did, would it attack them? Or, would it just hover before like it did a few hours ago when it entered through the window? They didn't know. So, all they could do was wait.

"Pulsing on the solar panels has stopped," informed Janice.

"What is it doing now?" asked Alina.

"I do not know. I cannot detect it."

"Are you still sending the sequence?" asked Zeke.

"Affirmative."

Their forced waiting was torturous. Would it accept their invitation to come to the bridge? Or would the sensors trigger an attack? All they could do was look at each other with blank expressions.

"This is crazy," said Hahn, but no one responded.

The creature was trying to communicate with them, and they were trying to communicate with it. But for now, nothing. They continued to wait, half expecting an attack, half expecting a possible peaceful encounter. It was interminable.

"I have a bad feeling about this," said Finn after a minute.

"Be patient."

"Maybe it has to decide what to do," said Alina. "I'm sure it's being as cautious as we are."

"Captain?" interrupted Janice.

"Yes?"

"There has been a change in the doctor's condition. She is regaining consciousness."

Zeke forced a breath out through his nostrils. The news was good, but the timing was bad. "Is the creature doing anything to her?"

"Nothing that I can detect."

"Do you know where it is?"

"No, Captain."

"That means that it could attack at any moment," said Hahn.

Her perpetual negativity brought another annoyed glance from Zeke.

"Is the doc awake now?"

"Yes. I've spoken with her, and she is asking where everyone is."

"Inform her that I will be right there."

"Yes, Captain."

"Keep sending the signals. If it shows up, let me know. But for now, we need to get to the doctor. Alina, you come with me. Finn and Hahn, you two stay here."

"Yes, Captain."

"Let's go," he said to Alina as he nodded his head towards the door. They disappeared into the hallway walking at a fast pace.

As they hurried, Alina spoke up. "From what you told me about the sequence of events, the doc doesn't know I'm alive."

"Yeah, that'll be a shock. But, I'd rather she find out sooner than later. So, let's see how she does and get back to the bridge as soon as possible."

"How do you think she'll handle it?"

"Actually, I think she'll do well. She's an intelligent woman."

The doctor was sitting up-right on the table, rubbing her forehead, taking several purposely deep breaths. She looked over at the body bag that she assumed still held Alina's body. She put her feet on the floor, then stood up and held onto it for balance. She lifted her head up and rotated it on her neck then looked around for the creature.

"Where's Oleg," she said to herself.

She took a wobbly step but was distracted by the sound of footsteps in the hallway, so she waited. Zeke and Alina walked in.

"Doc!" said Zeke. "How are you doing?"

She just looked back and forth at both of them, a blank stare scrawled on her face.

"Hi, Doc," said Alina.

"What the hell?"

Alina took a step closer and smiled.

The doctor moved her head back on her shoulders. What she was seeing wasn't possible.

Zeke moved closer, but Alina stayed back just a bit.

The doc kept staring, squinting. She shook her head once trying to clear her mind. "I'm hallucinating."

"No, you're not," said Zeke as he walked up to her.

The doc kept her gaze on Alina. "The hell I'm not!"

Zeke smiled slightly. "You're not seeing things. She's alive. We don't understand it. But after the creature attacked you, you went into some coma just like Oleg. Then, well, Alina's body disappeared and," he looked over at her and then back to the doc, "she then just walked into medical."

The doc blinked hard as she shook her head again. "I'm hallucinating you, two. I was attacked, and now I'm seeing things. I need to run some tests." She started to look around the room.

"You're not hallucinating," said Zeke.

"She's dead, and you are a figment of my imagination. People don't rise from the dead."

"Yes, they do," said Alina. "It's me."

The doc stared and scowled at the incongruity before her. Then, after a few seconds, she cautiously reached out and grabbed Alina's hand.

"It was the creature. Somehow it brought me back."

The doc dropped her arm and turned to Zeke. "You're not a hallucination?"

"No."

"She's back from the dead?"

Yes."

The doc blinked hard again, and as she took two steps backward and butted up against the table, then took two deep breaths. "Is it too early for a drink?"

Zeke smiled. "Lately, it seems that anytime has been a good time for a drink. But, for now, we could always get you a cup of coffee."

"Doc?" asked Alina. "I know this is hard to accept. But are you going to be okay?"

She just stared back in silence. There they were, real, not a hallucination. She rubbed her face with her hands and then ran her fingers through her hair.

"I know it's hard," he said. "And I know you will need time to process this. We certainly did. She's alive. We don't know how or why it brought her back, but for now, we need to get back to the bridge. We're trying to communicate with it."

The doctor opened her eyes wide once more and tilted her head to the side. "Can you say that again?"

"You heard me right. We devised a method, well at least we think we have, on how to communicate with it. We're trying to get it to show up on the bridge."

With that, the doc rubbed her temples with her fingertips. "Okay." Then after another few seconds. "Okay. Yeah, I need that drink now." She laughed weakly. "And you're trying to bring it *to* the bridge?"

"You heard me right."

Zeke and Alina waited and gave her time to absorb everything. She inhaled deeply then let it out slowly. She started to speak to herself.

"How long was I out?"

"A few hours."

The doc looked at Alina again and then the floor. "Okay, okay. We are in space. We just encountered an alien creature. The ship's power was gone, and we got it restored. Now Alina is back from the dead." She exhaled hard. "Yeah, that makes sense. Sure, why not?"

She took another breath and sat up straight as she stared at Alina. "You're alive."

"Yes, I am."

The doc slowly approached her and smiled. "Amazing." She then reached out and grabbed Alina by the shoulders. "Well, I guess you're real." Then, she hugged her.

After pulling back, she said, "Well, I guess your resurrection is gonna be a great read in the medical journals. That is if we ever get back home." She looked at Zeke. "As far as communicating with the creature, I definitely want to hear about this. But, somehow, it all makes sense in a weird way, resurrection, talking to aliens. Sure, why not?" Then one more breath. "Okay, now what? Anything significant happen while I was unconscious, other than the obvious?" She looked back at Alina.

"Yeah," said Zeke. "Two more things. First, Janice is back online."

The doc smiled. "Janice?"

"Yes, Doc, I am here. Welcome back."

"Welcome back to you, too."

"Well, that is definitely good news. Has she got any advice on the creature?"

"Yes," said Zeke. "But there's one more thing he said as he looked over at the body bag. "It's about Oleg."

She followed his eyes and frowned. "What? No, wait. That's right. When I first came to, I saw the bag, but I thought it was Alina. Then when Alina showed up, I was just in shock." She looked at it. "Oleg?"

Zeke approached her and put his hand on her shoulder. "He died a few hours ago."

She exhaled and squeezed her eyes shut as she rubbed her forehead and dropped her head. Once again, Zeke and Alina gave her time to absorb the new reality.

"Damn," she said after a bit.

"Yeah," said Zeke. "I know this is a time to take in, but you've got to know it all."

"Of course," the doc stared at the body bag. "Of course, it's Oleg. I should have put it together more quickly."

"You're doing fine," said Alina. "You just woke up and were bombarded with some pretty heavy stuff. I'm impressed."

Janice interrupted. "I anticipated this encounter with the doc, and preemptively gave her a medicine that would calm her and make her more open to dealing with stress."

The doc looked up at the ceiling. "I don't know whether to thank you or get pissed off."

"Doc?" said Zeke in a caring tone. "I'm sorry, but we don't have much time. I know this is a lot to process. But, like I said, we need to get back to the bridge."

The doc didn't acknowledge his words. Her patient was dead, and that preoccupied her doctor's heart. She took another deep breath and raised her head up. After a pause, she turned back to Zeke and in a slightly quivering voice, said, "Yeah, of course. But, I'm still a bit groggy, and, well, dealing with all of this isn't exactly easy." She looked up to the ceiling. "Even with the drugs."

She steadied herself. "When did Janice come back online?"

"A few hours ago," answered Zeke. "A lot's happened while you were in a coma. But, it was Janice who helped get you back on your feet."

The doc looked up to the ceiling again, "Thanks again, Janice."

"You are welcome, Doctor."

She rubbed her forehead and moved away from the table as she spoke to Janice. "I'd be interested in your diagnosis and treatment of me when we have some free time."

"Yes, Doctor. I would be happy to fill you in."

She looked at Zeke. "That is *if* we have free time."

She let out another breath and accompanied it with a good stretch. I'll be okay in a bit." She looked at the body bag. "A few hours ago, huh?"

"Give or take," he responded.

"How about Finn and Hahn? How are they doing?"

"They're fine. But, the stress is taking a toll on them, on all of us actually. We're exhausted. Finn and Hahn don't like the idea of us trying to communicate with the creature. They have more hostile intentions for it."

"Well, can you blame them? I mean, it has a tendency to break things and kill people."

"That's true. But, trying to open up a dialogue with it might be the best hope we have of survival. We're stranded out here. So, we've got to try and talk to it."

The doc looked at Zeke with a half-smile and a chuckle. "Really? And what are you going to use, sign language?"

"None of us knows sign language, so that's not gonna work," responded Zeke sarcastically.

"Oh, yeah, I didn't think of that."

"In fact, according to Janice, it was using the solar panels to produce prime number sequences. I guess it was doing it by blocking the light at varying intervals."

"Really?"

"Yeah. But we have something set up on the bridge that we're going to use to try and get it to show up so Janice can do her number pattern thing as she tries to set up a rudimentary kind of language."

The doc jerked a dubious look at him. "Okay… Sure, why not. Nothing can go wrong with that."

"It can't get much worse."

She looked at Alina and smiled. "Amazing. I mean, wow. Lazarus, come forth."

"Huh?" responded Alina.

"Forget it."

"Ready, Doc? We need to get to the bridge."

"Yeah, sure. But, hold on for a minute while I check my vitals. It'll be quick."

Zeke forced out an impatient, "One minute."

She walked to a set of drawers and pulled one open. She grabbed an instrument and flipped the switch on. She then ran it from her forehead down to her stomach and checked the readout. After 10 seconds, she said, "Good. I'm alive. I had to make sure."

Zeke looked at Alina. "I guess she's back."

"Appears so." She then walked over to the doc. "They'll be glad to see you."

"Really? I thought you all didn't like my bedside manner. But, now that I know you care about me, I won't be as nice."

Alina shook her head and looked at Zeke. "Can we put her back in a coma?"

Zeke chuckled. "Let's get back to the bridge."

The creature was no longer interfering with the solar panels, nor could Janice detect it anywhere. So, there was really nothing to do but wait until Zeke and Alina returned, hopefully with the doc. But, the interruption in their plans only served to raise their agitation. The constant unknown and the steady anticipation grated on their nerves. Their fatigue wasn't helping.

"I still don't think trying to talk to it is a good idea," said Hahn.

"I hear you. But those are the Cap's orders right now. Maybe it's the right thing to do. Maybe it isn't. I don't know."

"It can't be. It's stranded us out here in the middle of nowhere. It's killed, and yeah, I know it brought Alina back. But still, it's dangerous. And you and I both know incredible pain it can inflict on us. I don't trust it."

"Me either. If I knew how to destroy it, I would."

"Yeah, I'm in total agreement with…"

They heard the approaching sounds from the hallway. Zeke entered first, followed by the doc, and then Alina.

Hahn was closest to the door and walked over to the doc. "Welcome back. How are you feeling?" The doc smiled weakly. "I'm fine." She headed towards Finn.

"I'm glad you're okay," he said in a calm tone.

"Well, here I am. I still feel a little groggy, but I'm glad to be back."

"Do you remember that thing attacking you?" asked Hahn.

The doc thought for a moment. "I'm not sure. I know I was attacked, but…" Her words trailed off as she tried to remember. "I was going to say that it felt like I was floating. There wasn't any pain…but I was floating, and it was dark. It is almost as though it was…comfortable." She shook herself free from the memories. "And then I woke up in medical." She looked at Hahn. "When I hear myself speak about it, it sounds strange."

"That's not what I experienced," said Hahn tersely.

"I know. I can't explain it. That's just the sensation I had. To be honest, I don't know if it was real or not. Maybe it was some dream state. But for now, I'm here. Anyway, Zeke brought me up to speed on Oleg and Alina. Of course, I'm sorry to hear about him. When I saw Alina, I thought I was hallucinating. It took a while for them to convince me I wasn't." She looked over at Alina. "It's still hard to get used to seeing you."

"It was the same for us," said Finn. "The creature brought her back, and we have no idea why."

"Maybe it'll bring back Oleg," said the doc optimistically.

They just looked around at each other.

"If I may interrupt," said Janice. "But something has happened."

"What?" asked Zeke as he took a step towards the A.I. panel.

"All three of the sensors have stopped sending signals. I did not stop them. They just quit."

Finn furrowed his brow and walked over to them. He immediately went into diagnostic mode, moving from sensor to sensor. After a bit, he turned to the captain. "Without running tests, I can't tell you why they are not working."

Zeke shook his head. "That's great. Janice? Do you know what's wrong with them?"

"No, Captain. I suggest that Finn run a diagnostic on each one and then attempt to repair or replace them."

Finn looked at Hahn then to Zeke. "If Hahn goes with me, I can head back to engineering and get some tools. If I can't figure it out, I'll build some more. But diagnostics should only take a half-hour for all three."

"Alright, go ahead and…"

The distortion in the room was too obvious to miss. Within the triangular boundary of the sensors, they could see movement. Everyone backed away and watched as the creature slowly manifested. It was nebulous, grayish, and undulating, about a meter across and a meter high. Then, after it seemed to reach its completed state of development, it displayed a pulse of soft light before it went black and once again showed the Drake solar system.

Chapter 21
Communication

Even though they had invited the alien to the bridge, its arrival was still unsettling. But there it was, hovering, displaying the Drake solar system, staying within the three sensors.

"Janice," said Zeke in a calm voice. "Are you able to analyze it?"

"No, Captain. It does not register sufficiently for my sensors to determine its composition."

Then as before, it displayed a line that represented the Cascade's trajectory to the fourth planet.

All they could do was watch the other-worldly display.

They were face to face with a creature of unimaginable power. Obviously, it could kill them all. But for now, and for reasons they did not understand, it appeared to be cooperating.

"Okay, Janice. Now is as good a time as any."

Janice produced an image of Drakus about a meter in diameter on the holographic table and held it there for 10 seconds after which, it dissolved into nothing. Everyone waited. The creature continued to show the Drake system. Once again, she displayed the same image for 10 seconds before removing it.

The creature continued to show the Drake system.

Janice once again displayed the fourth planet and held it there.

After a few seconds, within the creature's form, an image of Drakus appeared.

"It's working," said Alina as she looked at Hahn.

Janice then produced a sphere about a half a meter in diameter. Within a few seconds, the creature copied it. Janice then produced a pyramid, which it also reproduced. Janice generated a total of 11 geometric images, all of which the creature matched.

The crew continued to watch in silent fascination.

Janice then changed from geometric images to those of objects found on the Cascade. It matched each one.

"The creature is not only matching the images that I am displaying, but it is mimicking exactly the slight variations of time that I've held each image in place."

She then stopped producing the images. The creature likewise stopped its mimicry.

"I will now display images that produce both positive and negative emotions in humans. Those images that we consider positive I will display for twice as long as those images that we consider negative."

Janice then produced three-dimensional images of waterfalls, sunsets, flowers, trees, and ocean waves. She held each one for 2 seconds. She then showed images of skeletal remains of dead animals, a meteor destroying a spaceship, collapsing buildings, and someone in pain. She held each one of those for 1 second. She did this for 101 images. As she was producing them, she informed the crew that there was a 2-to-1 time ratio which reflected binary, on and off, and, she hoped, would eventually represent positive and negative.

The scene before them was both mind-boggling and surreal. They were in the presence of an alien and an advanced artificial intelligence that were trying to communicate with each other by using pictures and prime numbers arranged in two different time intervals. It was an amazing spectacle.

Then, she stopped and spoke to the crew. "I displayed 101 images at two and one-second intervals comprised of two main categories: positive and negative. I do not know if it understands my intention. Also, since it has continued to limit its size and location within the sensors, we can conclude that it is cooperating. Since it is matching the images, I believe it understands that we are trying to communicate."

Zeke nodded absentmindedly but did not take his eyes off the creature. No one did.

Finally, after about half a minute, the creature produced seven two-second pulses of soft light, another prime number. Janice then responded with seven pulses, two seconds each on the holographic table.

They waited. Half a minute passed.

"I believe its pause is an invitation for me to continue." Janice showed more of these same kinds of images, still keeping the 2 to 1 ratio. This exchange went on for several minutes. She spoke to the crew during the image display.

"I am sure that you are intrigued as am I. So that I may keep you informed while I am carrying out this experiment, I will continue to speak with you. Presently, I am attempting to get it to recognize the positive-negative pattern. I will stop again shortly and wait for it to respond."

After five more images, she finished.

Ten seconds later, the creature pulsed two times at one-second intervals, paused, and then produced a one-second pulse of light.

"Very well," said Janice. "The creature has set a pattern of two pulses and one pulse. This is a good sign. Our first form of communication is a two to one ratio. Of course, we have a long way to go. I will now alter the pattern slightly in an attempt to see how much it understands."

With that, Janice displayed a single pleasant image, one of those previously shown, and let it stay in place.

After about five seconds, the creature responded with a double pulse of light.

The crew immediately picked up on this.

"Fascinating," said the doc, interrupting the crew's silence.

She then slowly reproduced 11 more previously used images, both positive and negative. In each case, it responded correctly with one or two pulses of light.

"So far, it can recall patterns associated with each image. But, I do not know if it understands the values we are placing on them. Therefore, in order to ascertain if it understands our concept of positive and negative associations, I will now introduce new images that are thematically consistent with the two categories without pulses and see how it responds. I hope that it will be able to deduce proper associations with the new images."

Then, on the holographic table, she produced an image of a human baby and waited.

The creature did nothing.

Janice continued to hold the image in place.

It still did nothing.

"I guess it doesn't understand," said Hahn softly and then in a sarcastic tone, "Show it a dead body, and see if it likes that."

Zeke turned and looked at her hard. She pressed her lips together and gazed back at the image.

Everyone else kept quiet.

Then after a few more seconds, it produced two pulses of light.

Hahn scoffed.

Janice then produced two adult people sitting on a rock in an open field.

Two pulses appeared in less time than before.

An image of trees falling into the ocean after being struck by a massive wave.

One pulse.

A drought-ridden crop.

One pulse.

A butterfly.

Two pulses.

Janice paused. "I did not expect it to so quickly understand the two primary categories. But it has accurately assigned positive and negative values to each image. I will now pause to see what the creature will do if anything."

The wide-eyed crew waited, staring at the grayish creature hovering between the sensors, slowly undulating. They continued to wait, but nothing happened.

"I don't think it understands," said Finn.

"Give it some time," responded Alina. "It obviously wants to communicate with us, so we must be patient. It isn't going to be a perfect process."

Finally, after another 15 seconds, the creature produced the image of the Drake solar system.

"I will produce two pulses of light to signal affirmation and approval," Janice said to the crew.

Two pulses of light appeared over the holo-table.

The image of the Drake system disappeared from within the creature's vague boundary.

The crew watched the two nonhuman intelligences work to develop, what they knew, would be a new language.

Then the creature produced what appeared to be an image of an asteroid.

Janice spoke. "The asteroid is neither positive or negative to us. Therefore, I will produce three pulses in an attempt to signify that it falls outside of our one-two parameter."

Three pulses of light appeared over the holo-table.

The creature reproduced the image of the Drake system. Janice responded with two pulses of light. It produced an image of the Cascade. Janice again generated two pulses. It produced the fourth planet in the Drake system. Two pulses. Then, to everyone's surprise, it produced the image of the Cascade without lights. Janice signaled with one pulse.

Janice then produced an image of Zeke with two pulses, followed by images of each person with two pulses. However, when Janice produce an image of Oleg, she produced one pulse. Then she generated an image of Alina but did not accompany it with any pulses. She let the image of Alina slowly fade away.

"I do not believe it is merely mimicking the patterns. It understands a great deal."

"Let's hope so," added Zeke.

The creature was inactive for about half a minute. When it started again, it produced images of the ship's solar panels, the quantum drive without energy, medical, the galley, the bridge, and an airlock.

Janice would reply with a single or double pulse for each image.

Then there was another roughly half-minute pause, after which the creature produced images of the crew. But it did so at a much slower rate. So far, it had been creating two-dimensional images, but now their faces were three dimensional.

"I think this is significant," said Janice. "The change from two to three dimensions, and the slower image pattern of the crew implies that it understands the significance of the crew as compared to the ship."

Finally, the procession of images stopped on Oleg's body lying in medical.

Janice flashed one pulse of light.

They all watched.

They all waited.

The creature showed a picture of Alina, but it was of her standing there in the bridge. She reacted with a little surprise, which was then copied in the creature's image of her.

Janice flashed two pulses.

The creature then immediately showed a picture of the body bag in which Oleg was resting.

Hahn exhaled as she balled her fists. Finn looked away. The Doc kept staring, as did Zeke. Alina nodded.

Janice flashed one pulse.

The creature showed Alina's face again and then Oleg's. The images went back and forth rapidly for several seconds before abruptly stopping. Then it produced an image of the Cascade as it was moving through space from the vantage point of it passing by and continuing on towards the Drake sun. It generated an image of the quantum drive when it was operational and then replaced it with the Drake sun, which stayed in place. Then, several images appeared and disappeared rapidly, consisting of the galley, medical, Alina's quarters, the bridge, and the solar panels.

After a little bit, Zeke asked, "Janice? Does that make any sense to you?"

"I have several possible interpretations, but I do not know if any of them would be correct."

The creature abruptly disappeared.

"Whoa," said Finn. "What the hell was all that?".

"Do you sense it anywhere on the ship?" asked Zeke.

"I do not," responded Janice in her usual calm voice.

The crew looked around the room while glancing back to the three sensors and each other. They exchanged a few shoulder shrugs. Alina went over to the window and gazed outside. There was nothing there except empty space and distant stars.

"Well, that was weird," said Finn.

"It's all weird," said Hahn.

"It is in medical," interrupted Janice.

"Oleg!" said the doc. "What is it doing there?"

"It is hovering over Oleg's body."

"Finn, you're with me," ordered Zeke. "You two stay here in case it returns."

"Yeah, we'll just wait for the deadly creature to come back," yelled Hahn to Zeke. He ignored her comment.

Finn and Zeke rushed out of the bridge towards medical. They did not know what they would find. When they arrived and entered cautiously.

The body bag was empty.'

"Where is it?" asked Zeke as he stared at the empty container. "What did it do with Oleg's body?"

Finn didn't say anything. He headed to the office. Zeke looked into the storage room. There was no sign of it.

"What did it do?" asked Finn.

"I don't know," replied Zeke as he stared at Finn. They both paused.

"It took Alina's body earlier, and she came back to life. Do you think it's going to do the same thing with Oleg?"

"That's what I was wondering."

"Captain," interrupted the doc, via an embedded speaker in the room. Her voice carried an urgency. "Oleg is here!"

They bolted.

Chapter 22
The Bridge

Oleg had walked onto the bridge without warning. The doc froze and stared with wide eyes. Alina gasped at his unexpected entrance. Hahn took a step back. The impossible had happened again.

Zeke and Finn made short work of the hallway as they burst onto the bridge and almost collided with him. He was standing about a meter inside.

Everyone kept staring. They didn't know what to do.

"What's going on?" asked Oleg. "How did I get back inside the ship?" He was rubbing his head, shaking it a little. He squinted hard and stroked his temples with his fingertips.

It was Alina who took the first step. He looked at her. "Alina? What's going on?" His voice was hesitant. He squinted his eyes and rubbed them with his palms, then looked down to the floor as he shook his head slightly. "I feel funny."

Zeke walked towards him.

"Cap? What is going on?" He looked around the bridge. "The lights are on, and gravity is back. What happened? I was outside the ship, and now I'm here." His eyes seemed to clear. He blinked hard once, focused on him, then frowned.

Zeke approached Oleg. "Maybe you should sit down for this."

"I'll stand," he said slowly.

Zeke eyed the doc. She moved closer to him.

"How do you feel?" she asked.

"I'm okay, a little woozy, but okay." Lines formed between his eyebrows as he looked around the bridge. "Doc, am I hallucinating?" He took a deep breath, then forced it out through his nostrils.

"You're not hallucinating," she said gently.

Zeke jumped in. "Oleg, I'm just going to give it to you straight, and it's not going to be easy to process. But here it is. When you were outside the ship, you were attacked by the alien. Finn managed to get you back in, but you were in a coma. The doc couldn't do anything to help you. After a while..." he paused as he positioned himself slightly closer to Oleg, "...you died."

Oleg drew his head back, his face wrapped in a frown.

"Look, I know this is unbelievable. But it's true." He paused and then said in a different tone, "Right, Janice?"

"That is correct, Captain."

Oleg looked up at the ceiling looking for the voice. "Janice? You're online?"

"Yes, Oleg. After the solar panels deployed, there was sufficient energy to reboot me."

He stared back at Zeke and exhaled sharply as he squinted his eyes. "I was dead?"

Zeke nodded slowly. "Yes, and it brought you back. We don't know how, but we've concluded it relates to time very differently than we do. So, you being here has to have something to do with that. In fact, it attacked Alina. She died, too."

He looked at her with his eyebrows raised high.

"It's true," she said. "I remember being attacked in my quarters. It was bad, real bad. The pain was incredible. And then like you, I was suddenly okay, and power was back. So, yeah, I get your confusion. It isn't easy."

Oleg shook his head, "This is crazy."

"Crazy is a new norm," said Finn. "Heck, I'm not that surprised that you're alive. Especially after how it brought Alina back."

Oleg examined everyone's faces. They were serious. He furrowed his brow and looked at the floor for a few seconds. "Okay, I was outside. We had no power. Now, suddenly I am inside the ship, and we have power."

He moved his jaw sideways then pursed his lips. "I can tell I'm not dreaming."

He looked up at Zeke.

"I need a couple shots of vodka."

"That's the Oleg I know," chuckled Zeke slightly.

"Okay, so, you say I was dead?"

"Yeah," said the Doc. "It's true. You died in medical."

He took a large breath and let it out slowly. "Well... uh..." He pursed his lips again as he tried to remember. "I was outside the ship." He looked at Finn.

"You brought me back inside?" He asked, looking for verification.

"Yeah, buddy. It's true. The thing got you outside the ship, and I had brought you back inside. Then you just lingered in a coma for a while before...before you died."

Oleg rubbed his fingers on his chin as he looked past the crew and out to the window into space.

"Well, I've got my mag boots on. I was outside, and now I'm inside. Power is restored, and Janice is operational." He exhaled again. "I can't deny it. So, I guess what you say is true." He looked over at Alina. "Including what they said about you being dead."

She nodded, "Yep. It's freaky. But it's true." He looked at the cap, then Finn, Hahn, and back to Zeke.

"It's all true," interjected Hahn. "She was dead, and so were you." She took a few steps forward. "I don't know what this creature is capable of, but I do know it can cause incredible pain. It attacked me in the galley. As far as I'm concerned, we can't trust it, and we should get as far away from it as possible."

Zeke through another annoyed look her way.

"Pain." Oleg's eyes brightened as a new memory surfaced. "Yeah, I remember now. It just came back to me." He looked down at the floor again as he examined the memories. "The pain, it was, it was *incredible*. It was unbelievable. I couldn't move. I was out there, and it got me. I was suffocating. Yeah, I remember it!" His voice was getting louder. "It was unbearable. I couldn't move or breathe!"

Oleg was staring off into nothing as he frantically relived the experience. He took a step backward and gripped his hair with his hands. "It was, it was bad, really bad. It was horrible." He grimaced. "Why did it bring me back? Does it want to kill me again? I won't let it. I won't go through that again. What does it want?" He looked at Zeke. "What's going on? Why did it bring me back?"

"Oleg!" interrupted the captain. "If you can, calm down. I know that what you went through was hell. Hahn experienced it too, and we've got a pretty good idea that it was the worst thing you've ever felt in your life."

Oleg's contorted expression of misery lessened slightly as he looked at Zeke.

"I don't have answers for you. We're trying to figure things out. But right now, we're in the middle of something."

Oleg looked at him with a furrowed brow. "What?"

Zeke cleared his throat before beginning again.

"You and Alina were both dead. But somehow, the creature was able to bring you back to life. Earlier, it appeared on the bridge, but it didn't attack us. In medical, when we were all there, it showed us the Drake star system."

"What?" asked Oleg through his continually confused grimace.

"It can show images. It not only showed the Drake system, but it also showed our flight path. It knows where we're going."

Oleg was obviously trying to process everything as his baffled expression revealed.

204

"Anyway, we figured it wants to communicate." He then motioned to the three sensors on the bridge with a small sweep of his hand.

"So, Janice suggested we set up these sensors and send some more prime number signals hoping that it would come here so that we could try and learn to talk to it. And believe it or not, it worked. It was here."

Oleg's eyebrows shot up.

"Janice and it have been communicating through mathematical patterns and images. She's trying to develop a kind of basic language. She was showing it pictures of the crew, and she stopped with you. It disappeared. Then Janice said that your body disappeared in medical. The next thing we know, you showed up here."

Oleg's brow was squeezed tightly as he concentrated on every word. He looked around at everyone once again. Their obviously serious expressions only confirmed Zeke's words. "For real?" he asked.

They muttered back several comments of affirmation.

Oleg took another deep, calming breath and slowly looked around the room. He ran his fingers through his hair, then focused on the stars outside the large bridge window. He took several deep breaths and after a full minute, he relaxed his shoulders and turned around.

"Just tell me again why you want to bring it here?"

"Because it appears to want to talk. Besides, we're stranded. We figured the best thing we can do is to learn about it and maybe find a way to get back home or wait for rescue. But we don't know if that's possible. We don't know what it wants. But, it is intelligent, and like I said, it clearly wants to communicate. So, we have to learn about it, and the bridge was the best place to do it. Besides, it's either us now or another crew later that might show up in a few years. We gotta figure something out while we can."

Oleg nodded a couple of times slowly as he considered Zeke's words. Then, after one more deep breath, he looked at the doc. "So, I'm not having a psychotic episode?"

"No, you are not."

"Damn!" he said as he began to walk back to a group. "I think it would be easier if I was going crazy."

"We are here for you," said Alina softly. "I know it's a lot to process. It took me a while, too. But, you're just going…"

There was a movement. A blur of light caught their attention. Once again in between the three sensors, the cloud unexpectedly began to manifest. Oleg stepped back awkwardly. It appeared to take form slowly, morphing into a shape that resembled that same odd cloud, until it was fully visible. It stayed inside the boundaries of the sensors.

"Apparently, it wants to continue to communicate with us," said Janice.

"No, friggen' way," said Oleg. He backed away another step.

The creature was hovering above the floor, undulating in a slow-changing shape. Its interior was once again gray with a slight luminescent glow. Then, it showed a three-dimensional image of Oleg in real-time. His surprise was instantly copied.

Janice responded with two pulses of light.

Zeke turned to Oleg and said, "We're communicating with it using pulses of light and images."

"I'll fill him in," said the doc. She motioned for Oleg to join her. He paused, blinked hard, then followed her to the other side of the halo-table.

Zeke watched them for a bit, making sure Oleg was in good hands before he faced the sensors and took a few steps towards the creature.

Oleg's image disappeared.

"Stay away from it," said Hahn from behind the holo-table.

Zeke raised his right arm in a small wave of acknowledgment as he continued his slow approach. The creature's undulating movement slowed. Zeke likewise slowed then stopped. The creature gradually rotated on its axis and, though it was difficult to tell because of its lack of symmetry, it appeared to be facing Zeke.

He stood there.

The creature elongated vertically and matched Zeke's height. It shifted its ambiguous form and changed into something that vaguely resembled his proportions. It was as though if Zeke wanted to, he could step into it.

The creature continued with its edges slowly phasing in and out of visibility.

Zeke raised his right hand towards it and held it out, palm down, fingers close together, pointing towards it. Then he turned his palm upward. The creature slowly moved towards him, but only a few centimeters. Zeke lowered his hand. It continued to hover near one of the imaginary boundaries between two of the closest sensors.

Zeke turned back and looked at the group, "What do you make of that?"

Blank and confused stares were all he saw.

He faced the creature again and slowly raised his arm with his palm up, fingers slightly open, stopping at the horizontal.

The creature emitted two pulses of soft light.

Zeke lowered his hand.

"It looks like you have a new friend," said Alina.

"Janice? What do you think?" asked Zeke.

"If the creature wanted to kill you, it undoubtedly could. We know it can go anywhere on the ship, yet it has remained within the sensors. It is complying with our spatial arrangements though it does not need to. In addition, its resurrection of Oleg tells me it understands, to some degree, what we consider positive and negative. I am confident, given enough time, that we can establish more sophisticated communications with it. For now, it seems to respond positively to your open hand."

Janice's mention of Oleg led Zeke to turn around. "How are you doing?"

Oleg looked up. "Fine."

"You got anything you want to add?"

Oleg looked back in surprise. "No, why are you asking me?"

"I'm just checking on you. You've been through hell, and it's a lot to take in."

Oleg scoffed just a little. "Sorry, but I'm just a computer specialist who came back from the dead. Naw. I got nothing. And besides, I'm still not entirely convinced you're all real. Maybe this is some deep space psychosis." He paused and put his hand on his stomach. "Come to think of it, I'm not feeling very good."

The doc put her hand on his forehead as she looked into his eyes.

"This is a lot to take in quickly," she said. "So, it would be normal to become overwhelmed." She moved her hand down to his wrist and checked his pulse.

"How's he doing, Doc?" asked Zeke.

She smiled at Oleg. "He's doing very well considering the circumstances."

"I'd do better with vodka."

"Okay. Good." Zeke turned his attention back to the creature, which was still hovering in the triangular boundary. He took a couple of steps back towards the rest of the group.

"Captain," said Janice. "In light of this latest development with Oleg, I am now convinced that it understands a lot more than we initially thought."

"I agree."

"I also would like to comment that it has never made a sound. I do not know if that is significant, I thought I would just point it out."

"You're right," said Zeke with a tone of realization. "I guess that makes sense since out in space sound is not possible."

"With your permission, Captain, I would like to continue," said Janice calmly.

"Of course."

With that, Janice caused the holographic table to show Oleg standing next to a chair, with his hand on its headrest, and emitted two pulses of light. But, instead of repeating with a pulse, which they had now expected would occur, the creature showed Oleg sitting in the chair with his right hand on his forehead.

Oleg made a guttural noise. They all looked at him. "I think I'm going to puke." He was pale.

The doc nodded to Hahn and then to the chair. She quickly moved it into position. They both lowered him into it.

"You are still recovering. So, you just sit here." She put her hand on his wrist and checked his pulse. "You're a little clammy, too."

By then, Finn had managed to materialize, out of nowhere, a bag into which Oleg could vomit.

"Thanks," he said as he received it, dropped it to his lap, and laid his head back on the chair's headrest. "I'll be fine." He exhaled a few short breaths and continued to rub his stomach. "I'm feeling better. Sorry, everyone. It's a lot to take in." He looked at the captain. "I'm okay. Really." He then leaned forward and put his right hand on his forehead.

"Look!" Said Alina. "It's the image." She was pointing at the creature. "The image the creature produced was of Oleg sitting in the chair with his hand on his forehead. That's what he was just doing. It was the same. It knew Oleg was going to do that."

She was right. The image of Oleg rubbing his forehead was still displayed within the creature's form. In stunned silence, they stared at it before searching each other's faces for empathetic confusion.

"That's disturbing," said Finn, breaking the silence.

The image of Oleg disappeared and was replaced by that same dull grey.

The shock of it knowing the future, at least to some degree, was another alarming fact in their constantly changing worldview.

"If it knew what would happen with Oleg," said Alina, "how much does it know about us and our futures? And, how much of our past does it know? Maybe it already knows where Earth is."

Her last statement was sobering, as well as disturbing. It was one thing to be stranded out there by themselves, but if this creature might know about Earth, then that raised their concern to a whole new level.

"Janice?" asked Zeke. "Besides this thing being able to wreak havoc and scare the hell out of us, what do you think this thing is capable of?"

"Given the temporal paradox that we encountered in our communication with it before it arrived, and the fact that it showed us a glimpse of Oleg's future suggests that it may very well know our past. But, we cannot know how much of the future or how much of the past it might have access to. After all, it only showed Oleg's positioning in the chair a few seconds before it happened."

During this whole time, the creature didn't change. It remained within the sensors, hovering in its ghostlike form.

It was all a lot to take in. The crew was faced with one dilemma after another, and now a whole new problem was just thrown into the mix.

"Well," said Zeke. "We can sit here and stare at each other, or we can move forward. Considering the serious possibility of it knowing about Earth, we still have to try to communicate with it. We have got to try and find out what its intentions are." He approached them all. "This is the unknown that we're faced with. It's not some other crew we're hearing about. It's us. We're it. So let's step up and work through this."

He turned back to the creature. "Okay, Janice. Continue."

Once again, she produced two pulses of light on the holographic table. And once again, the creature returned with two.

"I'm going to string several images together next to each other and attempt to convey an idea."

On the table, there appeared an image of the Cascade. Next to it, the Drake solar system. Next to that was the fourth planet. Then, an image appeared of all six crewmembers in spacesuits standing on the planet's surface. After that, she produced an image of them with machinery performing various tasks. Then she showed the Drake system with an arc moving away from the fourth planet out into space, but the ark faded to nothing just beyond the solar system.

The creature mimicked the final sequence of images from Janice but projected the trajectory much further back out into space. Then it pulsed twice.

"It knows we came from deep space," said Hahn. "That's not good. We can't let it know where the earth is."

"She's right," said Finn. "We can't let it get back there."

Hahn continued. "I just thought of something. Maybe it's a dumb question, but since it can move in and out of the ship and Janice is part of the ship, do you think that somehow it can read her databanks and figure out where Earth is?"

Janice spoke up quickly.

"My inner machinations are tied to an incredibly complex system. No single point of data can make any sense unless it is joined with a large number of other data points, all of which form a single fact which, in turn, must be contextualized. It would have to be aware of all those data points, understand my circuitry, know how to combine them, and then extract the correct information. But even then, it does not know the programming language in which my consciousness resides. I am the product of the whole, not of individual circuits. Furthermore, it would have to do this without me

211

being aware of it. But since I am comprised of the very circuits it would have to activate, I do not believe it is possible. Nevertheless, one of the precautions that I implemented shortly after my re-initialization was to encrypt all my data. The encryption key is sufficiently complex that it would take a quantum computer as sophisticated as I am, more than 2 million years to unlock."

Hahn just kind of nodded as she raised her eyebrows slightly. "Yeah, but what if it just went back in time and read your encryption key?"

"It would have to know what the encryption key is for and how to administer it within my system. Even if it somehow could do that, once the key was entered, I would be aware of it and could take additional evasive actions. I am certain that it creature can not breach my security."

"Well, I guess that answers that," responded Hahn in a tone that did not exactly convey confidence.

Zeke turned back to the creature. It immediately started to morph into something resembling a horizontal oval. Then, an image of Alina appeared within it. Afterward, an image of Oleg formed. Then, it showed the one of Zeke reaching out his hand, but the last image was from the creature's perspective, which then stayed in full view.

"Got any idea what that means?" asked the doc.

"Beats me," replied Zeke. "What do you think, Janice?"

"I do not have sufficient information to draw any conclusions at this time. But perhaps it is trying to elicit a response from us. I will reply with two pulses of light. "

The holo-table flashed twice.

The images within the creature disappeared.

Alina jumped in. "It's one thing to produce images, but it's another thing to actually have a conversation. We don't even know if this thing has a language or for that matter if there are more of them out there with which it communicates."

Hahn jerked her head at Alina, suddenly realizing the terrifying possibilities of more creatures. "That's great! More of them! What do we do if they find us? Hell, no. We need to get the hell outta here as soon as possible." Her voice was rising in intensity as she spoke.

"Calm down," said Zeke. "One thing at a time."

"Even if we were to leave the area," added Janice, "there is no guarantee it will leave us alone. We certainly do not want to risk leading it back to Earth. We must consider our options. One is to send the Cascade into distant space. It would mean the eventual death of you all, but it would be an attempt to ensure it cannot find Earth. Or we stay in orbit around Drakus and wait for rescue. But, that might mean risking more lives and increasing the chance that it would learn of Earth's location should it encounter another crew. It is, after all, learning. Therefore, I think the best option is to communicate with it, acquire as much information as we can, and see if we can make peace with it. If not, we can send out radio warnings telling Earth to avoid this system. Perhaps a ship might pick them up. Of course, both options would mean that we would never return to Earth."

The crew had grown somewhat accustomed to staring blankly into the depths of ominous circumstances and impossible situations. This was no different. Janice's options were a dismal reality.

"Well," said Zeke. "The company is most probably going to send another expedition out here when we don't return. Drakus is too valuable a resource to ignore. So, we have to work with what we've got and figure out a way to communicate with it. We have to know if it's peaceful or hostile or just accidentally dangerous. We don't want the next crew going through what we've gone through, and we certainly don't want them to inadvertently lead it back to Earth. So, the best option is to continue. Maybe, if we're lucky, we can convince it that we mean it no harm, and it'll leave us alone."

"That's pretty hopeful speculation," said the doc from the other side of the table next to Oleg.

"Yes, it is."

"The captain's assessment is sound," interjected Janice. "We must continue in our efforts to communicate with it."

Zeke looked back at the crew. He raised his eyebrows as if asking for comments. A couple of them shrugged their shoulders. He turned back to the creature.

"Okay, Janice, let's keep going."

"At this time, I would like to change the direction of communication. Captain, since the creature has replayed your extended hand, I will use you as my primary actor for the next segment."

Over the holographic table, Janice projected an image of Zeke standing. He then sat down at a desk. The picture zoomed into his right hand that held a pen. Zeke then pointed to a plant with his left hand. He then printed the word 'plant.' Then the word and the plant disappeared. In place of it, she produced a ball. Zeke then wrote the word 'ball.' The ball and the word faded away, and the Cascade appeared. Zeke printed the word 'ship.' This went on, image after image where the imaginary Zeke would write word after word that corresponded to a variety of objects.

"Clever," said Alina. "Perhaps this thing can communicate back to us via writing."

"What about producing more complex scenarios and their corresponding words?" asked Zeke.

"That is my intention. However, I am giving it a lot of information and want to proceed slowly. Nevertheless, thus far, it seems to retain everything."

Zeke disappeared from the holo-table.

"I will now produce images that correspond to actions."

The holographic table produced Zeke walking, and this time the word, 'walk' appeared near the bottom of the image. Then Zeke was running with the corresponding word, 'run.' Janice did this with images related to sitting, sleeping, coughing, drinking, swimming, standing, and eating.

Janice then waited.

After about 10 seconds, the creature, which had surprisingly become somewhat of a normal presence on the bridge, changed shape into a circle. A black canvass replaced its standard grey, and then various stars and a sun materialized. It was the Drake system again. The image then moved in towards the sun and planets, which filled the view, but it was obviously not to scale. Their orbits were sped up significantly as they traveled around the Drake star. Then, there appeared an undulating grayish cloud between the third and fourth planet. It orbited the sun and grew in size until it left the orbit and moved beyond the solar system. The image then faded away.

Alina, who had moved closer to Zeke, said it first. "Maybe the Drake system is its home."

"That's possible," said the doc, "but since Janice had displayed the concept of eating, perhaps it is correspondingly telling us that it derives energy from the sun."

"We can't assume it understands what eating is to us," said Janice.

"True," said Hahn. "But, what bothers me is how it left the solar system."

"Me, too," added Oleg. He was now standing up and appeared to be fully recovered. "Do you think it's telling us it wants to leave here and go with us?"

"Janice?" asked Zeke. "From what you could tell, as it projected an exit from the solar system, was it heading back towards Earth?"

"Yes, but it was off by several degrees."

"Then, that would imply that it doesn't know where we came from," said Finn.

"I agree," said Zeke.

The doc chimed in. "Do you think this place is its home? I mean the Drake system? Or, maybe it's a visitor here like we are."

"Both are possibilities," responded Alina. "But without more information, it is hard to tell what it really is trying to say." She turned to Zeke. "If it needs the sun for its energy, then if we were to head back into deep space away from sunlight, perhaps it could not follow."

"The image it produced had it leaving the solar system," said Zeke. "So, it appears to be able to travel in interstellar space, which is obvious since that's where we met it. But, if somehow the sun or the solar system is where it gets its energy from, then maybe it has a limit to how far out it can travel. But, again, without more information, we can't be sure."

"Maybe it was born here," said Finn. "Maybe it *is* somehow tied to this area."

"Or," said Alina, "maybe its food is motion or gravity. Or, maybe in some weird way, it doesn't need food. Heck, maybe it eats time."

"Eats time?" asked Finn.

"Well, I was joking. But let me run with that possibility. Janice said it had the ability to behave in a bizarre way relating to time. Maybe that's how it was able to raise me and Oleg back to life. Maybe it eats time, or lives in it, or swims through it the way we move through space. That could help explain how it projected an image of Oleg with his hand on his forehead before it happened."

She took a breath and made an expression that could only be interpreted as yes-I-know-it-sounds-crazy as she delivered her words. "I'm just entertaining an idea. After all, this thing is so completely different than us that we have to be careful not to make assumptions based on our understanding of how things work."

"She's right," said Finn. "We have no idea what this thing is capable of or how it can live in space. Like she said, maybe it could do some tricks with time. Maybe it shifts back and forth in time and derives energy that way, kinda like how alternating current works by deriving energy through shifting electrons back and forth. It would make as much sense as anything else right now. Janice, what do you think?"

"Given that we do not know very much about this radically different life form, I think what you and Alina have proposed is certainly possible. Such speculations can be productive. Nevertheless, we need to continue to communicate with it and develop, if possible, a vocabulary exchange."

"Have you guys noticed something?" interrupted Hahn. "When we're talking, it doesn't do anything. It waits."

Zeke stared at Hahn. He nodded. "Yeah, I noticed that, too."

He turned back to the creature and spoke to Janice. "You think it hears us or senses our voice vibrations in the air?"

"In space, there is no sound, so maybe it senses sound when we're talking and waits till we're finished."

"In that case," said Zeke, "instead of writing images, what if you spoke to it?"

"That is the next logical progression in our communication, given this new consideration. I would like to add, Hahn and Zeke, that your observations were very good. I, too, had noticed this, but was waiting for further confirmation."

Hahn tilted her head to one side. "Don't get the idea that I'm trying to help it. I still want it..." she paused. "...gone."

"What if it understands us?" said Oleg out of the blue. "Hahn has already said she wants it dead."

"It is not very likely," interrupted Janice. "In our situation, spoken language is a set of sounds in which meaning and communication are derived via context. I do not believe it has had anywhere near the necessary time to begin developing an understanding between our sound-symbols and their meaning. Furthermore, it lives in space where sound is impossible, which would suggest that it cannot hear. That does not mean it can't observe us facing each other and talking or experience sound vibrations in some way, the way you might experience heat or cold. Nevertheless, it does tend to continue its communication with us when we all stop talking, and you face it."

They had all bristled at the thought that it might be understanding them. Hahn, in particular, showed more concern than the others. "It makes me nervous just *thinking* that it can understand us," she said tersely. "But, I agree with Janice. I don't think that's the case."

Zeke turned back to the creature. He took a step towards it. "Do you understand what I'm saying?"

Did it understand? Or, was it only capable of mimicry? How long had it been watching them, maybe listening?

Zeke took another step forward.

Immediately, it morphed into the silhouetted form that resembled the proportions and size of Zeke. Then within it, Zeke's image appeared, standing.

"Whoa," he said. "What you think *that* means?"

"It appears interested in you," said Finn with a suspicious tone. "But stay away. If it touches you, the pain will be the worst you've ever felt in your life. You'll probably end up in a coma or worse. Don't even think about getting too close to it."

"I second that," said Oleg. "Finn is right. The pain is, is worse than bad."

Zeke took another step back. The creature's image of him changed to include his extended hand.

"It looks like an invitation," said Alina.

"Invitation to what?" retorted Hahn. "…to be tortured? You know what it can do. You know it can kill."

"We already know that," said Oleg. "Heck, maybe it's trying to communicate its peaceful intent."

"Or," retorted Hahn, "it's completely misinterpreting things and considers Zeke's extended hand a threat and is warning us to leave. We just don't know."

"It has been cooperating with us," said the doc. "I don't think it is seeing us as a threat."

"If it doesn't, then why did it kill you and Oleg and attack me?" snapped Hahn.

"We don't know," she responded. "And we don't know why it brought you back, either."

"Alright," interrupted Zeke with a wave of his hand. "Things have changed. It's learning, and we're learning. We've been communicating with it, and it's cooperating by staying within the sensors. So, we need to continue trying to communicate." He spoke into the air. "Janice? You got anything you want to add?"

"Yes. As you have said, the creature is staying within the boundaries, has brought back Alina and Oleg, and is now returning the image of your extended hand. Also, it has changed its proportions to match yours when you approached. So, your closer proximity appears to be what it is seeking. Though I do not know why. Of course, I recommend extreme caution. And finally, it could be merely a sophisticated mimicry."

Zeke stood silently, pondering Janice's words for a few moments. He turned and looked at the creature. It was hoving within the sensors.

"Janice, do you think you could use the imagery of the solar system that it produced in order to suggest that it return in about an hour? Could you zoom in on Drakus and have it move slightly, something that would correspond to about an hour? I want to sit and think about this."

"Captain. You can't seriously be thinking about it." Hahn was adamant.

"We don't know what it wants," he said.

"Exactly! This isn't a game. If it is trying to get you to come closer to it, you should not do it. It's deadly."

"Yes, I know that. But what choice do we have? We can't go back to Earth, and we have to make sure that the next crew that comes out here doesn't fall victim to it. Either way, we're probably gonna die. So, we have to move forward."

Hahn moved her head back on her shoulders. "So that's it? We're gonna die anyway, so that makes it okay for you to take a huge risk? You're not thinking clearly."

"I have to agree with Hahn," said the doc. "It's a bad idea."

He ignored their negative comments. "Janice? Can you attempt to convey the idea of an hour?"

"Captain," said Finn. "Are you sure?"

"No, which is why I want to talk about it."

"It might be our only chance," said Oleg, surprising everyone. He was standing up next to the chair. "I don't know why I'm saying this, but something tells me that we should consider this possible invitation seriously."

"Invitation? What makes you think its an invitation?" asked the doc.

"It just makes sense to me," responded Oleg. "I think it's trying to do something, and it's being cautious."

"That's a laugh," snorted Hahn. "It'll probably attack him and then us."

"And what if it doesn't?" responded Oleg. "It could do that anyway whether Zeke gets close to it or not."

Hahn looked at him. Her brows were knitted into a frown.

"We all know it's dangerous," interrupted Zeke. "We've already rehashed this plenty of times. The reality is that we're stranded out here, and we may never make it back home. We know that the company will probably send another team once it believes that we are lost. And, of course, I agree that we cannot let it know about Earth's location, which another crew might inadvertently reveal. This thing is smart and is learning. So, for now, it's up to us to do as much as possible to figure out what it wants, even if it means taking huge risks."

The captain was right, but the crew bristled, nonetheless.

"Janice, can you produce that image, please?"

"Yes, Captain"

With that, Janice created a likeness of the Drake system the way the creature had displayed it. Then, she zoomed in to Drakus and showed some stars behind it. Then, she made Drakus move forward the equivalent of one hour before repeating it several times. She then stopped the projection.

The gray undulating form stayed.

Janice produced the image again.

After a few seconds, the creature disappeared.

Chapter 23
Disagreement

"Don't do it," said Hahn in a strained calm. "It's too big of a risk."

"I get it, Hahn," said Zeke, "I know that your experience was horrible, and I know this is risky. But our situation is serious, and we have to move forward, one way or another."

Hahn just shook her head and let out a disapproving sigh.

He continued, speaking to everyone. "This isn't easy for any of us. We know we have to try and communicate with it for our sake, the sake of the next crew, and maybe even for Earth. So, we're moving forward with communication, one way or another."

"Do you mind if I add something?" asked Alina.

Zeke motioned with a slow, open hand.

"I agree with the cap. We have to think this through." She eyed Hahn. "But we don't know why it is doing what it is. Maybe it killed accidentally, the way we step on ants and don't even realize it. But that doesn't mean it's evil. Besides, isn't my own coming back from the dead, as well as Oleg's, enough evidence that there's more to it than mere malicious intent? I mean, look at *all* of the evidence, not just some of it. It has stayed inside the sensor boundaries and responded to images. It's cooperating. It wants to talk."

Hahn took a half step towards Alina and, with a voice that strained of suppressed anger, spoke. "But why? We might be a threat to it, and it is smart enough to realize more of us might be coming. It could just be gathering intel."

Excuse me," interrupted the doc, trying to disarm a potential conflict. "Hahn, we get it. But, I'm with the cap on this."

Hahn just shook her head and looked at Zeke. "I think you're being too easy and taking too many risks. Sure, talk to it, but slow down. Be cautious. And, if you want my opinion, I think we should look for a way to fight it."

"Not so fast," said Zeke. "We don't know if fighting it would only make things worse. So, the more we know, the better off we are."

"I understand," said Hahn. "But for now, we're supposed to be discussing your potential suicide. I think you're moving way too fast."

Alina jumped in. "We don't have any other real option. Cap is right. We have to try and talk to it. Think about how it stayed inside the three sensors, which it most certainly doesn't need to do, and it apparently understood the idea of coming back in an hour. I'm telling you this thing is smart, really smart, so we better pay attention to it. I don't think it is intentionally malicious."

"Yeah, well, maybe you're right. But, maybe not." said Finn. "We still don't know what it wants."

"All the more reason to find out," Alina retorted as she looked at Finn, then turned her attention to Zeke. "I don't know if it was inviting you to get closer or if it was just mimicking you. But trying to work with it is the best option we have right now. And, yeah, I know it's risky, and you're the one taking the risk, but hell, I think we need to find out what it wants if we can, while we can."

Zeke had his arms crossed and had been strumming his fingers above his elbow. "Finn," he asked. "What do you think?"

"Well, first of all, you've already made up your mind. You're going through with this invitation, or whatever it is. But, you better be sure. Come on. I mean, think about it. It looked like a whole in space that was your size, and it played your open hand back to you. It looks like it wants you to step inside of it."

Zeke straightened his arms. "I didn't say anything about stepping inside of it. I just want to know what you think."

"I just told you. And, what amazes me is that you're considering risking your life by... by maybe even coming in contact with it. Yeah, it has stayed in the sensors and imitated your general proportions while showing an open hand. I mean, crap! Do you really want to see what it wants? Not me. I'd steer clear of it and learn what you can from a safe distance."

Zeke walked over to a chair next to the holo-table and lowered himself into it, answering the call of fatigue that had been plaguing him for some time. "Okay, look. You're right. I've already decided I'm going to… to move forward with our interaction and, I guess, get closer to it and see what happens. But that's it. Heck, if we're going to die out here, I want to go out trying to make things better, not worse. And of course, I could be wrong. That's why I want to hear from you all because maybe someone has thought of something that I haven't. Besides, this is way too important to screw up."

"Well, there's honesty for you," said Finn. He then found a chair, grabbed the backrest, and guided it over towards Zeke, and then he slowly sat down opposite him. "Okay, let's talk about it." He leaned back and rested his ankle over his knee.

They all found chairs and pretty soon were sitting as a group.

Hahn, of course, was more resistant and moved slowly. She was the last to join the ill-formed circle. She stared past them at a wall.

"All right. Let's hear it. Speak freely."

"Don't do it," said Hahn with emphasized syllables. She shifted her body weight in her chair. "We need to fight it."

"Okay, that is an option." Zeke looked at the doc and raised his eyebrows. "What do you have to say?"

"I'm not exactly sure. I mean, here we are stuck in the middle of nowhere trying to communicate with a new life form. But what exactly are we trying to decide here? Sure, it makes sense to try and talk to it, but we don't know what it wants. Besides, we don't know if we *can* establish any meaningful communication. Does it want you to get inside the sensors, so it can attack you? I don't think so. But it could do that outside the sensors, and yet it doesn't, so I'm not sure what to make of it. On the other hand, is something new and unexpected going to happen? Again, I don't know, and I can't recommend anything except that we continue to try and learn about it." She looked at Hahn. "In case we have to fight it." She looked back at Zeke. "There, you heard my ramblings."

"Oleg?"

He looked around at his crewmates. "We can't run from it. So, we either work with it or, like Hahn says, we fight it. But, if we do, we would have to figure out some way to defeat it. I don't think that'll be easy. In fact, I don't believe its possible. It's too powerful. Heck, it ate all the quantum drive energy and didn't even burp. So, where would we even begin to figure out how to fight it? So, I say talk to it. Go for it."

"The bone scanner," said Hahn. "It doesn't like it. So, we need to look into that." She was a little calmer this time.

The doc leaned forward in her chair and put her elbows on the armrests. "Look, we're just talking in circles. We're marooned. They are probably going to send another mission. The next crew will be the same position we are now, maybe even worse. So, we have to continue to talk to it and learn whatever we can." She looked at Zeke. "So, if it is an invitation to you, whatever that means, I say go for it."

"Acknowledged," responded Zeke and then with a lackluster smile, he said. "But then, maybe it will bring me back if it kills me."

No one responded to his slight attempt at humor.

"I have another idea," said Finn. "I think it's something that we need to consider." He paused for a few of seconds. "We can blow up the Cascade and it with us."

Oleg was the one who broke the residual silence left after Finn's proposal. "So, you're saying our suicide would be a noble effort to save the earth?"

"Something like that. There's enough chemical fuel in the standard engines for us to go supernova. Now, I know there's no guarantee that blowing up the Cascade will kill it, but it's an option we have to consider." He paused for a moment before adding, "Trust me. It's not an option I like. I'd rather find a way to neutralize it and get back to Earth. My family is there."

Zeke leaned back in his chair and put his hands behind his head. "I've thought about that, too. But it is something we'll have to agree to if there are no other options. But, since Finn's suggestion is on the table, what do you all think?"

Silence claimed the room as they eyed each other.

"I vote yes," said the doc after a while. "As much as I hate the idea of self-destruction, if communication fails and things go bad, then we are obligated to try and destroy it, for Earth's sake."

They pondered her words carefully.

"I agree," said Hahn in a somber tone.

"Me too," added Oleg.

"I'm in," said Finn as he gently hammered the chair armrest.

"Yeah, me too," said Alina.

Zeke lowered his arms and placed them in his lap as he intertwined his fingers. "Okay, it's unanimous. If things go south and we run out of options, we destroy the Cascade and try to take it with us. But, let's hope it doesn't come to that."

He looked over at Finn. "Since the Quantum drive is dead, the self-destruct option is useless. So, how easy would it be to ignite the chemical fuel?"

"Not that easy. It would require making a detonator. Janice could help us with the design. There's plenty of explosives in the cargo bay that we were going to use for mining on Drakus. Then it would just be a matter of getting them close enough to the main fuel-cell, and if I remember correctly, that would probably require cutting through a bulkhead or two. But that shouldn't be a big deal. So yeah, it's doable."

"How long do you think it would take to set it up?"

Finn pursed his lips a little as he thought about it. "If all goes well, I think we could have it set up in three or four hours. We could set up a detonator that Janice could activate remotely. Then, voilà. We become a mini-star for a few seconds."

Janice interrupted their conversation. "I would like to remind you that since the creature has free reign of the ship and is often undetectable, it might become aware of your plans to destroy the ship. Therefore it is possible that it could neutralize your efforts. I say this only as a possibility worth considering."

Zeke leaned forward in his chair and put his elbows on the table. "Yeah, that's true. But, either way, we have to try something. So, let's do it. We'll set the ship for possible self-destruction. We'll also continue to try and communicate with it. I don't know why, but it seems to have focused on me a little bit. If it kills me or I'm incapacitated, then Finn, it will be up to you all to decide when to implement the final plan."

"Aye, Cap," responded Finn as he looked at the other crew members.

Zeke slapped the armrests with his palm. "Okay, let's talk about this so-called invitation again. What do you think?"

Finn piped in immediately. "Since we're low on options, if it is an invitation aimed at you, and since we're probably going to end up dying out here anyway, why not? I say go for it. Just make sure I'm in your will."

"You can have the box of grass on my desk."

"Finally!"

"Anyone else?"

Oleg jumped in. "Look, all of this is surreal. You tell me that Alina and I were dead, and I'm still processing that." He looked at her and back to Zeke. "So, that tells me we're dealing with an incredibly powerful being. It is too important and dangerous to ignore. We're in the middle of nowhere, and we have to try to communicate with it. Maybe we'll become best buddies. But if not, it's either gonna kill us, or we're going to end up obliterating ourselves trying to kill it. Either way, it'll suck. So, we need to take risks. Hell, it's all a big risk, anyway."

Zeke nodded to Oleg then turned to Alina. "What do you think? Do you see any other options?"

She looked down and scratched her nose before speaking. "Oleg's right. I say we do our best to learn about it now. Maybe in the process we might find a way to defend ourselves. So, I would consider communication to be a strategic move. Accept its invitation, if that is what it is. Get close to it. Blow it a kiss, and let's find out what happens."

"Anyone else?"

Hahn shook her head and looked at Finn. She stood up, pushing the chair back with her legs before heading towards an empty area of the room. She folded her arms before finally turning to Zeke and took a step toward him. "I agree that we should learn what we can about it, so we can fight it. But you might want to consider that it's thinking the same thing about us. Moving forward might be helping it discover our weaknesses. Maybe our mere presence injures it, and it wants to make sure that no one from Earth ever comes here again. So, my vote is for destroying it. Oh, and we're all probably going to die horrible deaths."

Zeke shifted his head back and exhaled slowly in response to her gloomy outlook. "I really hope you're wrong."

"The only thing we should be doing, she continued, "is finding out how to kill it, not talk to it. The bone scanner thing is our clue. We should work with Janice to figure out how to use it and develop a weapon. If we can destroy it, we can get into the parking orbit and wait for rescue – provided there aren't any more of those things floating around. With any luck, it might only be a few years. But it's a better option than committing cosmic suicide. So, there. I've said my piece. I'm done."

Zeke slowly stood up, then turned around and grabbed his chair with both hands as he stood behind it. He strummed his fingertips on its back. "Finn, what do you think about Hahn's suggestion of developing a weapon based on the bone scanner?"

"Well, given we don't know much about it and we don't know how that thing affected it, we would probably be wasting our time. But on the other hand, you never know. It might work. If it doesn't, then we could always go with plan B and self-destruct."

Zeke looked over at Hahn. "All right, I think we need to consider making a weapon, but *after* we set the ship for self-destruct."

"Finally!" said Hahn.

"Janice?" said Zeke into the air. "How much time do we have remaining in the hour."

"27 minutes."

"All right, we'll wait for it to show up again, and if it does, I'll accept its invitation, whatever that means. Hopefully, it won't kill me. But, if it does, then Finn, rig the ship to explode. After that, see about making a weapon. If things continue to go bad and you can't develop anything that's effective against it, then destroy the ship when it's onboard."

He took a breath and let it out slowly. "Janice, I want you to compile all the information you have gained about the creature and whatever else you learn through our interactions with it and send it via standard radio towards Earth. I know it will not get there for 22 years. But, I want you to do that now and then at regular intervals with any additional information that you decide might be beneficial."

"Yes, Captain. But, I have already been sending updates to Earth via radio."

"Of course, you have." He took another breath and walked over to the bridge window. He let his mind fall into the depths of starlit darkness as he tried to prepare himself for what was to come.

"I wonder what else is out there."

Chapter 24
Taken

It had been a little more than an hour since the creature disappeared. After their initial meeting, they went to the galley for something to eat before heading back to the bridge. They mostly kept themselves occupied with stories of Earth. Finn and doc were both resting in chairs. He had his legs propped up. She was semi-snoozing. The others meandered around the bridge, glancing at the three sensors, walking up to the large window, peering out, pacing by the holo-table.

"Janice?" asked Zeke. "How long has it been since it disappeared?"

"One hour, 17 minutes."

"Maybe it did not understand. Or maybe we sent it the wrong message."

"It is possible that the lack of precision in producing an image that is supposed to represent one hour is the reason it has not yet returned. Though my calculations were accurate, I do not know if the creature understood it the way we intended."

Zeke walked over to the window. Just a meter beyond him was the emptiness of space. The infinite black sprinkled with a myriad stars had always helped him to clear his mind and think things through. It was a beautiful distraction. But now, not so much.

There was a pulse of light between the sensors that drew their attention. Over several seconds, the creature manifested. Everyone moved into a group about three meters away from it, near the holo-table.

Its form was the same as before, but this time it contained the starry background visible from the bridge window that shifted back and forth as if they were underwater.

"All right," said Zeke. "That's different."

"I wonder what it means," asked Alina.

"I have no idea. Maybe that's how it shows it's eager to talk."

"Or that it's angry," said Hahn.

They watched quietly as Zeke moved to about two meters from the triangular array. The creature responded by morphing the starscape into the Drake system.

"Janice? If you have anything to say, now would be a good time."

"Since it has returned and is voluntarily remaining within the triangle, I must interpret this as a sign towards continued communication."

Zeke was staring into the representation of the Drake system. It was not exact because it couldn't be. The creature had enlarged the planets and shortened the orbit distance from the sun in order to make the Drake system recognizable and fit within its boundaries. Zeke found himself wondering if it was capable of art.

He exhaled deeply. "Here goes." He took one small step towards it.

The image of the Drake system disappeared.

He waited.

It then again showed the image of him holding out his hand. Zeke stood in one place, not sure what to do. Was it merely associating an image with his presence? Was it an invitation, or was it misunderstanding everything? For that matter, maybe it wasn't an invitation at all. Perhaps it was a warning. But, he had no way of knowing.

The creature began to increase in height and stopped at about 2 meters tall.

The image of Zeke holding his hand out slowly faded away until the only thing left was an empty, dark gray.

Zeke continued to stay where he was and watch the alien that had no real form or symmetry. It had an undulating water-like appearance that was surprisingly pleasant to look at. He studied it. It was somehow beautiful.

The dryness of his mouth made it difficult for him to swallow. His heart pounded, and he noticed he was taking short breaths. *Relax,* he said to himself and then scoffed internally at his own suggestion. There was no way he could. He was two meters away from an incredibly powerful and deadly alien creature. He wondered who would blink first.

It did not change. It did nothing. It merely hovered, elongated vertically. Zeke looked back at the crew. Their silent expressions displayed a mixture of fear and concern.

He turned at the creature and waited a few seconds before he took another step, a very small one.

His heart pounded, eyes wide, muscles tense.

It elongated a little more.

"The closer you get," said Alina, "the more its shape matches yours."

The obvious correspondence between his approach and its form was clear. "Yeah, I picked up on that."

He took a step backward.

The creature's mimicking proportions lessened slightly.

"Crap. This is scary as hell," said Zeke in a cracking voice.

"Get away from it," said Hahn in a surprisingly calm tone. "It's not worth the risk."

"Everything's a risk at this point," said Zeke quickly.

His breathing was shallow and quick. He flexed his fingers and rubbed his fingertips on his pants. It was hard to swallow.

She stepped a few centimeters closer.

He tried to swallow again, but his mouth was dry. He could hear the pounding of blood in his ears.

The creature grew in size until it once again matched Zeke's proportions.

He stopped about a meter and a half from it.

The dark grey slowly turned to pure blackness.

"That can't be good," said Finn.

Zeke didn't move. What did the blackness mean? His heart was pounding, and a trickle of sweat ran down his temple.

He was face-to-face with a creature so different, so completely other than him, that everything it did and appeared to be was an ominous mystery, and he was risking his life to learn about it.

The blackness was replaced by the beautiful starry background once again.

Zeke stayed in place.

Then within the canvas of the creature, the image of Zeke with his hand out appeared yet again.

Adrenaline surged through his body. His hands shook, and his mouth was dry. An ache crept into his throat.

Though he did not want to take his eyes off it, once again, he turned and looked at the crew. Worried and concerned expressions met him. He turned back and waited.

In an instant, the creature engulfed him, and both disappeared.

Hahn gasped in horror, "Zeke!" She rushed forward as did Finn and the Oleg. The doc stood without expression, stunned. Alina was covering her open mouth with both hands, eyes wide open.

Chapter 25
The Here

Blackness.

Empty nothingness.

There was no up, no down, no direction. There were no points of reference by which movement or time could be determined. There was only complete and total unfilled space. He could feel no warmth nor cold. It was neutral. It was as if he was in the midst of nothing.

He could not breathe, but he realized he did not need to. Why not? He tried to look at his own hands, but his eyes were useless here. That is when he realized that he did not have the sense of his physical body. Maybe he didn't have eyes anymore, or a mouth, or arms and legs. Was he disembodied? Or dead?

He remembered that the creature had killed twice. But, it had brought them back. Was this where they were taken? No, that can't be since they didn't say anything about it, or maybe they just didn't remember. He tried to look around again, but his effort to move was useless. Where was he?

This isn't a place.

Why did he think that? He existed. He had to exist in a place. But, somehow, this wasn't a place.

He wrestled with the enigma of existence without a location. Yet, that's what it was. It was existence without a location.

How do I know that? He asked himself. *That makes no sense.*

Just moments ago, the creature had engulfed him. Or *was* it moments ago? How long had he been here? Seconds? Hours?

He did not know. His sense of time seemed to be affected, yet he felt as though a long time had passed – but then again, it had not.

The truth seemed to come from outside of him, yet also from within. It had been both.

Both?

How long?

This doesn't make sense, he thought. *It has not been that long, but it was. Somehow space and time were different here. But where is 'here'?*

Again, he puzzled at how he knew this, at how he recognized what was true.

His physical senses were not working because there was nothing *to* sense. Was his mind playing tricks on him? Was it creating sensations somehow pretending to know something? He had read accounts of people in sensory deprivation chambers whose minds quickly began to manufacture images and sounds. The brain needs stimulation. So, maybe he was imagining that space and time were different here because of the complete sensory deprivation.

He could *see* blackness. Or was that simply the absence of seeing? But, if he were not in his body, then he wouldn't have eyes to see with. How then, could blackness be what he was seeing?

This does not make sense. Am I seeing or not seeing?

There was no warmth, no cold, no balance, no sight, no sound, no breathing, no touch...nothing. But he needed them. He could feel an inner desire to be in touch with existence. But there was nothing in this place.

He wanted to exhale, but could not. He tried to speak, but there was no movement of his chest, no exhaling, no sound, no sensation of having a body.

He was trapped, trapped in nothingness, trapped in a nightmare of confusing absence.

He listened for any sound, for anything at all. But there was nothing to hear. Pure silence.

He realized he had never heard complete silence before.

He strained to sense something, anything. But, there was nothing at all.

It was disorienting. He shook his mind free from the unpleasant nonexistence of everything and focused on doing something.

He tried to put his hands together, but they did not move or touch each other. He did not sense their movement.

Where are my hands? Where is my body?

He wanted to feel something, anything. He tried to speak again, but nothing.

Then he wondered if his mind had been completely disconnected from his body by the creature's attack. Was he still on the bridge, only disengaged somehow from everything, completely disconnected from his senses?

The thought brought with it the beginnings of dread and panic.

Don't think about it, he told himself as he pushed himself away from the thought.

Resist it, he said to himself. *Focus.* He tried to close his eyes, but he quickly realized the effort was useless.

What is going on? He asked himself.

He tried to move again, but nothing happened. His body wasn't there to move. Instead, there was this horrible numbness of disconnection. He knew where his arms and legs were supposed to be, but he could not feel thim.

Then the feeling of panic he had so quickly suppressed, came back. He resisted it again, but it was being fed by the disorienting absence of everything. He fought against it.

What did that creature do to me?

He paused from his thoughts, forcing back the fear and anxiety that were scraping against his soul.

Then a horrifying thought came to him, which caused him to convulse mentally and emotionally.

What if I'm here forever? What if this is where I'll be without end?

He was instantly shocked at the incredible anxiety such a prospect brought. If he could have moaned, he would have. If he could have fled, he would have. This place had already become hell, and the reality of his complete helplessness was growing into a foreboding monster.

It had come upon him quickly, and he realized how easily he was unraveling.

No, he thought in defiance. *No.*

He forced the emptiness away and strained to focus on something better, something, anything. He thought of the Cascade and the crew. He remembered them, their faces, their voices. That helped, but only momentarily. The blackness was what he 'saw' more than anything else, and pushing it away was like trying to push away the ocean.

He decided to sense his own self. At least he could do that. Yes, that's it. He would survey his own existence.

Did he have a physical form? It felt as though he did, but only the way a shadow existed as the absence of light. Hands? He could not tell. A mouth? Arms? Legs? They weren't there, but he somehow sensed them. Or was it a figment, a residual effect of physical existence.

I am absent from space and time.

Why did he think that? Why would he contemplate such a thing? But somehow, the thought seemed true, and he had no idea why he knew it was.

Relax, he said to himself. *Relax. Relax.*

Yes. Thinking to himself helped. It was pseudo sensory, but it was something.

Relax Zeke. Focus. Think. The creature did this. It's going to end. It has to end. Calm yourself. Think logically. Maybe you're dead. Maybe you're on the bridge in a helpless state of disconnection. They crew will be working to help me.

He paused for a moment before continuing. *Is death nothingness,* he wondered? *Is death complete and total aloneness? Is this the penalty for my sins?*

Then this inner sensation manifested again. He was not dead. Somehow, he knew he was not, but he did not know how. Then another truth came to him. He was not on the bridge. Again, how did he know that? Or did he? Was it his mind falling apart and playing tricks on him?

Then the same horrifying thought hit him again.

What if I can never get away from here?

He fought against the thought.

No, don't go there. You'll make it out. You'll get out of here.

Then an idea came to him, almost as though it wasn't his. This *was* a place. But, it wasn't a three-dimensional place. It was more than that.

But the thought made no sense. He tried to rip his mind free from the spiral of confusion and helpless solitude. *No,* he thought to himself. *This can't be real.*

He focused on the blackness, on the sense-less reality.

Nothing was all around him. Nothing had become something, a terrifying certainty that robbed him of hope and was attacking his sanity.

He fought against the black nothingness. But it was too strong. It was too oppressive.

No, he thought. *Fight it!*

He tried to move again.

Nothing, but futility.

The oppressive dread lashed out at him. He tried to mentally push back against the relentless and terrifying reality of his helpless situation.

He closed his eyes. Or did he? He didn't know. His attempt made no difference in the disorienting blackness.

This can't be real. Please, it can't be real.

Then, another thought seemed to appear on its own.

It *is* real.

Was that him? He did not know. It was in his mind, but it was different. Maybe his mind was unraveling in this sense-deprived hell. He tried to moan again. Anything would be better than nothingness. Even the sound of his own agonized cries would be preferable to this profound and intense deprivation. He would welcome physical pain. He would cherish it. Anything! Anything but this!

"Help," he tried to say into the nothingness. He heard no sound.

He tried to yell. But, there was only the same dominating, empty silence. He was slipping. He needed something, anything to escape this complete sensory void. He could feel the twisting insanity growing inside. He was aware of his breaking of becoming deranged.

No, he thought. *This is worse than death!*

He tried to break himself free but was met with a profound sense of hopeless failure. It rattled him to his core.

He could not bear to watch himself slide into lunacy. But there was nothing he could do. He felt it crawling in him.

No! he cried internally.

He tried to resist.

Hell, he thought, as he wailed internally. *I am in hell.*

His resistance was weakening. It was useless to fight against the profound nothing that surrounded him. That is when he realized the complete futility. There was nothing to fight against because there was nothing there.

And so, as a dam begins to break, he felt himself weakening in the face of the menacing, empty, aloneness. It was too powerful.

It was too much. He knew he could not fight against the nothingness that permeated this place.

And so, under the realization of the hopeless before him, he knew would eventually collapse under the weight of his dreadful experience. He whimpered internally in agony.

Wait! What was that?

He pushed himself to focus. *Was there something there?*

Or was his mind deceiving him?

There it was again. What was that?

He latched onto it. Did he see something? Did he sense something?

He forced himself to believe against all hope that he was not alone.

There it was again. He did not know how, but he was aware of something else.

Yes! There it was again. Yes. Yes, it is real.

Elation! Pure elation!

The blackness. It was changing.

Was that light? He could not tell. Maybe it was. But, he *was* seeing something. Or, he dreaded the thought, was his mind already gone and he had not yet realized it? He waited. Looking. Hoping.

Yes, the blackness *was* changing.

He wanted to cry. He wanted to break down and sob. *Please let it be real!*

He could see it. Yes! Yes! He could see! It was wonderful. He wanted to yell into the darkness. But, he could not. So, he forced himself to concentrate. It took all of his strength.

Look at it! He yelled to himself. *It's real!*

Something was there. It was in front of him. Was it close or far? He could not tell. What was it? Was it moving?

Yes, it was moving.

It was getting closer.

But how did he know that? There were no spatial references.

241

He didn't care. Somehow he knew it was approaching.

Then, suddenly, in front of him manifested the silhouetted form of the creature.

He could see it. He could focus on it.

His mind grasped at the sensation of sight.

Yes, thought Zeke. *Yes. I can see!*

The relief was almost as overwhelming as the agony he had just been experiencing.

He did not know how he knew, but again, from within, he realized that it had brought him here to communicate. And, with that, all the panic and fear began to subside as his mind quickly regained its composure.

Then another thought manifested about the Cascade and those in it. They were not on the bridge. But he didn't know if the thought was his own.

Is it in my mind?

The idea seemed to appear by itself. Was his mind playing tricks on him? No. That was not it. His mind was clearing. The agony, the frustration, the aloneness, the fear, the hell were all slipping rapidly away.

But then, maybe he was crazy.

No, he was not.

How do I know that?

But there it was. He was seeing the creature, and somehow it was also in his mind.

As strange as it was, relief washed over him and brought a feeling of incredible elation. Hope was back. He could experience again, even if it were only with one sense, sight. He could see, and with that seeing, he understood that he was in the place where the creature existed. This was its realm, a realm of altered space and time.

It was, 'the here.'

Chapter 26
Time and Space

He could see it, the creature's grey form with its faint glow of light. Seeing it was so incredibly welcome. His mind had something to focus on, and in so doing, the impending psychosis was chased away far quicker than it took to arrive.

Then images began to flash across his mind of the Cascade, the crew, medical, hallways, eating, showering. It all flooded in a disordered yet almost simultaneous rush. It was too much for him. He recoiled internally. The images stopped.

How did that happen? How did the images become so real, so vivid?

He looked at the creature. Was it doing that? Was it somehow in his mind? Or, maybe he was rebounding from the horror of isolation and sensory deprivation.

Then, after a moment, they resumed, but at a slower pace. He saw Alina and Oleg. Their figures seemed to emerge from his imagination. Still, he had a distinct impression that his mind was somehow passive in the display.

Is this what a vision is like, he wondered.

More images from the past two days came into his awareness. They were disjointed, confusing. And once again, he recoiled.

They stopped.

It wasn't him. It *was* the creature. He knew it now. The creature was in his mind. But how was that possible?

Maybe, he thought. *In this place, it is able to be in more than one place at a time. It is there and in my mind.*

But, he still wondered if his brain had somehow been so traumatized that it had cracked and he was too far gone to realize it.

The images began again but at a slower pace. This time, however, they were ordered, which enabled him to focus.

What do they mean?

They were sequential. He was on the bridge talking to Finn. He was in the galley, eating with the crew. Then, he was showering, sleeping, waking up, working, and recording his captain's log. The order made sense, and he absorbed them, relishing in their vividness.

But it was also tiring. The movement of images through his mind wasn't natural. It was awkward, and in a strange way, he could feel the strain of remembering, almost as if his mind was being forced. Once again, he asked himself. *Is this is because I'm recovering from the trauma of nothingness?*

He'd already been to the edge of insanity, and now he was being assailed with images that he could not control. But, didn't *that* mean he was crazy?

But no, he wasn't.

It *had* to be the creature. And, to his surprise, that is what he hoped it would be. So, he decided to accept it and endure the strangeness of being in 'the here' with an alien that could somehow be in his mind.

The images had stopped while he was contemplating his mental state and situation.

Was that because he was thinking? Did it react to his internal state and wait?

Is it aware of my thoughts?

Zeke paused while he considered the possibility. Then it occurred to him that maybe he could manifest an idea and see what happened.

He thought of the Cascade.

Nothing happened.

He thought of it again.

A faraway image of the ship materialized, but it seemed to appear on its own, not by his will. It was as if it was put into his mind. And, it was more vivid than a memory.

He saw a series of single images of the ship that progressed from one place to another and then stopped. It was vivid yet also possessed the same vagueness of memories retrieved.

Somehow, someway he knew it was the creature doing this. But to his surprise, it was surprisingly easy to accept.

The image stayed. When he thought of the Cascade, the creature produced a series of single moments in time where the ship had been traveling through space. They all stayed there simultaneously.

Is that how it sees us as different moments of time all at once? Absolutely fascinating.

The series of still frames disappeared.

Maybe it is trying to figure out how we relate to time. We perceive it sequentially. But perhaps it perceives time all at once, or something close to it.

Then a thought flashed into his mind. He remembered how the creature was disrupted when it had been attacking Alina and Oleg. It has something to do with time?

Was how it relates to time so different than how we do, that there are not compatible in some way? When it was attacking them, and they put something into its field, it was a different time reference. So it left. Yes, that's got to be it. Somehow it makes sense.

He looked at the grey form before him and wondered if his assessment was accurate. He did not know what he believed it was true.

Immediately, new images moved into his awareness, but they were of him moving about in his quarters right after awakening from hyper sleep. They were not a sequence of still images. They were of him moving.

Wait! How could that be?

He had not yet encountered the creature, so how could it have those images? But it did, and with them came a disturbing thought. How far back did its knowledge go? Did it already know where Earth was?

The realization disturbed him. Instantly the images stopped. Then he rebuked himself for thinking of Earth. But, an image of Earth did not manifest. Why? Maybe it was because the creature is not aware of it. Maybe there is a limit to its ability to move backward in time. He thought about it, which caused him to recall the 3D Earth model in his quarters.

Instantly, it appeared in his mind, vivid and distinct.

He scolded himself again for thinking of it. *Stupid!*

He decided to push that idea away. He had to protect his home world.

Zeke thought of eating in the galley, and instantly an image of the crew eating popped into his mind.

Yes, he thought with slight relief. *It knows. It knows what I'm thinking. I must be careful. But it doesn't know where we came from... I must think of other things.*

No image formed.

But, how did it manifest images of me before our encounter? Maybe because it can only retrieve time so far back. That has to be it.

Zeke purposely thought of his house on the lake. It was a pleasant memory, a beautiful image. But, it manifested by *his* effort. Somehow he could tell the difference between his own retrieval of his memories and those brought up by the creature. It had to be that they were both mentally there in the same place, interacting, somehow knowing each other's thoughts.

Amazing.

Zeke wondered why the creature was so interested in them.

The image of the earth manifested in his mind. But, it was of the earth model from his quarters. Without a doubt, it knew his mind…and he knew its, at least to some degree.

The image stayed.

Why that image? He wondered. *Maybe it can't recall too far back.*

It stayed.

Did it want to know about Earth? Did it need the Cascade to travel there? Was the earth in danger? Was it just curious? Or was it calculating and manipulative? The questions arose and fell without answers.

If it knows my thoughts, does it understand my questions and worries about it and us?

An image of the Cascade orbiting the fourth planet formed. It was something that hovered in the realm of vague awareness. It was different. Perhaps it was because it had not yet happened.

It slowly faded away.

He thought of the bridge.

Instantly he could see it. But to his surprise, it was not in his mind. It was in front of him. He saw it with his eyes. The sudden shift in perception caught him off guard, and he needed a moment to adjust.

Was he really seeing it, or was the creature able to affect his optic nerves and create images? Or, did it create them in this place and he was seeing them.

The Bridge with the crew was there. It *appeared* real. But, to his surprise, he was outside the ship looking in. He could see them moving about, gesturing, speaking, occasionally pointing towards the three sensors. Hahn was pounding her fist on the holo-table. Oleg was standing, barking something back at her.

I can't hear them.

Their voices suddenly became clear.

"No, I don't agree," said Hahn.

"You don't know why it took him," replied Alina, jumping in. "We have to wait. It's only been a couple of minutes."

A couple of minutes? That can't be right? It's been hours.

His confusion on how long he had been gone, somehow broke the audio and they became silent once more.

It's been hours, not minutes.

It *had* been a long time, or so he thought. He remembered back to the utter aloneness of the empty realm. It had seemed such a long time. But maybe it wasn't. Could he have started to lose his mind that quickly? It's possible. He didn't know. But there had to be a difference in time and space with the creature and wherever he was. So, even though he was shocked to hear it had only been a short time, he was able to accept it.

Wait, maybe that was just a replay of something that happened earlier. Perhaps he *had* been gone for a much longer time. But how would he know?

It was mentally tiring. The thought was simply another possibility he had to keep track of. With all the unanswered questions, he decided to refocus on what was happening.

Time is different here. In here, things are not the same.

The image of the bridge was still there. He refocused on it and wanted to be back with them. But it was not to be, at least not now. So, he continued to watch. Alina said something to the doc and threw her hands in the air. He watched her.

He tried to speak her name, but nothing happened. So he called to her in his mind. *Alina*

She stopped talking as if something had distracted her. Then, she slowly turned and looked out of the portal window into the depths of space. Hahn and Finn seemed to be surprised and annoyed by her sudden departure from their conversation.

She took a step towards the window and paused.

Alina! He thought.

She moved closer and stared into the darkness. He watched her as she peered outward, looking right at him. Then she slowly placed her hand on the glass.

In an instant, he was back in that dark place, void of sight and sound. The unexpected visual shift shocked him, and he recoiled.

What had happened? Was it real? Or, was it another projection into his mind?

It felt so real. It had to be real.

He knew the creature could affect space-time. If he were actually outside the ship without a spacesuit, then he had to be outside of his body. Was that even possible? Or, maybe it *was* an image projected into his awareness. He could *not* have been outside the ship. Could he? Or did it place him there in a bubble of space in which he could survive?

I don't know what to think.

The intensity of his contemplation was taxing. For him, it had been hours of terror, confusion, elation, and trying to interpret images. It took a moment to regroup his thoughts. Maybe in some way, his thinking of Alina had influenced her. Or, the creature influenced her because it knew his thoughts. Then again, maybe it was just her. Either way, he hoped it was real. He remembered Alina putting her hand on the window and realized how desperately he wanted to be back with them.

Zeke shook his mind free from the memory.

How could it do that in my mind? How could it respond to my thoughts?

He resented the idea of an invasion into his being where his thoughts and fears could be laid bare. But, then, since he had a sense of its thoughts, maybe the feeling was mutual. Perhaps his thoughts were just as perplexing to it.

But how could he know? It was all so difficult to comprehend as he hovered on the verge of continued incomprehensibility and concentrated examination. So, he thought of something pleasant. He thought of a time when he was resting on a beach, listening to the waves, feeling the warm breeze. Rest. He needed a break from this constant invasion of images, the ceaseless deprivation of senses, and perpetual uncertainty.

But, he had to press on.

Since the creature was not physical, it can probably occupy the same space as other objects.

That seemed true. The creature was not corporeal, and it existed in a different space-time realm, so why couldn't it be in his mind? His brain was physical, but his mind was not. But, his thoughts? How could it know them? Or did it just sense them?

Another unanswered set of questions.

Okay. There is no way I am going to figure this out. It's no use.

He directed his thoughts to the creature. Instantly an image of the featureless cloud appeared. As he pondered it, he tried to sense it, to understand its intention. So, he let go. He opened his mind to its presence.

He waited. Then, something emerged. But, it was not an image. It was a sensation, a feeling.

What is that?

It grew, and the word 'time' entered his mind as if he was seeing the letters.

Time, he thought.

Then, the word *home*.

Then nothing.

Words? He thought. *It can manifest words?*

Wait a minute. He remembered that Janice had associated pictures with words, hundreds, and hundreds of them. It was using them. That had to be it. The creature was somehow using words that it had already encountered in its communication with Janice.

Okay, good. That makes sense. But what do they mean, time and home?

Then, an image of empty space with stars formed.

Was that its home? He wondered. *Of course, that is its home. It lives in space. Space is its home. But why time?*

And once again, the same image of star-studded space emerged.

He considered the three concepts: space, time, and home. He decided that instead of interpreting them, he would just accept them. Time and space were where it lived.

A double pulse of light flashed across his awareness. He reeled from its unexpected manifestation. Then he remembered that Janice had established one pulse for no, and two for yes.

It was revelatory. It was exciting.

An image of the bridge with him speaking to the crew popped into his mind.

Yes, without a doubt, it knows my thoughts.

He wondered how intelligent it was. What were its capabilities? What could humans learn from it? He wanted to know more, and surprisingly, he realized he was comfortable with all of this.

Comfortable?

He almost laughed to himself about how easy it was to accept that he was in a strange place with an alien creature reading his mind, communicating with him via images and basic words.

Instantly a visage manifested of him on the bridge holding his hand out towards the creature. Its desire to communicate with him did not seem like the actions of a malevolent being.

It does not intend to harm, he thought. *But it also does not intend not to harm. It is just alive, different, seeking to understand things that are so unlike itself.*

He broke free from the train of thought. Was his reasoning his own, or was it the creature?

Either way, he believed it was true.

I can understand it in a basic way, he said to himself. *Its language, if I can call it that, is by displaying different images at different times. Their time-context is what carries meaning. Yes, that's it.*

Again, the image of him with his extended hand manifested accompanied by two pulses of light.

That was confirmation, at least it seemed to be.

He reviewed what he knew about it. He knew it could live in space and time, the same as him. But, unlike him, it can travel through time the way we travel down a road. Just as we can move back and forth on a road, it can move back and forth in time.

Was that me or the creature?

It didn't matter. His understanding seemed to be a blend of his own reasoning and something else. He let his thoughts continue.

Perhaps the reason the creature was dangerous to people was because it was trying to experience their time-frame all at once. Maybe that's why they died. Perhaps it had something to do with the fact that we are physical beings and are limited to linear space-time, where the creature is not. It engulfed them in relation to its own space-time existence, and it injured them in the process. Time to it is referential, but to us, it is sequential.

He turned his attention to the creature and thought, *I do not know if my thinking is right or wrong, but perhaps this is why they died. We can't live time all at once like you do.*

Three pulses of soft light appeared, but they weren't in his mind. They registered via his eyes.

Okay, he thought. *I think I'm getting it. That was neither yes or no. The creature had killed not out of malevolence, but by accident. It was curious about us and did not know that time is different for us. Our time-references are incompatible.*

Then, the images of Alina and Oleg flashed across his mind. He saw them in sequence: alive, dead, and alive again.

This had to be it, he thought to himself. *It's the only thing that makes sense. But how could the creature bring them back to life?*

Instantly an image of a hallway inside the Cascade appeared where both Alina and Oleg were walking. Behind them was a duplicate image of them walking. Then the front image was replaced with both Alina and Oleg lying on gurneys. They disappeared, and the second image of them walking continued past where they had been lying.

It can travel back and forth in time, he thought. *It can restart a person's timeline… so it restarted their time-line earlier than their deaths and brought them back.*

Two pulses of light.

Yes, that makes sense, …but…

He thought for a moment. *If it restarted their lives, then why did they remember the pain even though it seemed that they were brought back from a time before they were attacked?*

An image of Alina walking behind herself appeared in his mind. Then the two met each other and were blurry for a moment. Then there was only one Alina.

It combines their timeline, and part of it was their pain. I get it. It is like overlapping images of a sequence for a movie.

He marveled at the ease of communication. It was exciting and surprisingly enjoyable.

Yes, I think I understand.

This thing was so different, so utterly different, that it was entirely enigmatic. Time to it is a series of reference points that it can move between.

Amazing.

A surprising flush of mental fatigue washed over him.

Why the sudden exhaustion?

The creature was in his mind, and he was having to experience both his own thoughts and its at the same time. He let his mind go blank for a moment, not thinking, not analyzing. Rest. He needed rest.

But exhaustion would relate to a physical condition, not just mental. That implies I'm still in my physical body, tied to it.

This experience of constant, deep concentration, and an apparent sharing of his mind was a lot to endure. But it was necessary. He waited a few seconds, and purposely did not think.

After a short while, he refocused on the creature. Then he reviewed what he had learned. *It communicates by experiencing past and possibly future events that are represented by images, and it combines these images as a form of language.*

But again, he did not know if it was his own thoughts or the creature's. Or, maybe it was a cooperative effort a kind of symbiotic language. He suspected that almost anything was possible in this strange place with a non-corporeal alien intelligence.

If it has a language, does that imply there are others like it that it communicates with?

The image of his extended hand entered his mind again, and two pulses of light, clearly visible.

There are others, he realized. *There are more of them out there!*

The Drake solar system appeared in his mind, dotted with what appeared to be many clouds.

The thought was instantly disturbing. Dealing with one had been terrifying. What would it be like to encounter more? What if they were curious, too. Would they inadvertently kill the crew or others that came later?

One flash of light appeared.

No? They will not harm us?

Two pulses of light appeared before him.

The sudden trepidation was replaced by intense relief.

Good. Two means that they will not harm us. But that would mean it would have to communicate with them about the crew. Then he wondered. *If they are as different as people are, perhaps there can be good ones and bad ones.* But, the thought only brought up more questions. He could not go down that rabbit trail. Besides, he realized that he did not know if the creature was telling the truth or not. *Could it be deceiving him?*

One pulse of light appeared before him.

He rebuked himself for not being more careful in his thoughts. He was slipping. He wondered if he could think without thinking. One thing was for sure. It was hard to focus and keep his train of thought and not go where he shouldn't. He'd had no break for… for how long? It seemed like hours, but maybe it wasn't. He didn't know and decided not to worry about it, at least not for now.

He stopped for a moment and considered how he was in some strange ultra-dimensional place where his thoughts and the alien's were somehow intermeshed and where pulses of light were part of the means of communication. It was surreal.

How is this even possible?

He pondered the seemly ridiculous scenario that was happening before him. But, there was one more thing he wanted to know. What about the doc and the bone scanner?

Immediately an image of the doc with the bone scanner filled his mind along with his extended hand from the bridge.

I see, he said to himself. *It was able to project a frequency. Maybe the creature saw it as an opportunity to communicate and so moved upon the doc, but it realized that it could not, so it left.*

Amazing. That makes sense.

He paused for another moment to regroup his thoughts.

But why the intense light?

Three pulses of light manifested before him.

No answer.

Why was there no answer? Why the light?

Then, slowly, the words home and time entered his mind again. But, with them, the image of the Drake solar system appeared, speeded up. The Drake sun grew brighter.

What does that mean?

He thought about it. Home. Time. The solar system sped up. The Drake sun was growing brighter.

I don't understand.

The images vanished and were replaced by three pulses of light. The image of him on the bridge with his hand extended appeared in front of him. It was not in his mind. He could see it. It stayed and hovered in front of him.

Maybe the bone scanner was somehow mistaken for an attempt to communicate, and so it poured images towards them at incredible speed. Perhaps, that is why there was light. It was trying to present images in its time frame, but it was too many all at once.

The creature remained silent.

He continued to review the pseudo-memory of his own image with his extended hand. He had meant it as a non-threatening gesture. Perhaps that is what the creature understood.

Two pulses of light.

Zeke added it all up. He thought he understood the creature enough now. It was not malicious. It was merely curious and ignorant about them and had inadvertently injured Oleg, Alina, and the doc. It was intrigued by the biological creatures that could only move one direction through time and had entered its realm in a strange ship.

Yes. I think I understand.

There was a double pulse of light clearly visible in front of him. Then the creature began to fade until finally, it disappeared.

It was unexpected.

Then with that same ominous blackness, the same automatic dread began to reemerge. But it only lasted for a moment.

He felt something like motion, but he was not moving. He could see the bridge again and along with it the heaviness of gravity and the warmth of the temperature upon his skin. He squinted at the brightness of the lights as he seemed to move from outside to inside the ship.

"Zeke!" shouted the doc.

They all jerked to attention. He was standing in the center of the three sensors.

Chapter 27
Exhaustion

They fumbled over themselves. Oleg collided with the doc as they all rushed towards him. Finn had turned around sharply and bumped into a chair. Alina and Hahn got as close as they dared, stopping just short of the sensors' boundaries.

Zeke felt the warmth of the air, the brightness of the lights, and the pull of gravity. He moved both hands to his face and fingered his stubble. The familiarity of movement and sensation was confirmation that he really was back. He closed his eyes and took a breath of real air and smiled.

Finn spoke first. "Zeke?"

He scanned the room. "You're real," he said as he looked at them all.

"Hell, yes," responded Hahn. She approached him. "Are you?"

The doc braved the sensors and moved within them, putting her hand on his shoulder. She looked into his eyes and checked his pupils then grabbed his wrist. Zeke did not resist. Her touch was wonderful. He grabbed her hand with both of his, savoring the smoothness of her skin.

He exhaled hard as he let his head fall backward. Another heavy sigh seeped passed his lips. He then straightened out and focused on the doc.

"How long was I gone?"

"Maybe five minutes," she responded.

"Janice, how long was I gone?"

"Four minutes, 38 seconds."

"That can't be right. It was hours." He took another breath of the marvelous air and smiled.

The doc looked at Finn and Alina with obvious concern. "Have a seat," she said to Zeke. "Doctor's orders." She gently pulled him by the arm towards a chair that Oleg had pushed towards them. Zeke willingly complied.

He rested one elbow on the armrest, dropped his forehead onto his fingertips, and massaged his skin. The crew waited patiently as she rechecked his pulse, then looked into his eyes, and watched his breathing.

"He seems okay," said the doc. "But, I want to get him into medical and do a full workup." She pulled at a chair close and sat down in front of him.

Hahn looked at Alina from behind a worried frown. Alina shrugged her shoulders. Oleg watched the doc, who was watching Zeke. Finn grabbed a chair and joined them. The sound of their movements was wonderful. His senses were active again, and the sheer joy of experiencing sight, sound, touch, and weight was all a spectacular pleasure. Endorphins flooded into his brain at the incredible delight of sensory experience. It was euphoric.

He smiled big. "You have no idea how good it feels to be here."

"Janice," said the doc, "Can you give us an assessment on Zeke's condition?"

"From what I can tell, he appears to be okay. But he is showing signs of exhaustion. His blood pressure is above normal, as is his heart rate, and there is a residue of adrenaline in his system. But, his condition is more consistent with someone who has been under high stress for hours, not minutes. Nevertheless, barring any unforeseen negative diagnosis, he should recover."

"Hours?" repeated Alina. "Doc? Is that consistent with what you see?"

"Well, he is stressed, and it could be from being under stress that long. Given how strange everything has been, who knows what really happened to him. For us, he was gone for only a few minutes, but maybe for him, it *was* hours."

She looked into Zeke's eyes. He was smiling.

"I love the sound of your voice." He spoke slowly.

She frowned as she stared at him. "Why are you smiling? What happened?"

"It took me somewhere," responded Zeke in an obviously exhausted delivery, almost slurring his words. "I was there for a long time." He dropped his head down a little bit.

"Wow... am I tired! I need to sleep." He lowered his head a little more before straining to keep his eyes open.

"It just hit me like a ton of bricks." His words were slow.

The doc grabbed his jaw with her hand and brought his eyes level to hers. "Look at me."

Zeke complied and smiled. "I'm just tired, really tired. I was there for a long time, and I'm exhausted." He slurred his words.

"Is he okay?" asked Finn.

"As far as I can tell, he is. He's just really drained."

Zeke spoke slowly and smiled as he spoke in groups of words between breaths. "I was there... for hours ... We talked ... But I need to sleep."

"You talked?" asked Finn. "What do you mean, you talked?"

"I'll tell you later...I need sleep." He was breathing in short breaths, dropping his head down, then jerking it up and raising his eyebrows in an attempt to keep his eyes open.

"Janice, what can you tell me about his physical condition? Is he in danger? Do I need to get him to medical right now?"

"As far as I can tell, Doctor, he is exhausted and needs sleep. But a thorough examination is warranted. All his vitals are consistent with being under high stress for a long time."

"Screw this, we're getting him to medical," she said as she stood up.

Zeke grabbed the doc's hand and looked at her. "Look, I'm fine. I'm just… Really tired… That's all… I need to sleep." He smiled and added, "It is so good to be back. It's wonderful."

She squeezed his hand.

"I'm also starving," he said.

"That's a good sign."

Zeke looked up at her and smiled.

"What happened?" she asked.

He knew he had to explain everything, but for now, he was exhausted. He let his body relax, and his mind abandon the fray of the contemplative stress he'd been undergoing for so long in the 'here.' Every breath was a pleasure. He looked at the crew and found Hahn's steely, worried glare. He looked at Oleg, who seemed surprisingly relaxed. Finn had worry written all over his face.

He smiled at no one, at everyone.

"You won't have to worry about the creature," said Zeke in a slow and mumbling voice. "It won't hurt us anymore."

Hahn responded quickly. "What do you mean? How do you know that?"

"I know," he said as he forced himself to speak more coherently, pushing back the fatigue. "We were communicating. It uses pictures." He inhaled again. "I love the air."

His words were surprising, to say the least. He was obviously exhausted, which suggested he had experienced something very stressful. But what?

Zeke inhaled again and let the weight of his own chest muscles force the air out.

"I'll explain… everything… later," he said slowly as he laid his head back in the chair and closed his eyes. His breaths were short.

"Sleep," he said in a breathy voice. "I need sleep." His words were slurred again.

The doc put her hand on his forehead. Then she rechecked his pulse and listened to his short labored breathing. "I need to get him to medical and check him out."

"I'm fine," he retorted in run-together words.

"I'll be the judge of that." She looked at Finn and Oleg. "Let's get him to medical."

"I'll explain everything…" he yawned. "…later, but for now, I just need sleep." His words were forced out, strained. He really *was* exhausted.

"Medical."

She nodded at the two men who obediently approached Zeke and lifted him up, one under each arm.

"Take me to my quarters," said Zeke. "That's an order. It doesn't want to hurt us." He nodded his head slightly as he spoke. "I'm so tired."

The doc looked at the two men and jerked her head towards the door. "Medical."

They nodded.

"Let's go," said Finn.

Zeke forced himself up under their sturdy guidance. "Take me to my quarters."

"No," said Oleg. "The doc outranks you when it comes to this. You're going to medical."

He slumped his head down in submission. "Okay, l will… let's get this over with," he said as he let the words blend together. "But I have a lot to tell you." He smiled. "It is so good to be here."

Of course, getting him to medical wasn't too difficult. Though Zeke was cooperating, his exhaustion was evident, and they had to guide him along the way, halfway lifting him to compensate for his wobbly legs. When they got to medical, and he saw the table, he aimed for it and, with their assistance, collapsed onto it. His breaths quickly became short. He dropped his hands to his side.

He was asleep.

"Is he really okay?" asked Hahn.

"I hope so." She grabbed some instruments out of a couple of drawers and quickly returned and aimed them at him. She then looked at the panel on the wall for his readouts. They showed heartbeat, brain activity, breathing, and weight. She walked over to it and swept her hand to the right. Another display manifested. There were brain waves and a bunch of technical terms that no one understood except her and Janice.

"Amygdala," she said. The display changed again, and some wavy lines moved rhythmically across the screen.

"Hmmm."

"What," asked Alina?

"Hippocampus." A different set of lines coursed across the monitor.

She answered without turning around. "It looks like the areas of his brain dealing with new memories have been very active. "She paused and thought for a few seconds." This is consistent with him being gone for hours, just like he said."

She turned around and faced them. "Whatever happened to him, it took a while."

She returned her gaze to the monitor.

"Adrenals." The display once again changed, and some initials appeared next to another line. "Check." The line changed and then returned to its original pattern.

"Heart rate and respiration." Again, the display changed, and she stared at the output. After about 15 seconds, she turned to the crew again.

"He seems okay."

"What do you think happened?" asked Hahn. "I mean, he was only gone for five minutes, then he comes back absolutely exhausted."

"Yeah," said Oleg. "Maybe it took him somewhere and did something to him."

Finn and Alina both examined Oleg's remark while looking at each other.

"Well," offered Alina. "He was smiling, so whatever happened, it wasn't bad. But what gets me is that he said he was gone for hours. So, for now, we have a mystery on our hands. Something happened to him, and we'll just have to wait to find out."

Finn looked at the doc. "Would you say he's been traumatized?"

She looked at him as she thought about it. "Possibly. Why do you ask?"

"Just curious."

Finn looked at Oleg and Hahn. "We all need to talk."

Chapter 28
The Plot

Except for Zeke, the entire crew had gathered in the galley. Their meeting naturally flowed around their eating.

"The cap was gone for a few minutes, not hours. Something's wrong with him." Hahn was determined as she spoke, raising her voice to be heard." We don't know what that thing did to him. I'm telling you, we can't trust it. And, now, maybe we can't trust him."

"Hold on, Hahn," said Finn. "You don't know that. We have to find out what happened first before we jump to conclusions. Maybe he *was* gone for hours. That creature has some weird time thing going on, so who knows. Besides both the doc and Janice said his condition was consistent with being gone longer than a few minutes. That's why we have to wait and get more information."

"It killed Alina and Oleg," she retorted. "And it hurt me bad, and you too, Finn."

"And brought us back," responded Oleg.

"For what reason?" Hahn adjusted herself in her chair and twirled a glass of water in her fingertips, causing a slight scraping sound on the table. "What we know so far is that it has stranded us here. Think about it. It took all of the energy out of the ship, and we're stuck with no way to get home. She looked at Alina and Oleg before continuing. "It killed them and brought them back. But we don't know why. Maybe it's toying with us." She pushed the glass of water away and sank back into her chair. "If it can bring you back, then why didn't it restore the energy to the ship? I'll tell you why. Because it doesn't want us to leave. It has plans for us."

"Look," said Oleg. "I agree we need to be cautious, but we don't always have to assume the worst."

She threw a look of angry disbelief at him as she dismissed his comment. "Does anyone else feel like it has done what it's done so it can keep us here and study us or maybe even play with us like rats in a cage?"

"I must admit," said Finn. "The thought has crossed my mind. It can kill us, yet it's keeping us alive, and we can't go anywhere. So, yeah, I have wondered the same thing. But, Cap says that it's not gonna hurt us. So for now, I'd consider that as a possibility. At least until after we hear what he says."

"Not going to hurt us?" responded Hahn again as she sat forward, putting her elbows on the table and crossing her arms. "What the hell do you think it's already done? Like I said, it has stranded us, killed, brought back to life, and inflicted pain. The Quantum drive is *still* useless. Is that the behavior of something that is friendly?"

Finn raised his eyebrows briefly and sat back as he shook his head. "No."

"Hold on," interjected the doc. "I'm not siding with the thing. But, Zeke, he was obviously gone for longer than a few minutes. So, if he says it is not going to hurt us, then we need to entertain the possibility. Maybe it's learning. Maybe it *is* friendly. After all, it hasn't attacked anyone for quite a while. Maybe he's right."

"Maybe," responded Finn. "But we don't know what it did to the cap. A creature as powerful as it can do who knows what. We have to be very careful and very cautious."

"Look," added Hahn. "I say we find a way to blast it into oblivion and get ourselves outta here." She paused and looked around. "But if we can't, then as much as I hate to say it, we have to prepare the ship for self-destruction."

"The orders were to do that only if the captain didn't come back. He's back," said the doc.

"Yeah, but did you see him? He was exhausted and smiling? Does that make sense to you? Is that normal? Look, we're in a very serious situation, and he's having a good time? I'm telling you he's not right in the head. We either kill this thing or get the hell out of here, head back towards Earth, and take our chances.."

Alina jumped in. "But we have to hear from the cap. Then we decide what we do. There's no need to go off half-cocked right now. It's true that we've all been under great deal of stress, so let's think this through carefully and slowly. After all, this is a new life form we're dealing with, and it's either us or the next crew that's gotta face it."

Hahn looked directly at Finn, brushing aside Alina's comment. "You know I'm right."

He sat back in his chair. "Whatever happens, we can't let it get back to Earth." He looked at each of the crew, leaned forward, and intertwined his fingers as he placed his hands on the table.

"Am I the only one here who thinks that something's wrong with the captain?" asked Hahn.

They checked each other, but no one was sure what to say. "Doc?"

"I don't know. I have to admit, it was a little strange how he came back and was all smiles while at the same time being exhausted. That concerns me. But like I said, we don't know what happened. We have to wait to find out."

"I agree with Hahn," said Oleg. "I have to admit, that *was* weird."

Finn readjusted himself in his seat. "Alright. We all agree that the captain's behavior is a concern. So, yeah. I think we need to consider all our options."

He leaned back in his chair.

"We can go into a parking orbit around the fourth planet and wait for rescue. Who knows how long that will be, if ever. The solar panels will keep us powered indefinitely so food won't be a problem as long as the generators don't break down."

He reached for his glass of water and took a brief sip.

"But I don't like that option because even if we survive until rescue, what's this alien thing going to do to us in the meantime, not to mention the next crew? Maybe it won't sap all their energy. Maybe it's learned enough to be more patient. Perhaps it wants to find a way back to Earth? Who knows. But, that's not something that we can risk happening."

"Okay," said Oleg in a slow, deliberate tone, "then that leads us to option two."

"Yeah, option two. We lure the thing onto our ship and blow ourselves and it to the next galaxy."

"So," said Oleg. "We destroy the ship to save the earth."

Finn sat back and nodded slowly.

"But, there's a third option," said Oleg.

"And what's that?"

"We talk to it."

"Wrong," exclaimed Hahn. "The more we talk to it, the more it learns our weaknesses. It's bad strategy. So we fight it." She looked at Finn. "Right?"

He paused. They all waited for his response.

"The bone scanner apparently did something to it. So, like we talked about before, we can look into using it as a basis for a weapon. If we can modify some sensors or create an array to try to fight this thing, then maybe we can have a chance of coming out of this alive."

Hahn and Oleg were nodding.

"What do you think, Janice? How realistic is it to try and create a weapon based on the bone scanner?"

"I do not have enough information to determine whether or not a weapon could be produced. We do not know how it affected the creature. Perhaps it was deadly to it, or only an irritation. We do not know. But, there is also the possibility that the bone scanner had a negative effect on it."

"Damn right," said Hahn. "I say a small chance is better than no chance."

"If I may continue," said Janice. They went silent. "There are too many unknowns. As I have said, we do not know if such a weapon will have any effect on it. Also, we do not know if destroying the ship with it aboard will kill it. However, what we do know is that the longer you are alive, the more chance there is it might discover the location of Earth. In fact, if you were all dead, it might pursue me for more information. Therefore, because we do not have answers and because of the great potential risk to our home world, it is a legitimate option to attempt to destroy it by detonating the Cascade. And, perhaps as the next crew approaches and receives our radio transmission, they will avoid this system."

The sobering words left them with little to say. The doc took another sip of coffee. Alina forced herself to stand up and get some, too. Oleg sat back in his chair and put his hands behind his head.

"I don't want to die," said Hahn. "But it's our best plan."

"But what if it brings us back? What if we blow ourselves up, and it brings us back?" asked Oleg. "Think about it. It brought Alina and me back. So, if it brings the ship back after we blow it up, then what if it starts things over and we don't remember it? What'll that lead to?"

His question proposed a possibility they had not yet considered.

"Well," said Finn. "We can't base our plans on what-ifs. Maybe it can bring us back, but the only way that would work is if it also brought back the entire ship. Even it must have limits. So, I still think that's a necessary option."

"I agree," said the doc. "We can't let it get to Earth, and we have to do whatever we can to make sure it doesn't." She looked around at them. "Even after we hear from the captain."

"As much as I hate to admit it," said Finn. "I will be suspicious of what he says when he wakes up. If he is unstable, then we'll have to take action. To do that, we will have to get the ship ready for self-destruction, just in case."

"Janice?" asked Finn into the air.

"Yes, Finn?"

"Can you give us an estimate on how long before the captain wakes up."

"He could wake up at any time. However, judging from his biometrics, he should be unconscious for several more hours."

Finn strummed his fingers on the table. "We have plenty of explosives in the cargo bay. They are designed for blasting rocks on Drakus, so they're powerful. We can strategically place them near the main fuel-cells. The combined detonation of all explosives along with the fuel will reduce everything to vapor."

"Yeah," said the doc in a somber tone. "At least it'll be quick. If it comes to that, I hope it works."

"You got a better idea? Do you want to risk it getting back to Earth? We're probably gonna die out here anyway, so we might as well go out swinging."

The doc sat there and shook her head as she looked blankly at her coffee. "I hate to say it, but I think that's our best option. I still think we should try and communicate with it, though." She looked at Hahn. "Maybe we can learn some of its weaknesses and radio them back towards Earth."

Alina spoke into the air. "Janice?"

"Yes, Alina."

"Do you agree with Finn's assessment?"

"Yes." Her quick answer was a sad confirmation of Finn's proposal. "But, I also agree with the doc. We should try to communicate with it, cautiously, of course."

Alina continued. "Do you have any directive that would prevent us from carrying out Finn's plan?"

"I am programmed for the safety of the crew and for carrying out the mission. But given the present situation, any other crew that arrives is equally at risk. Furthermore, as we have already stated, we cannot risk it getting back to Earth. So, I concur with the option of attempting to destroy the creature as a means to protect the earth, and I will carry out the order to do so. However, I still recommend we continue to communicate with it."

Finn gently tapped his fingertips on the table. He looked around the room. "Are we all in agreement? We prep the ship?"

There was no quick affirmation. Each person looked back silently as they contemplated the possibility of their own deaths.

"All right then," he said in a soft voice. "As much as I hate the idea of committing cosmic suicide, we just can't let it get back home. We can't risk it. We have to try to stop it."

"No matter what the captain says after wakes up?" asked Oleg.

"It'd have to be pretty damn convincing. And you saw him. He wasn't acting right."

Oleg nodded slowly as he looked down and stared at the dreadful truth before them.

Finn sat back in his chair. "Alight, unless anyone wants to disagree, I'll assume the vote is unanimous."

He waited for a few seconds.

"Okay, then. We'll prepare to destroy the ship and see what the captain has to say when he wakes up. We will consider his words, but we must be ready to act." He spoke in a calm, resolute manner.

"Do we tell him what we are planning?" asked Oleg.

"No. We keep it to ourselves. After all, we don't know if he's been compromised or not, or if he's stable. Do you agree, Janice?"

"I agree."

Finn looked around the room.

They all gave subdued nods.

"Let's get this done."

He stood up, moved behind his chair, and put his hands on it.

"Janice?"

"Yes?"

"I want to confirm. Since you agree with my assessment that the number one priority is the safety of Earth, if I were to give you the order to detonate the explosives, would you carry out that order?"

"Yes, Finn."

"All right, then, let's hope it doesn't come to that. But, in the meantime, let's prep for the worst."

One by one, they all stood up and pushed their chairs back with their legs. They looked around at each other, sober-minded, but determined.

"Let's all meet back here in the galley when we're done."

Chapter 29
Awake

Zeke opened his eyes and squinted. He had been jolted awake by a dream of floating in darkness, disconnected from everything, alone. It was terrifying. He groaned as he pushed the memory away, along with its residual fear and panic.

Then it came back to him. He had communicated with the creature. It was extraordinary, and the crew had to know.

He tried to move, but his body felt like it was wrapped in lead.

"Janice? How long have I been asleep?"

"Three hours and twenty-two minutes."

"That explains why I feel like crap." He ran his fingers through his hair and yawned as he threw his legs over the side of the table and managed to sit up, but only after considerable effort.

"Wow, it feels like gravity is doubled."

He forced himself to sit up straight. A stretch manifested along with a good yawn.

"Where's the crew?"

"They are all in the galley."

"Perfect. I'm starving. I could eat a couple of steaks."

"Would you like me to program the food generator to have them ready when you get there?"

"No, well, yeah. I guess so." He yawned once again and arched his spine backward.

"Could you let them know that I'm on my way?"

"Yes, Captain."

Zeke smiled as he looked at the floor, watching his feet dangle above it. He flexed his toes inside his shoes.

"I'm glad to be back, but hell, I feel like I've been dragged over a pile of rocks."

He pushed himself off the table and fought back against the weight of his own body, a little weak and woozy.

"I could use a stiff drink and a long bath," he said. He stretched and twisted. "Has the doc done an assessment on me?"

"Yes. She says you are fine and in need of rest."

"Where is she?"

"She is in the galley with everyone else."

"Oh yeah. Right."

"The doctor was here with you for the first hour and monitored you. She then rested in her quarters for an hour and a half before joining the others in the galley."

"Good." He leaned forward and plodded out of medical, swaying to one side just a little as he walked.

The two minutes it took to get there were enough for him to shake his mind and body free from the fog of sleep. By the time he arrived, he was awake and ready to fill them in. As he entered the room, he smelled the steaks. Someone had retrieved them and put them on a table in a strategic location so that everybody could talk to him.

He wandered in. "Thanks for letting me sleep." He sat down in the chair in front of the food. There was a large cup of water which he grabbed and downed half of it in one breath. The smell of the two steaks was all the more incredible as he remembered the sense-less realm in which he had been trapped. Sensation. It felt so good to experience gravity, to smell the steaks, and enjoy the delight of breathing. He smiled.

"Cap?" asked the doc. "I asked Janice for an update on your vitals. You're fine. You still need some more sleep. But how do you feel?"

"I'm good." Of course, that wasn't exactly telling the truth. He was still fatigued, and yes, she was right. He needed more sleep.

"You gonna fill us in?" asked Finn.

Zeke grabbed a steak with both hands and shoved it into his mouth. He ripped free a large chunk. It was stunningly good. He moaned in pleasure as he closed his eyes and savored the morsel. Its warmth in his hands was almost as pleasurable as the taste. "That is incredible," he mumbled, then he took another bite.

Both Oleg and Alina Hahn frowned at his feeding frenzy. Hahn shook her head as she looked at the doc, who was, by now, returning her stare.

"Cap?" said the doc. "What the hell happened to you?"

He stopped chewing for a moment and looked at her, the morsel puffing out his cheek. "The creature hasn't hurt anyone in several hours, has it?"

The doc fingered her coffee cup as she stared at him. "No, it hasn't."

"And it's not going to," he said confidently as swallowed and tore off another piece of steak.

"How do you know that?" asked Hahn.

He stopped chewing and stared her directly in the eye. "Because I spent time talking to it, and it was a lot longer than a few minutes, I can tell you that."

The doc looked at Alina and then Hahn and back to him.

Zeke grabbed the glass of water and finished it off in one breath. He set it down hard as he leaned back in his chair after grabbing a napkin, wiping his hands, and tossing it on the table.

"I know it sounds crazy," he said as he surveyed the crew. "But I spent a long time with it. I was in a different place, a different time." He eyed the steak.

He used his tongue to free a piece of meat from between his teeth as he considered another bite. But, of course, he knew how important it was to tell the crew what happened.

"What I'm gonna tell you is not going to make much sense. But you have to believe me. You have to understand that I'm not crazy." He adjusted himself in his chair.

"It took me to some strange place. At first, it was this, this empty blackness. There was no light. There was no sound. There wasn't any up or down, no gravity, no sensation at all. It was the weirdest frigging thing I've ever experienced in my entire life. I don't know how long I was there, but it was a while. I don't want to ever experience that again. It's not good. Our minds are made to experience, not to be isolated. And man, am I enjoying sensing everything again. It's wonderful." He smiled hugely before staring absentmindedly down at the table, remembering the trauma of pure emptiness. He glanced up at the doc and Finn. They had matching frowns, which warned him that he needed to be careful. He took a deep breath before continuing.

"Okay. I know it sounds ridiculous, and if I were you, I don't know if I'd believe me, either. But, I was in this place of darkness, and it was complete aloneness, total aloneness. It was horrible, and like I said, I never want to experience that again. But, it showed up after a while, and…" he looked past them all. "How do I explain this?"

He opened his hand, palms facing forward. "It lives in time. It travels through time the way we travel down a road. But it can go back and forth. It can start things over. It kind of sees everything at once. That's what it communicated to me. And, it's just curious about us because we are so completely different than it is."

"And," interrupted Hahn. "how do you know this?"

He leaned his right elbow on his armrest and stared back at her as he considered the best way to respond.

"Remember how Janice and it were developing a means of communication using images and some words?" His eyebrows were raised as he looked around.

He saw some half nods.

276

"Well, that's what we did. We were in this place, this same black emptiness, but it was there, too. And, well…" He reached for that another glass of water and took a large drink before continuing.

"It was in my head."

He waited for the words to sink in. Obviously, they couldn't understand, and as he heard himself speak, he sounded irrational. "I know it doesn't make any sense. But, we weren't in normal space. And, I suspect that somehow we were in a different time-frame, too. I, I don't know how to explain it."

He exhaled and closed his eyes for a few seconds before opening them again. They weren't convinced.

"Look, it was like an exchange of images. At first, it was too fast, but it slowed down. I mean, the creature was feeding me these images. That's how I knew it wasn't me."

He looked at the crew and could see their continued concerned and doubtful expressions. He took a breath and decided to just say it.

"I would think of something, and it had this way of projecting an image into my own mind that represented what I was thinking. I thought I was going crazy at first, so I tested it. I started thinking of different things, and the images would just show up in my head. But, they were more vivid than a memory. It was like seeing, but not really seeing." He pounded his fist gently on the armrest. "It's just difficult to explain."

He took another breath and purposely slowed himself down.

"At first, I didn't know if it was my own mind that was playing tricks on me or not. So, I just, I just kept trying to talk to it and figure things out. I mean, I would imagine things, and these images would just pop into my head. But, like I said somehow, I knew it wasn't me. It was the creature that was doing it."

Zeke could read the suspicion from the crew in their scrambled, and skeptical expressions.

"Yeah, crazy. I know." He looked at Alina. "Alina, I saw you walk over to the window on the bridge and put your hand on the glass."

She immediately stiffened up. "What?"

"While I was in that place, I thought of the bridge, and well, could then see all of you. I was outside the bridge window looking in."

Most of them checked with the doc, who returned an I-don't-know-what-to-say expression.

"I saw you on the bridge, Alina."

"Yeah, that's right," she said. "We were scrambling about after you disappeared, and, out of nowhere, I had this sensation, this impression that you were watching me. It didn't make sense. It was as though…" She stopped talking and stared at him.

"What?" asked Hahn.

Alina looked at Hahn and then to the doc. "I had this feeling that Zeke was there, outside. It was the strangest thing, and so I reached out and put my hand on the window."

"Why didn't you say anything?" asked Finn.

"Because I knew it would have sounded like I was losing it. Besides, everything happened so fast, and we were all pretty shaken up." She tilted her head forward and nodded as she looked at Zeke. "I remember it well."

"Which hand was it?" asked the doc to Zeke.

He thought for a moment. "Her right hand, and she put it about level with her head."

Everyone looked at Alina.

"Yeah, that's right." Alina's confirmation had disrupted the flow of the conversation. "Maybe what he's saying is true."

Hahn immediately jumped in. "He knows you're right-handed. It could have been a lucky guess."

Zeke scoffed.

278

"I don't know," responded Alina. "But, I did feel something."

"So you're saying that what he's saying might be true because you had a feeling? Really?"

"Do what you want with it. I'm only telling you what I felt, and yes, I admit it's not much to go on. But it matches what he said."

"Doc?" asked Hahn. "Is it possible that the captain here is unstable and has been compromised?" She looked at Zeke and offered a slightly apologetic expression.

"Yes, it's possible. But it's also possible that he is telling the truth. After all, it was just like Alina said. So, I think we have to accept it at face value."

Zeke nodded as he looked around.

"All right, let me just cut to the chase," said Zeke. "This creature is smart. And, it's just as curious about us as we are about it. But we are completely different lifeforms. It doesn't want to harm us. But it doesn't want to not harm us, either. It's just neutral, curious. And, get this. It can take images from different periods of time and put them together. Those images have a context, and by arranging them in a certain way, that's how it communicates."

Alina jumped in. "Communicates?"

Zeke clenched his jaw and fingered the empty glass he had commandeered. "Yeah," he said cautiously, "It says there are others like it out there."

That, of course, was not what anyone wanted to hear.

"What?" asked Hahn forcefully as she leaned back in her chair. "There are more of those killers out there?"

"So, you do believe me?" Zeke asked Hahn.

She glared back through the corner she had painted herself into.

"And I thought things couldn't get any worse," said Finn.

Zeke put his hands up a little to quiet them down. "Yeah, there are others like it, and it's able to communicate with them by putting time referenced images in a particular combination to convey ideas. That's what it was doing with me."

"That's great," said Hahn. "Oh man, that's just, that's just great. We are so screwed. That thing is going to bring more of them, and they're going to end up torturing us."

"Stow that," ordered Zeke. Hahn was startled. Up to that moment, he had been submitting to their questions as he had tried calmly to communicate what he had learned. But he needed to get control of the situation once again. "You weren't there. You don't know."

He continued. "I was concerned about that as well. So I asked it if they were going to come here to do the same thing. And just like it did on the bridge talking to Janice, it produced a single flash of light. It meant no."

He cleared his throat and spread his fingers apart on the table as he tried to explain. "Look, it's just curious. It hurt people because it did not know that we can't experience time, the past, the present, and the future all at once, the way it does. So, when it was engulfing Alina and Oleg and Hahn," he looked over at the doc, "and the doc, it was just trying to communicate in the only way it knew how. But, to do that, it had the experience our time all at once. It's like putting us in its time reference where it sees all our time at once, but that messes with us badly, and we end up in pain and dying."

His last words were delivered with a softer and slower pace.

"Why did it bring us back," asked Alina.

"Well, it brought back Alina on its own, and I don't know why. But maybe it realized her time-path had ended and just restarted it. And, our earlier communication hinted at Oleg being brought back, and it responded. Hell, I don't even know if it understands what death is to us. Anyway, it just, it just went to another place in your timeline where you were alive, and restarted you at that moment."

When he spoke the last couple of sentences, he had slowed his pace down even more. He was straining to put his thoughts into words and make them sound reasonable.

"I know you're skeptical. I get it. But that's what I learned. And this means we can continue to communicate with it."

Finn looked knowingly at the rest of the crew before speaking up. "If it could do that with people, could it do it with the Cascade and restore our energy, restore the quantum drive?"

"I don't know. That didn't come up in our communication."

"Why did it drain the ship's energy?" asked Oleg.

"I don't know. It didn't come up, either."

"It didn't come up?" blurted out Hahn. "Are you kidding me!"

"I think that's a pretty important question," added Oleg. "And you didn't think of asking it?"

Zeke shook his head and exhaled hard. "Well, no. I was just trying to figure out what was happening and why it was doing what it did. I didn't think to ask it, and besides, I was getting exhausted."

Hahn looked over at Finn and flexed her eyebrows up.

Finn leaned forward onto the table. "Maybe we could ask it."

Zeke examined Finn just for a moment. It was almost imperceptible, but there was a difference in his tone and body language. Was he just imagining it because of his fatigue?

Zeke took a few more seconds before considering Finn's statement. "Yes, I suppose so." Zeke leaned back in his chair. "If it can bring people back to life, maybe it can do the same thing for the Cascade. I say let's give it a shot."

Zeke looked upward. "Janice?"

"Sir."

"From what you have heard me tell you about the creature, and what you have already learned from it in your communication

281

with it, do you think you could establish a series of images to convey the message to restore the quantum drive?"

"I believe it is possible, but it would take more time," responded Janice with her usual calm feminine voice.

"Good. Let's get to the bridge and activate the sensors." He looked at Finn. "They are still working, right?"

Finn nodded slowly.

Zeke looked at the two steaks on the plate. He grabbed the knife and fork and quickly cut off a large chunk. He then grabbed the fullest cup of water he could find and headed out the door as he said, "You coming?"

Everyone moved slowly as they started to comply.

Finn and Hahn stalled a little long. They left together.

"What do you think?" she asked.

"Not good. How could he have forgotten to ask about restoring the quantum drive if what he said was true?"

"Exactly. I don't like it."

"Me, either."

"Maybe it was controlling him somehow, keeping his thoughts away from it."

"It's possible."

"Yeah, and that would mean it doesn't want us to leave."

Chapter 30
Responsibility

"Janice, activate the sensors."

"Activated, Captain."

All six of them stood about two meters away from the triangle. They divided their attention between it and the captain, who seemed unusually calm.

"How long do you think it'll take?" asked Alina.

"I have no idea," he responded. "It operates on its own schedule. Maybe it won't show up at all. Maybe it's satisfied and got all the information it needed from us, never to return."

"And left us stranded," said Hahn.

Finn looked at the doc, but his expression was more of a subtle frown than anything else. "What concerns me is what you said about there being more of these things out there. If it *is* gone then maybe it went back to let them know about us and get reinforcements."

"Reinforcements?" asked Zeke. "Do you think something that powerful needs reinforcements?"

Finn withdrew his comment with a sweep of his hand, but added, "This thing can be aggressive, and since we appear to be in its territory, maybe it considers us a threat. Maybe it doesn't know right from wrong the way we do. Or maybe it's curiosity will get the best of it, and it goes all cat-and-mouse on us. Whatever the case, as far as I'm concerned, I want it gone."

"I hear that," said Hahn.

"Yeah," said the doc. "And, we can't let it find out about Earth."

"You're right," said Zeke clearly. "We're expendable. Earth is not."

The doc had her usual cup of coffee and took a silent sip but once again clanked it on the holo-table next to where she was standing.

"You know," said Zeke. "I think they have clinics where you can break coffee addictions. They shouldn't be too expensive."

She took another sip before saying, "If we get back home, I'll consider it." She noted Zeke's relaxed manner and looked at Finn out of the corner of her eye. He nodded.

In between the sensors, a small pulse of light caught their attention. A few seconds later, another one. A few seconds after that, a third. They watched.

It was slow in appearing, but the creature manifested with its usual gray, undulating form and kept itself within the boundaries of the triangle.

"See?" said Zeke. "It hasn't hurt anyone for a long time, and it comes when called. It's learning and is cooperating."

"Yeah, it's learning alright," said Hahn in a sarcastic tone.

After a few more seconds, the doc spoke up. "Does anyone else besides me realize that we're strangely comfortable with this thing appearing on the bridge?"

"Yeah," said Oleg. "Come to think of it, you're right."

Though they had seen it before, it was still quite a spectacle to behold. Its undulating form with a slight luminescent gray seemed to resemble, somehow, a hole in space. It had killed and brought back to life. It had sucked all the energy out of the ship. It was huge outside and small inside the Cascade. And, here they were, welcoming it.

"Ok," said Hahn to Zeke. "You're friends with it, so you talk to it."

"Friends? Hardly."

"It seems to like you and you it. So, the ball's in your court."

"When I was in that other place, things were different, and communicating was, well, strange. Here we have to work with images and pulses and stuff. So that's how we'll proceed."

He took a step towards the creature.

"Janice, would you please project an image of the Cascade on the hollow table before we lost power?"

Instantly an image of the Cascade appeared. It had its lights on.

"Now, could you flash two pulses of light?"

Two pulses of light.

"Now, could you display the Drake solar system?"

"Do you want me to replace the image of the Cascade?"

"Yes."

It appeared on the holo-table.

"Good. Could you alternate between them, say three times, and then stop and flash twice."

Janice did as he requested.

"I don't get it," said Alina.

"When I was in the other place with it, it was able to communicate to me that the Drake solar system is its home. So I'm trying to convey the same idea of home to the Cascade."

Janice, who understood his intention, displayed the sequence again and ended it with two flashes of light.

Zeke continued. "Display an image of the creature intersecting the Cascade with the power going out and follow it by a single pulse of light."

Just as the captain requested, the scenario manifested over the holo-table.

They all waited.

"Now what?" asked the doc.

"I don't know," responded Zeke.

After a few seconds, the creature repeated what Janice had displayed, including the pulses of light. The image faded until it disappeared.

After 20 seconds, Zeke spoke. "Janice, I'm open to any suggestions."

"Captain, I suggest that we display the trajectory of the Cascade towards the Drake system. I will then reverse the images so that we are heading backward in time. The display will show, in reverse, lights on, deploying the solar panels, lights off, the arrival of the creature, and lights on before the arrival of the creature. I will also show the quantum drive in a fully functioning condition. I will then pulse two lights on the restored quantum drive and a single pulse accompanying the drive in its dead state."

"Yes, that makes sense. Go for it."

"Wait a minute," said Oleg. "If it restores the ship to its original state, what happens to us? I mean, think about it. We're inside the ship. Does that mean that all of us will have our minds wiped since we're starting over? If that's the case, then we have to go through this all over again."

Oleg was right. What would happen to them?

Zeke looked over at Alina. "What do you think?"

She shrugged her shoulders as she said, "I have no idea."

"Maybe we've already been through this?" said Oleg. "Maybe we're caught in some time trap, and we've been doing this over and over again for years."

His comment had a very chilling effect on everyone's already bleak mood. "Thanks, Oleg," said Hahn. "If you're right, that means I get to experience the agony over and over again. Yeah, thanks for that." She looked over at Finn knowingly.

He nodded back slowly and then looked over at the doc and Alina.

"Well," said Zeke. "I don't believe that's the case. We gotta keep moving forward, and we have to communicate with it, no matter what."

"Janice, please continue with your images."

Just as Janice had described, the images displayed over the holo-table for about 20 seconds. Then, the image of a functioning quantum drive with two pulses of light associated with it hovered in the middle of the table.

They waited. It had responded before, but would it respond now? Did it understand?

"Wait," interrupted Alina. "When you were in this so-called place with it, you said you didn't ask about the Quantum drive."

"No, I didn't. Like I said. It never entered my mind."

Finn once again looked at the doc and then to Oleg with that same expressionless stare.

"Maybe it needs our energy," said Hahn. "Maybe it wants more. Could it have kept the idea from you?"

Zeke froze and furrowed his brow. "I have to admit that I suppose it's possible."

She shook her head and looked at Finn again. "If more ships end up coming here, maybe they will just be more food for it. Maybe that's what it's after. Maybe this whole thing is a trick."

Zeke held his hand up to stop her runaway thoughts. "I did not get that sense. Or at least I mean, I did not get that sense when I was with it."

"But," said Finn, "what if Hahn is right? In the conversation you had with it, why did the energy issue not come up? We asked you that before, and you didn't have an answer. Maybe she's right. Maybe it kept you from asking the question. Maybe it was controlling you more than you realize."

"So you believe me now that I was with it and that we were communicating?"

Finn tilted his head slightly as he stared at Zeke. "I'm not sure. Maybe. But, I can't dismiss it."

Their stern and worried expressions only emphasized the seriousness of Alina's comments. Had he been tricked? Was it after their energy? All living things need energy to survive. So, maybe she was right.

"Janice. Do you think there's any way to form some pictures to ask about its energy source so that we can learn if it needs the quantum drive for food?"

"I will try."

The image of the quantum drive was replaced by the image of the arrival of the creature at the Cascade. Then Janice projected the Cascade and zoomed into engineering, into the walls, and to the quantum drive. She then moved it outside of the ship and intersected it with the creature's image. She then flashed three pulses of light."

"Why three lights?" asked the doc.

Janice responded in her usual, calm tone. "Three pulses of light is neither yes nor no. I am hoping that the creature will understand I am asking a question."

Again for another 20 seconds, the creature did nothing. The image that associated it with the quantum drive still hovered over the holo-table.

"I hope it doesn't misunderstand what we're asking," said Hahn. "Because I have a bad feeling about this. What if it thinks we're offering it the quantum drive?"

"I don't think so," said Zeke. "It must know that the quantum drive is dead. Since it has seen images of the Cascade before its arrival and the quantum drive in full power with it, I think it'll understand what we're asking."

"And what if it does?" asked Finn. "What if it gets the point and somehow restores the quantum drive and the anti-matter. That would mean we could go home. But would we want to? If it follows us, we will be leading it right back to Earth and, we just can't do that. We *can't* go back. Even if it restores the quantum drive, we *have* to stay here. We can never go home. It is our responsibility to safeguard Earth."

The crew bristled at Finn's comments. He was right.

"I don't think its intentions are malevolent," said Zeke.

"You don't know that, and we can't risk it," responded Finn.

"I spent time with it. It doesn't intend to harm us."

"Maybe you're right," responded Finn in a stronger tone. "Maybe it's done playing with us and needs some new toys. Then again, maybe it's benevolent. But I think it's suspicious that you never thought of asking it to restore the quantum drive when you are with it. And now, you two are all chummy."

"What are you saying?"

"You know what I'm saying. We just can't risk it getting back to Earth, no matter what."

Zeke stared at him for a moment, narrowing his eyes. Then he widened them. "I agree. We can't risk it getting back to Earth. We need to be careful. But we also need to communicate with it." His voice was growing more firm. "We have to. More people will come. What will happen to them? We have to figure this out now for their sake and for Earth."

"If we can destroy it, then just maybe they'll be safe, and Earth will be safe."

Zeke shook his head once. "Destroy it? Why? I'm telling you it's peaceful."

Hahn scoffed loudly enough for all to hear.

"I know it hurt us. But it hasn't for quite a while. It doesn't want to harm us. I'm telling you that it's learning and only wants to communicate."

"That's my concern," said Finn. "The more it learns, the less safe we and Earth are. Unless, of course, we can all be convinced beyond a shadow of a doubt that it isn't going to hurt anyone ever again."

"It still hasn't restored the quantum drive," said Hahn. "We're still stranded."

"Yeah, I know. But, one thing at a time." Zeke's tone had a slight tinge of desperation in it. "It didn't mean to hurt us, which is why it hasn't anymore."

Finn countered. "It might be because it is just getting smarter with how to deal with us. As you said, it's learning. And, that is what scares me." He adjusted his posture. "Look, cap. I know you've been through a lot with this thing, and maybe what you say is true. But we just don't know. It is real smart, and as Hahn has said, it hasn't restored the quantum drive. Why not? That is a serious problem."

"Finn's got a point," said the doc interrupting their flow. "We have to consider a way to destroy it in order to keep it away from Earth."

"That's short-sighted. It is aware of us, which means that if there are others, then they are probably aware of us, too. Do you think destroying it is going to help? Do you really think that is how you want to introduce this new species to humanity? You'll be labeling us as hostile. It's foolish to try it. We don't want it or them if there are others to be our enemies."

"We don't agree," piped in Hahn again. "For the sake of Earth, we have to be extremely careful. Janice has already been sending radio summaries back to Earth about everything, about its power and how big of a potential threat it is to us and Earth. They'll be picked up by the next approaching ship, and, if they're smart, they'll abandon their mission once they get all the facts."

"If you try and destroy it or if you succeed in destroying it, you might be unleashing hell on anyone else who comes here from the others like it. Or, if you try and fail and it brings us back, then what? You'll have pissed it off!"

"You don't know if it was telling the truth," said Hahn. "If there are others, why didn't they show up."

"I don't know," said Zeke.

"Then where did it come from? Has it lived forever, or did it pop into existence out of some energy cloud?"

"If we talk to it, maybe we can get those answers," responded Zeke with a dismissive wave of the hand.

"And it can learn about us if we do," said Hahn. "I don't like that idea. Time to it isn't the same for us. So, maybe it already knows what we are going to do, just like the picture of Oleg it showed earlier when he wasn't feeling well. Think about it. Something as different as it is, could wreak havoc with us and Earth."

"Those are all valid concerns," interjected Alina. "But I have to admit, I'm very curious about talking to it."

A bright flash of light emanated from the creature. They looked, and it was gone.

"Janice?" said Zeke. "Do you know where it is?"

"It is in engineering at the quantum drive."

Zeke looked at Finn. "You're with me." They immediately hurried out of the bridge towards engineering. Everyone else followed.

It only took about a minute, but they arrived to find the creature occupying a large space of the room, shimmering like the surface of water the way it did on the bridge so many hours ago.

"The quantum drive," said Finn. "It's doing something to it." He looked over at Zeke. "Maybe it's restoring the drive."

Without warning, another bright light flashed that forced them all to wince backward and shield their eyes. Then, as quickly as it appeared, the light vanished. The creature stopped its shimmering and reduced in size to the standard gray, undulating form that it had maintained inside the sensors.

"Captain," said Janice. "It appears that the quantum drive has been restored."

He jerked his head towards the drive and then at Finn. "Check it."

Finn took a couple of steps forward, but the creature was still hovering in place. He stopped, not wanting to get close. After a few moments, it moved aside.

Finn cautious approached the quantum drive display next to the main viewing door as he repeatedly glanced over at the cloud. The Drive showed 100% operational. He looked through the view portal, stayed there for 20 seconds, and then turned around. He eyed the creature and then moved back over towards Zeke and the others.

"I have no idea how it did it, but it looks like the drive is back. It's restored, along with the antimatter." Finn's tone conveyed genuine amazement. "That is supposed to be impossible."

"Then we can go home," said Zeke.

Finn countered him. "We have to ask ourselves if we *should* go home. Maybe it restored the drive so it could follow us. We don't know it's true intentions, and we can't risk it getting back there. We can stay here and talk to it some more, but that has the risk of it discovering where Earth is. Or, we could send ourselves into deep space, and it won't learn where Earth is."

"It could just follow us and keep doing the same thing to us," said Hahn. "That idea won't work."

"Or," he continued, "we could destroy the ship and it with us. I don't see any other options."

"Or we stay out here and communicate with it until we realize its true intentions."

Finn's expression was resolute. "And how long will that take? Years? And if we're convinced it's benevolent, then how do we know it isn't a trick?"

"It's a no-win situation with you, Finn. No matter what the options, you'll deny the possibility that it can work with us."

Finn stared back with a stiff expression.

"Think about this," continued Zeke. "The company will send another crew, and this whole scenario might repeat itself."

"Not if it gets the radio transmissions in time," said Hahn.

Zeke looked down to the ground for a moment as he took a breath before looking back at them. "I'm the captain, and this mission is my responsibility. It is either us, here, now, or another crew later. And yeah, I know you hope the radio transmissions are received in time. But if they're not, then even by your thinking, the risk is too great. Therefore, we need to stay here and talk to it and send more information back. We don't have to go home, and to be honest, I agree we should not."

"Talking to it could somehow lead it to Earth," said Finn in a calm tone. "We can't risk it."

Zeke looked at Finn for a few seconds then around the room. All eyes were on him. "I've seen you all eyeing each other. You've already discussed this, haven't you?"

"Yeah," interrupted the doc. "We did. Finn is right. Unless we're absolutely sure it's benevolent, we can't risk leading it back home. That means we either learn to talk to it and discover its true motives, which I don't believe is possible, or we try to destroy it."

"What about ignoring it?" asked Oleg. Everyone looked at him. "I'm just saying. It's an option that no one's brought up. Maybe, ignoring it will cause it to go away."

"If it goes away," responded Hahn, "How can we verify that? We've already seen how it can elude the ship's sensors. It could be waiting for us to go back home and just follow us. You're right. It's an option we have not considered but, it can't work. The risk is too high." She looked at Finn. "We have to destroy it."

"How do you plan to do that?" asked Zeke.

No one responded.

He examined his crew and knew they had something up their collective sleeve. "Talk to me. What have you got planned?"

Again silence.

"Janice? Update me on what they're planning."

"The destruction of the Cascade along with the creature."

"How?"

"Explosives have already been planted in an area next to the fuel cells in order to detonate them."

Zeke scanned them all. After a few long seconds, he spoke. "And what about the next crew? If you destroy the Cascade, it'll just start over with them."

"It wouldn't be a problem if it were destroyed," responded Finn. He looked over at the creature, which was still hovering a few meters away. She shook his head. "Besides, I'm sure Janice has already sent back all information about what's happened, now that we have full power. That means they would know not to come here." He glanced up towards the ceiling. "Right, Janice?"

"That is correct, Finn. The moment the quantum drive was restored, I sent back all information via subspace. I am sure they would be very hesitant to send any further missions to this area."

"Maybe they will anyway," interjected Oleg. "You know how the company is, money first. And besides, what if Space Force sees this thing as a potential weapon and decides to try and capture it or try to figure out how to time travel? I wouldn't put it past them."

"Now that's a comforting thought," said the doc.

"We must talk to it," said Zeke. He looked over at the creature. "Look, it's right there. It has not attacked us. It just restored the drive. And, as crazy as it sounds, here we are talking about it with the right there!" He nodded to the creature. "We're becoming comfortable with it being here. Do you really think it's malevolent?"

"That's just it," said Finn. "With Earth at risk, we can't get comfortable."

Zeke showed his annoyance at being countered at every comment. "It's learning and becoming easier to work with. It knows the general area where we came from. Have you thought that maybe our self-destruction will mean it turns its attention to finding Earth, and your fears would be realized?"

"But, we don't know that would happen," said Finn. "Besides, Janice said she doesn't think its possible for it to find Earth. Right, Janice?"

"That is correct."

"Now who's guilty of wishful thinking," responded Zeke with a slightly mocking tone. "We're going to stay here and talk to it. Those are my orders."

"And risk it learning where Earth is? I don't think you've thought this through." Finn took a step towards Zeke and spoke in a calm, self-assured tone. "The ship is rigged with explosives. But now that we have the quantum drive back, we don't need them. All Janice has to do is override the safety protocols and release the antimatter."

"You're not thinking right," said Zeke. His voice was a mixture of tension and anger. "I'm telling you it's not malevolent. We are going to stay here. We can communicate with it, and we can send back what we learn to Earth. The more Earth learns of it, the safer it will be. So, we're staying."

"For how long?" said Finn. "Even if we get convinced its not going to harm us, can we really trust it afterward? It's too powerful. It's too dangerous. How are we going to know its true intention and that it isn't just biding its time until it finds out where Earth is?"

"Like I've been telling you. It's friendly. It's learning about us and doesn't want to harm us." Zeke's tone was self-assured.

"To be perfectly honest, Captain," said the doc. "We have to consider the possibility that you've been compromised. After all, it had you someplace and was able to control you. That is a huge concern. And, you seem to want to spend time with it, get to know it. Even after all it's done. You trust it, and we don't. You see our concern?"

Zeke looked over at the creature. *Did it do something to me while I was with it?* He pushed away the thought.

"I'm fine," he said directly to the doc.

"He then looked back at Finn. "My orders are that we talk to it and send what we learn back to Earth."

"The more we do that," said Finn, "the more information it will have. It's too risky. It's here right now, and we have an opportunity to take action. We can try and destroy it by destroying the Cascade." He glanced over at the alien. "With the quantum drive restored, we can make this ship go supernova. Nothing will be left, not even vapor. It is what we must do for the sake of Earth. There is simply no way that we could return home. We can't risk it."

"It's not your decision," retorted Zeke. "It's mine."

"Not if you've been compromised," responded Finn quickly.

"I'm the captain. Not you. Look, you've been under a great deal of stress, and you haven't had nearly enough sleep for a few days now. How do you know *you're* the one not thinking rationally?"

"Really? Let's let Janice decide." He took a step back and glanced upward. "Janice, is destroying ourselves in an attempt to destroy it the best option to ensure the safety of Earth?"

"In my estimation, yes," she said quickly.

Zeke took a deep breath. He forced his eyes shut and rubbed his forehead before forcing the air out through his nostrils. He stared at Finn. "Look, I've been with it. I'm telling you it's not malevolent. We have to study it, communicate with it, and maybe even learn from it." His words were coming strong and steady. "I understand your logic. But, this is space. We're going to encounter things that are difficult to deal with. I'm telling you, sooner or later we are going to have to face this thing."

He looked around the room at his crew.

"Is anyone with me on this?"

No one responded.

"It doesn't matter. I've heard what you'll have to say, but the final decision is mine. We're going to try and talk to it and learn what we can and send the information back to Earth." He paused for a moment before adding, "It's not hostile."

"You don't know that for sure," said Hahn.

"Yes, I do. I was with it. It was in my mind." He flinched at how bad the words sounded. "I was able to understand it and sense it. It does not intend us harm." He emphasized the last sentence.

"Janice?" said Hahn, "do you think it's possible that this thing was in the cap's mind and that it could be influencing him now."

"It is possible, but I cannot know for sure."

Zeke looked around the room and found no sympathetic eyes. "Alina? You've got a good head on your shoulders. Don't you think we should learn as much as we can about it?"

They looked at her. She lowered her head down, staring blankly at the floor before finally looking back at him. "I think we should find out what it wants if we can. But, I don't know what happened to you when you were away, and that concerns me. So, I think we all need to be very cautious. But, as much as I hate to say it, we're expendable. Earth is not."

Zeke stared at her with an expression of being betrayed.

"Alina's right," said Finn. "We have to act. It's here now. We have to do what we can." He glanced again at the creature, which was still hovering in place. He looked at the doc, then to Hahn, Oleg, and Alina. Hahn took a long breath and nodded. Oleg did too. The doc took a big sip of coffee, but would not look at Zeke. Her hands were trembling.

"We don't have any choice," said Finn. "We can't take any chances. We have to destroy it. We have to." He swallowed hard. "I'm scared as hell. But, we have to do this for Earth."

"Mutiny?" said Zeke. "I won't let you do this."

Finn relaxed. "We have to. I don't want to. I'm scared the same as everyone else. But, we've experienced its power and pain. We have to protect Earth. We can't risk it getting back there. We have to destroy it."

Zeke spoke into the air. "Janice, I'm ordering you to ignore any orders given to you by Finn or anybody else, Priority Order Alpha One Alpha One."

Janice did not respond.

"Janice, I'm ordering you to ignore any orders given to you by Finn! Priority Order Alpha One Alpha One. Comply!"

Janice did not respond.

Zeke looked over at the creature and walked right up to it. "Get out of here!" The creature mimicked his proportions once again and replayed the image of him with his open hand."

Zeke looked at Finn, a hopeless expression of defeat scraped across his face. "No, Finn! Don't do this!"

Finn looked into Zeke's eyes. A fearful expression accompanied his words. "Sorry, Cap. Janice. Execute," said Finn in a quivering voice.

Everyone closed their eyes except Zeke. He looked at the creature.

From deep space near the Drake system, what appeared to be a faint star suddenly flared for two minutes and then slowly faded away.

Chapter 31
Captain's Log

The door to the captain's quarters slid open. Zeke walked in. It closed silently behind him as he walked to his chair and let himself drop down into plush comfort. After a huge exhale, he threw his legs onto his desk and leaned back. Across the room, there was a model of the earth. It slowly rotated on its stand. His hometown was on the dark side, hidden in the beauty of a thousand city lights.

On his desk was a small shallow box full of live grass. He ran his fingers through the blades. After staring at it for a few seconds, he slid his legs off of the desk and swung his chair to the right. With the bottom of his hand, he smacked a nob on a door. It popped open. He reached in, grabbed a beer, and twisted off the cap.

"I need this," he said. Then he leaned forward and placed his elbows on his desk and dropped his head down.

"Janice?"

"Yes, Captain."

"Begin the first video log."

"Yes, Captain."

He set the beer out of view and looked at the large screen on the wall. August 7, 2158, automatically showed up. His image stared back.

"We woke from hyper-sleep three days ago. It took a few hours to get rid of the shakes, then two days to verify that the ship's systems, including…" He stopped talking.

There was a slight movement in the room next to the rotating globe of the earth.

"What the hell?" he muttered to himself.

He pushed back his chair as he stood up, then walked around his desk. The model of Earth was encased in a kind of shimmering light that resembled the surface of water.

"Janice? What is wrong with the globe?"

"I am not aware of any problems with it, Captain."

He took a step back and watched. Then over several seconds, the shimmering slowly turned into a slightly gray, luminescent cloud engulfing the entire Earth.